I dedicate this book to Sarah Beck and Danny Gallagher. Friends from different worlds, who kept me alive and in good company throughout my twenties. (We really need to get together.) Cheers!

This is a work of fiction. All names and characters are either invented or used fictitiously. (Except for the toast to Fisherman Russ, who I have never met and yet saluted on dozens of occasions with the traditional woo-woo shot.) As for my North Carolina coast line; yeah, I tweaked it a bit, and added gambling and Great White Sharks. Tippany Ridge was inspired by numerous visits to my sister's A-frame cottage on Topsail Island.

Jen Purcell, Publisher, in association with CreateSpace, a subsidiary of Amazon.com.

Published in the United States in association with CreateSpace, a subsidiary of Amazon.com

ISBN-10: 1475068360
ISBN-13: 978-1475068368

Manufactured in the United States of America

Prologue

"I was speed walking on the beach, my arms swinging ridiculously, hair wild, trapped in my thoughts. The setting sun, an orange pink blaze, reflected off the ocean spray and turned the water gold. A golden yellow so bright it blinded me! My eyes burned and yet I couldn't look away.

"Then I saw it. Thousands of tiny fish splashing about like raindrops. They were tracking something. And it was *huge*! I followed it best I could, but it was quick. One minute it flashed a hundred yards to my left, and before my eyes could adjust it popped up fifty feet to my right. I walked straight at it, into the ocean like a flippin' zombie…

"IT WAS *HER!*" The woman cried. "Shaken, I fell back into the surf and got pummeled by a wave. I coughed and wheezed, tasting salt and feeling the sandy grit of the ocean floor between my teeth. Remember what I said about my dreams? How they felt so FLIPPIN' real I never wanted to wake up.

"Minutes later, I came back to myself. What in the world was I doing soaking wet, standing knee deep in the surf? And in my cross trainers no less! I must be mad!

"Right then…as I inspected my sneaker, she broke through the waves. My baby GLOWED like a piece of GOLD! She shot straight up, about twenty feet in the air, arched her back and flipped into a dive. SPLASH!"

A fragile smile passed over Bird Lady's trembling lips. "The moment lasted less than a second, but like a photograph snapped in my memory, I can still see her.

"My baby was a mermaid…"

The Dirty Mermaid

By Jen Purcell

Chapter 1 (Present Day)

I figured Sarah must have blown town when I got the call. If it was me, I would've high-tailed it out of there months ago. That's me. Not Sarah. Sarah had been off the radar for days. After seventy-two hours the police made it official. On the sixth day I got a call.

"Have you seen her? Has she come by? Called? Emailed? She's your best friend Maggie, or at least, well, she was."

I didn't recognize the caller at first. The voice sounded weathered and gruff. Tired. But there was only one guy in the world that would be searching so frantically for Sarah Fox. Or should I say, Sarah Harrison. The same man who made her run.

It was Tuesday night. Scotty McCreery and Tim McGraw were belting out *"Live Like You Were Dying"* on *American Idol.* I contemplated whether or not to smack on some make-up and hit the Pavilion. Tuesday was cheapo wine night and usually I went, but I'd been in a funk since my fight with Buddy and thought maybe it'd be better if I just skipped the drama altogether. Drinking too much on a work night, pretending to flirt with anyone in kissing distance, while I watched the little bastard make a move on every available girl in the joint was just plain stupid. And I didn't want to sleep with him, either. That's another thing that always happened. Pitiful really. Here I was twenty-five years old, trying to keep a twenty-one year old hard body interested, wasting time on a friggin' *baby*. *Sheeiit*. I wish Sarah had called me. We could've hauled ass together.

Work wasn't any better. My job at the newspaper was so pathetic I was forced to waitress on Thursday nights just to cover the bills. Every morning I'd wake to the alarm and immediately question my existence. I'd brush my teeth, eat toast, and contemplate ways of escaping. I could move to Hawaii or join the Coast Guard, maybe take a road trip or cocktail in Vegas? I had no ties, no serious relationships! Why the hell *not*?

By lunchtime, under a stack of paperwork and a boss crowing in my ear, these dreams would dissipate and the day would get away from me. By six p.m. I'd drop on the couch like dead weight, down a box of doughnuts and then run for two hours, guilty about the calories. Some nights I'd sit at the computer and attempt my version of *The Great American Novel*. Then the phone would ring or the dryer would buzz. Instead of creating something fabulous, I'd spend the time folding towels and blabbing to my mother about coupon deals and bad hair.

I'd run into Buddy around mid-week at the one deli in town. He'd offer to buy me a sandwich, and we'd eat together in the front seat of his pickup. He'd be so sweet and apologetic and then, before I could finish my chips, he'd have me in the back of the cab half-naked and late for another deadline. My stories usually involved coupon deals from the local *Piggly Wiggly*, or tips to keep bugs from killing the springtime roses — real life changing material. Hey, in the newspaper business, a deadline was a deadline.

Buddy would always promise to call. I'd wait by the phone for a day or two and then get really pissed when he reneged. Saturday I'd be sucking face in downtown Raleigh with some NC State student for a little morale booster, and Sunday I'd be hung-the-frick-over. By Monday, at the sound of my alarm, I'd be back at the breakfast table eating toast and talking to myself, once again questioning my very existence.

All these thoughts jumped around my brain as I moved to the bathroom and inspected my reflection in the mirror. Mechanically, I pulled out some cover up and smeared it over my face. I was working the mascara brush when the phone rang.

"Maggie?" The voice tired. Urgent.

"Speaking."

"I know it's been awhile, but I'm calling about Sarah."

Pausing the mascara wand, I replied. "Sarah *who*?"

"Your roommate, that's who."

"I...uh...don't have a roommate." I caught myself, thinking it wasn't such a good idea offering this information to a stranger. "Uh, that's available right now. You must have the wrong number."

"*College*, you idiot! Your *college* roommate."

"Did you call me an idiot?"

"I'm *sorry*, okay. But I need to find her!"

The phone lay quiet for a minute as my mind rushed back to a different time, when I did have a friend named Sarah. We were college roommates for the better part of three years. It was in our junior year that Sarah landed her man, and that was pretty much the end of our relationship. She quit painting, partying, and stopped running with me at the gym. She spent every available second with an ear clamped to the phone because three days every single weekend was never enough.

Off the phone, she wasn't any better. Sarah was constantly playing a collection of her boyfriend's favorite tunes. Underground Music she called it — a mix of rock-n-roll, country and jazz. Local bands like *The Filipino Cowboy*, *Rendition* and *The Saddle Bruzers*, who played every coastal bar from Washington, D.C. to Myrtle Beach. I used to love *The Filipino Cowboy*, but after hearing the CD in-and-flipping-out, ten hours a day, weeks at a time, all I wanted to do was smash it or put a bullet in my head. I finally broke down and purchased Sarah a pair of earphones. Best ten bucks I ever spent.

*

It was a week after the headset purchase that shit went down. I finished my last class for the day and was off to happy hour. Technically, most of my friends sprouted from my relationship with Sarah. We used to be inseparable. I can't count how many Fridays we knocked on random doors, searching for a willing senior to beg off a fake I.D. or pretended to pledge a sorority just to get into a free beer party.

We tailgated every football game, spent long afternoons playing pool in the student common room, smoked pot and ate pizza. There was cow tipping and barn dancing; even studying was fun with Sarah. Pointing out hot guys between chapters, having life changing girl talks in the library bathroom, simple coffee breaks were a hoot. She found joy in everything. All that changed when Sarah landed the man of her dreams, and delivering the gift wrapped earphones didn't help. Sarah was, in my overly zealous opinion, fucked in love.

The Crew was sitting at a corner table hovering over a pitcher of beer and an ashtray littered with butts. They waved me over and handed me a plastic cup. Already in deep conversation about a shared writing class, I immediately jumped in.

"Is Miss Fox planning to join us?" Drew asked.

"Doubt it."

"Maybe I should give her a call." He added casually.

"It won't do any good. I'm sure she's in our room packing for yet another long weekend with old Blue eyes, probably on the phone while she's folding. God forbid she does anything without his permission. Barely leaves the dorm. Never paints. Jets every Thursday and doesn't return until Monday morning. Back in the dorm for five minutes and she's on the phone or cranking that freaky music. To hear Zeppelin again would be heaven!"

Drew grinned. "And to think, Maggie, you used to hate rock-n-roll."

"Well now I hate the Filipino-friggin'-COWBOY!"

"Go easy, Mags. Sarah's in love."

"No shit, dork. But it's more than that. You can be in love and still have a life. Jimmy's got her all screwed up. He hooked up with his old girlfriend last week by *accident*." I flinched my fingers to enunciate. "How the hell can you call tongue jamming an accident? Give me a break. It's because he's trying to *control* her, getting back at her for attempting to be someone, for actually having a *life*. He called and begged for an apology, blamed it on her absence. Said he missed her too much. What *bullshit!*

"Sarah's been an absolute basket case, weeping like a baby, playing that friggin' underground music. *Holy cripes!* I can't handle it. Had to go out and buy her a set of headphones. Problem is that I can't even console her because I *want* them to break up."

"Get her on the phone. Let me talk. "

Drew was in la-la land, but I handed over my cell just the same. Maybe he could convince her. I was starting to feel guilty about the earphones.

"Hey darlin'? It's me...*me*! No silly, *Drew.*" The jukebox was blaring so loudly he had to scream into the receiver. "BUT IT'S *WEDNESDAY*! COME OUT AND MEET US!"

Drew held up a finger and pointed to the exit, conversing as he went. I turned back to Jeannie, a grad student who dressed as such with long silky hair parted down the middle. She took a drag off one of those fake metal cigarettes they advertise on late night television (forever an earth cruncher) and asked me if I'd consider writing for the school paper. Since she was the editor, getting the job would be simple. "It looks great on a resume."

"I'd *love* to Jeannie! Oh, but what would I write about? Can I have a column?"

Before I knew it, Drew was tapping me on the shoulder, his movements abrupt and excitable. "I think she's going for it."

Still in a tizzy about my possible newspaper job, I had forgotten about Sarah. "Come out? Really?"

"No, no, no...not *that*!" He glowed, ecstatic that he received the information first. "She's going to elope."

Forgetting about Jeannie and the paper, I ripped the phone out of his hand and snapped, "That's *ridiculous*! She's barely twenty-one! Did she tell you that? Did you really say she wanted to marry that asshole?"

"Not in so many words, Maggie. But...well, Sarah's gone."

"*Home*? It's only Wednesday. See what I'm saying? Can't even make it three days!"

"No." He shook his head solemnly. "She's packed her things. *All* of them." Drew lit another smoke. "She quit school, Maggie. Sarah's gone for good."

I smacked at him playfully and offered an exaggerated laugh. When he didn't join in I tensed and pulled away. The bar was now jam packed so I had to shove and beat my way to the exit. I struggled to push open the door and then broke into a run.

It was February, mid winter in North Carolina. The sky had already darkened but the temperature remained a balmy fifty degrees. A chilly wind sliced through a strip of Carolina pines bringing with it a fragrance that always reminded me of clean linoleum. Anxious to disprove Drew's statement, I continued to sprint but the beer and cigarettes quickly proved a hindrance. Dizzy and out of breath, I reached the room eleven minutes later and twisted the knob. Locked. A bitch move for sure. Sarah knew I never carried a key. I slid my card into the crevice and manipulated the latch. Thankfully, it was just a button. The door snapped open. I flipped on the light and stopped short.

One side of the room looked amazingly clean, like Sarah finally decided to pick up her shit. Her mattress laid battered and naked, the sheets completely stripped. This wasn't uncommon. Sarah was known to bring laundry home on weekends. *But not on Wednesday. Never on Wednesday.*

Sarah's comforter was missing off the futon couch. I jerked open her closet and found a bunch of hangers. Empty. You'd think this would be enough to believe Drew's gossip, but still I remained skeptical. Sheets, clothes, and even comforters needed cleaning.

It was the poster that clinched it. Sarah and Jimmy picked it up at their very first concert together, when The

Cowboy opened for Kenny Chesney at the RBC. Flashing six pack abs and tight Levi jeans, Stetson hat shadowing a sculpted jaw as he jammed an electric guitar in a field of blue grass—autographed by the Filipino himself.

I glared at the empty tattered wall space and my head began to spin. Only then was I convinced. My sweet little Sarah had gone off and eloped with a monster.

Chapter 2 (College)

Sarah spent every summer on the North Carolina coast, in a town called Tippany Ridge. (Or *Tipp* or *Ridge* depending on whom you asked.) A slice of heaven, she liked to call it, located just north of Wilmington that got its share of summer tourists even without cool waterslides and snazzy hotels. Technically, it was an inlet shaped like a giant pointy icicle. There was only one way in, over a metal causeway that rotated every thirty minutes for water traffic. Most folks referred to it as an island. An island famous for three things — fishing, surfing and the third...well, I'll get to that in a minute.

First, Tippany Ridge was a fishing town. The southern part of the island literally surrounded by one continuous dock, crammed full of every make and model boat. From Makos and Sea Rays, to Boston Whalers, flat boards and deck boats, there were even a couple of yachts; all geared for the same purpose — trolling The Ridge. A large portion of the crafts were for private use only, while others advertised fishing trips and offshore excursions.

For everyone else, with an angler's heart and a pauper's purse, unable to shell out $850 bucks (the average gas bill for a day at sea) there was South Pier. Located ocean side on the southeast tip, the pier was always packed. Men, women and children alike, lounging in fold-up chairs or leaning against the rail, loaded with coolers, shrimp bait, flashlights and tackle boxes. Some socialized while others sat stock still, forever watching, waiting for the poles to dance. Folks say that if you ever need anything specific on Tippany Ridge, perhaps a new exhaust system put on your Chevy or plumbing fixed in the washroom, your best bet was to pick up a pole and head for the pier.

As for town, most of the commercial businesses were

located in the southern vicinity just over the bridge. There were a handful of restaurants and shops, one pizza delivery place and a Quick Stop, that sold gas and expensive condiments. Food Lion, McDonald's, Taco Bell, even the Laundromat was located on the mainland. For this reason alone, very few people stuck out winters on Tippany Ridge. These were the true island folk, those who believed in reading the sky, sensing the wind, and tracking weather changes with the lick of a finger.

The island was a popular place for surfers as well, offering a lengthy coastline with powerful tides. Tippany Ridge has been sighted in many a travel magazine as producing what long boarders considered the "perfect surfable wave". Early March always brought with it a two-week surge of rowdy spring breakers.

As for swimming, well, that wasn't as common. It has been explained that the Atlantic side of the northern tip catches a western wind that isn't barricaded by the Outer Banks. Therefore, the ocean, even during low tide, has a rip current that can pull under even the most adept of swimmers. With this in mind, most folks keep their belly surfing extremely close to shore.

Although winters on island were quiet, when locals spent long days cleaning fishing tackle and drinking canned beer, the summer season promised excessive crowds and every type of beach junky. The shores continuously packed with vacationers, young and old, garbed in enormous shades and the thickest of sun block, trudging the surf for the most glorious of treasures. From shark's teeth to drift wood, sea glass and fully formed starfish, they lugged buckets and shovels; relaxed on blankets and chairs, while small children ran in circles squealing joyfully as they buried each other deep in the sand.

The island definitely had its share of young strapping lads. Paid well to maintain and maneuver the fishing boats by day and surf the Ridge any chance they could, usually as the sun dipped behind the skyline. These sultry nights brought out the college girls, draped in near transparent garb, just enough to display the skimpiest of swimsuits. They'd prance along the coastline pretending not to watch.

The teenage girls were less inconspicuous. They giggled in groups, carried radios and binoculars (always with the binoculars), and stationed themselves on water's edge so they could blatantly point and croon over the string of buff boarders.

Grammar girls, the youngest of sweethearts, also coveted binoculars, forever searching even more aggressively than their older counterparts. However, it wasn't boys they were hunting for…

***

Sarah was always talking about the Tipp as if she were standing knee-deep in ocean spray holding a monster conch shell in one hand. Especially that very first month at East Carolina University, when we were all trying just a little too hard. I blabbed on about life as an Army *Brat*, how we relocated every few years for my dad's military job. Complaining that I was born in Italy, but currently resided in Dixon, North Carolina.

Dixon was one of those little Bible belt towns just off of I-95, midway between Raleigh and Fayetteville, with lots of churches and limited night life. So it went that I was born in the same country as Leonardo Da Vinci, moved on to the surfing capital of San Diego, and then, well, the transfers became less glamorous and more pathetic. Next stop was Dallas, Texas way after the Cowboys were considered interesting, followed by Upstate New York with its excessive snow and frigid temperatures. I was actually happy when Dad got the call about North Carolina. But did we move somewhere hip like Chapel Hill or Boone? Uh, no. He goes and picks Dixon, The Trailer Park Capital of The World.

Sarah perked up when I mentioned Italy. After her beach monologue, I tried to milk it for all it was worth, but truthfully, we moved before I was three so my memories were limited.

"What about your summer, Maggie? Any cool vacations?"

"Camping," I scoffed. "My parents thought it would be a good bonding experience. It rained for two weeks and we all caught poison ivy." This got a laugh. "I'm also a life guard at the county pool. It's really fun, actually, but compared to the beach, well…"

"How far is Dixon from Cary? You'd think I'd know, seeing I went to high school out there."

"I thought you lived at the beach?"

"In the summers, yes. My parents are both doctors. When I was little we lived year-round on the Tipp in Gran's apartment. But during my father's first residency at Cape Fear, he almost got booted when the bridge defaulted and he was four hours late for surgery. So we moved to Wilmington. Then Mom landed this great job at Duke. They wanted her so badly they hired Dad as well. I cried when we had to move inland, but what could I do? That's when Gran stepped in and said I could live with her in the summers. My parents were okay with it since their jobs were so demanding. They understood that my only other alternative was a string of camps, so I got my dream. Every summer since I was fourteen I've been chillin' at the Tipp.

"And next year, Gran promised that I could live above the store. I can't wait! The apartment's right near South Pier, the restaurants and Larry's, of course, where I've been working since I was fifteen. I can't wait for next summer!"

My response was agreeable but I stewed on the inside. Never could I be so lucky. I was one of four children and although my father had a reasonably decent job and mom cut hair for a living, we were always, as my parents liked to say, one paycheck away from the soup kitchen. College tuition

21

didn't help. Our net family income totaled just enough for the government to screw me out of any possible college assistance. I couldn't even get a personal loan. This, of course, sucked the life out of vacations and summer get-a-ways. According to Dad, we were lucky to eat.

I picked ECU because it was one of the area's more reasonably priced State Schools and it took me ninety minutes away from home. *Go Pirates*! My father grumbled about this but Mom was insistent that I stay on campus for at least one year. "She needs to meet friends, Cal. You can't expect her to live at home forever!"

So off I went with a bucket of toiletries, two new outfits, laundry detergent and a squeaky tight bank account. My fourteen hundred dollar summer savings took a huge hit in the book store that very first day. I wondered how long it would take before I'd be forced into a part-time job. A jumble of cash deprived thoughts rushed my mind as Sarah spoke of her little island. Here I was starting college half broke, only to discover my roommate had doctors for parents and a coastal apartment for her leisurely use. Life just wasn't fair.

As Sarah sorted clothes and made up her loft, she sensed my oppression. (Tell me I didn't have one of those rich types who couldn't shut up about the money.) Standing there in her designer pants and silver hoops, hands pressed against her hips, she tilted her head sideways. "Maybe next year you come to the Tipp?"

Her comment startled me. "But...we've only just met. Technically, you may hate my guts by morning."

Sarah chuckled. "I doubt it. I'm pretty good at reading people, like my Gran. I can already sense that we're going to be excellent friends."

***

Sarah's skin was dark and golden, almost black in parts, and her eyes were light hazel, like a lioness, with purple flecks. She looked bi-racial to me. According to my mother, nobody had that kind of exotic complexion unless his or her parents were ethnically diverse. When Sarah showed me a picture of Mr. and Mrs. Doctor, I didn't know what to think.

Her father had blond hair and pale skin. Excluding his eyes, which were dark brown, almost Asian in appearance, he could've passed for Norwegian. Sarah's mother, pure Bostonian Wasp, had a strong bony build, sharp green eyes and pin-straight hair. Sarah may have inherited her mother's angular features and her father's almond shaped eyes, but that was about it. Truthfully, she looked adopted.

Sarah's hair was one big burst of ratty curls balled up in a scrunchy on the top of her head. I found myself thinking flat iron, or just the opposite, Grecian Formula and hot rollers. *Fix the locks and you will fix the girl.* I could hear my mother's hairdressing voice redefining Sarah's mane.

As I visualized her make-over, adding mascara and a personal trainer, Sarah pulled out a small plastic suitcase and flipped the latch. It was filled with cassette tapes, the real ancient kind people used to put in Boom Boxes. You'd think with rich parents she'd consider an MP3 player or possibly a phone. "Do you like Zeppelin? I know its Old School but, like my dad, I've got a thing for rock and roll."

I pointed over at the photo of *Dad* with his tucked in polo and shoulder-draped sweater. "*That* dad likes Led Zeppelin?"

Sarah grinned. "Mom cleaned him up for that picture. Usually he walks around in ripped shorts and concert t-shirts. He's a music junkie. We've been to so many shows together I can't even count! "

"Really? I've been to one, way back, when I was like ten."

"Who was it?"

"Errr...Brittany Spears."

"Not what you'd call head banging material but it's a start." Sarah nodded encouragingly. We both burst out laughing. "Are you hungry? The cafeteria opens in ten minutes and I'm starved."

I managed to locate my meal card and we followed the masses to the lunch room. The whole time Sarah rambled, detailing her extensive list of concert events, not excluding Aerosmith, The Rolling Stones (when she was five), Jimmy Buffett, AC/DC and Sugar Ray. If Sarah noticed that I was sizing her up, she deferred comment. After awhile I got absorbed in one of her stories, forgetting her frizzy locks and near perfect complexion that could use a touch of eyeliner and cinnamon lip gloss; or the fact that she had rich parents and a little apartment on the coast for summer getaways. She was just a funny, excitable girl with an agreeable personality. This was Sarah Fox, my soon-to-be best friend.

Chapter 3 (College)

That summer on Tippany Ridge was by far the best twelve weeks of my whole life. I didn't go that first year, my parents were still too panty twisted about money. Mom didn't want me giving up the lifeguard gig, a job that only surfaced once a decade. I couldn't convince her that I was responsible enough to live a vacation lifestyle and expand my bank account at the same time.

Besides, my mother harbored no love for the Carolina coast. Growing up in West Virginia, she spent her childhood in a countryside filled with *purple mountains majesty* and fresh water streams. Not once did Mom even consider a coastal vacation. She was fair skinned after all, milky white at best, with sandy brown hair (that she dyed because she couldn't stand) and a freckled face.

Whenever I asked about a day trip to the beach she would flat out refuse and say, "I'm helping you, Maggie, save your skin." And by that she meant literally. Mom was stone cold serious about ultra violet rays and skin deterioration. If I mentioned Coppertone or SPF 50 she'd rebut with, "Sun block clogs the pores, dear. Boys'll be calling you zit face."

Mom was hoping I'd go to Appalachian State. That way she could spend every weekend in her precious mountains trying to make me hike or eat tree bark, which of course was the very reason I headed east. When the decision was sealed in a check, Mom turned to Finn, my younger brother, and started pressing him with information about western schools. Finn loved hunting and fishing, spent half his time in a tree stand behind our house practicing his bow and arrow skills on the occasional varmint. He was a shoe-in for Appalachian.

It was Sarah who changed my mother's tune about the

second summer. She was staying with her parents in Cary over Christmas break, so it wasn't surprising that three days into the New Year she phoned and asked directions to my house. I snagged a job wrapping presents at the mall, a two-week gig just before Christmas, but after the holidays, I was bored senseless. Like Sarah, I was anxious to get back east, to my parties and fun and freedom.

Sarah rolled up in a white 1998 Volvo, a hand-me-down from her father, and jumped straight into blab mode. "The best part about this dinosaur is the radio." She preened. "It's got a dual cassette player and rocking speakers! Dad bought a new car last year and asked the guy to switch out the system. The dude laughed in his face and said *who puts a cassette player in a Lexus*? Lucky for the dealer my mother was with us or the new car would've been toast."

Sarah sprouted two inches over those first few years, stretching and reassembling her chubby features into a more womanly frame. In a world of cafeteria food and quart beers, Sarah retaliated, forever running and lifting, transforming baby fat into well-defined muscle. As for her hair, I have to pat myself on the back for that. The dark frizzy scrunched up mess now dropped below her shoulders in the most amazing curls. My mother hadn't seen Sarah since spring and wouldn't shut up about the transformation, enchanted I suspect by her dewy complexion and perfect locks.

She pranced into the kitchen carrying an armful of gifts—caramel strawberry cheese cake for my parents, a sequined *Doors* t-shirt for me, and carefully wrapped packages for each of my siblings.

Finn and Roman each received a tackle box filled with weird little weights and gadgets. "Maggie said you guys do a lot of stream fishing. I'm more of an ocean girl myself but Shrimper Sam tells me this gear can be used in both fresh and salt water."

My brothers hooted and howled, comparing hooks and weights as if they'd just won the state lottery, immediately conjuring up plans for a trip to the beach.

"I'll take you fishing on the pier," Sarah offered, "and trolling down the secret waterways. You want to catch some real muck monsters, that's where they like to hide."

Sarah was laying it on tremendously thick, working her magic to glamorize the beach. She then handed my nine-year-old sister, Scarlett, a thin square package. By its shape, I suspected a book. Scarlett's eyes twinkled as she ripped into the shiny silk paper and gasped at the cover. "Mommy! Mommy! Come see! It's a mermaid book!"

"Oh, I remember this book!" My mother exclaimed. "I had a copy when I was a kid."

"I thought you didn't like the ocean?"

Mom rolled her eyes. "I did when I was ten. My parents used to send us out in the hot sun slathered in baby oil! Can you imagine? It's no wonder I'm already a candidate for *Geritol* commercials."

"What's *Geritol*?" Scarlett asked.

"A vitamin dear, for *old* people! They don't make it anymore, it's so ancient. But this book! Oh, I loved the pictures, memorized all the mermaids and their stories. Twelve, as I recall."

"Thirteen." Sarah chimed. "The September Mermaids are twins."

"That's right. It reads like a calendar. I believe April was my favorite.

"April is everyone's favorite."

I leaned over my little sister who was hoarding her gift like a bag of M&M's. "*The Mermaids of Tippany Ridge?*" I turned to my friend. "Your beach town?"

"Yep. The very same."

Scarlett flipped through the pictures until she located the April Mermaid. *Miss Norma Jean was a queen...who loved to sing her songs...* The April Mermaid had platinum hair and wore a white sequined dress that transformed into a tail. Hundreds of metallic fish swam around her arms giving the impression of a feathery boa. The ocean floor lay scattered with diamond studded bubbles.

"Diamonds for April," Sarah announced.

"You know, she kind of resembles Marily…"

Sarah cut me off. "That's because it *is* Norma. Norma Jean."

"Norma *who*?" I asked.

Sarah chuckled. "You're lost, sister. *Google* Norma Jean and see what comes up." She turned to my mother. "One of the locals, Nicky Pearson, had a cousin who worked for the FBI. He was in town for a big fishing trip with a bunch of retired D.C. boys. Swears that she was lying in the surf slapping at an entourage of silvery fish with her big sequined tail. The way Nicky tells it, she blew him a kiss, flipped a double bird at the ex-secret servicemen, and disappeared."

"What in the world are you *talking* about?"

"The mermaid book, sweet heart," Mom replied. "It was written for children but the stories are based on myths. Legends. My friends and I went crazy trying to investigate the old pirate mermaids. I can remember at least a dozen dinner conversations about Miss April. Even my father had a theory."

"Gran says she painted her just like Nicky's cousin described."

I leaned over and inspected the April mermaid. "So your Gran's a painter?"

"Oh, she's more that that." Sarah flipped back to the front cover and pointed to the name in the bottom corner. "My grandmother *is* Viola Fox, author and illustrator of one of the most famous picture books of all time."

Chapter 4 (College)

On my first drive to school Mom couldn't help but comment on the vast North Carolina farm country. "You sure you want to move so far away, sweetie? You could go to State and then I'd visit every weekend. It seems so lonely out here."

I wasn't paying her any attention. With the window cranked, the cool breeze whipping steadily against my face, I found the miles of agricultural landscape calming. I especially loved the little A-frame shacks, with tiny porches and shade trees, that cropped up every few miles as if the house itself had been planted and not the corn.

The narrow road twisted and hundreds of acres opened up before us. They were covered in a blanket of...of snow? "What is that?"

"A cotton field, baby." My mother reported and pulled over. I scrambled out of the car and snatched a piece that had broken off and lay near the roadside. "Beautiful, isn't it?" She continued. "The plant starts out a bushy green but as the cotton matures the leaves wilt then turn brown. This is when the seeds pop. Wa-la! Carolina snow."

Sarah and I sped across a similar terrain in a southeast direction determined to hit sand by sundown. Cruising by cabbage fields already bursting with abundance, rows of chicken coops and rolling green meadows scattered with ten foot circular bales of hay, I was reminded of the cotton. How it resembled enormous popping corn, so white and fibrous, ripping into it and picking out the seeds felt oddly rewarding.

We passed a blueberry farm with rows upon rows of bountiful bushes. (Bladen County gloated *Blueberry Capital of the World* for a reason.) Every few miles we'd come across a clutter of printed advertisements and homemade signs reminding us of that fact.

"Let's pick some blueberries!" I yelled, already salivating.

"TOO EARLY!" Sarah hollered over the music. "June is the best month for picking. Got a friend named Dakater, runs a farm a bit closer to the beach. I'm talking the most voluptuous berries!"

"Voluptuous?"

"That's right!" Sarah winked. "You'll see!"

Those first few years, Sarah and I were inseparable. We could spend hours, side by side, without pissing each other off and monologue about anything, even stupid words like voluptuous. I'd be typing away at the computer trying to finish another story for Lit 222, every so often asking her opinion about a certain descriptive phrase. "Give me an adjective for lips? Plump? Juicy?"

Sarah would be elbow deep in work leaning into her easel as she concentrated. Her hair tattered and speckled with oil colors as she created another waterscape of magnified sea life engrossed in human activity. On this particular day, she painted a sea horse and a turtle at a tea party. The horse wearing a flowery cap and the turtle smeared in bright pink lipstick. She wiped a hand across her forehead, leaving a streak of magenta. I wasn't sure she heard me at all until she said, "How about voluptuous?"

I hashed it over and plugged it in, reading the phrase aloud. In a flash we were back on task, me the writer and Sarah the painter, a skill she so proudly inherited from her grandmother.

Sarah checked her watch as we whipped along the twisting country roads, passing the occasional rickety gas station and abandoned trailer, in the middle of nowhere. "Perfect timing. The bridge will be opening in two minutes."

"Bridge?"

"Yup. The Tipp isn't an island but it may as well be. The patch of dirt that connects the mainland is nothing more than a giant marsh. They dug it out when the bridge was built."

"How'd they manage before construction?"

"Beats me. That was like a hundred years ago. Maybe they used horses. You know, like Tonto."

"I'm pretty sure Tonto was an Indian."

Sarah ignored my comment and continued her narration. "The metal turn-bridge runs on a timer. Every half-hour it opens for boats. Right when you think you're home the bridge holds you hostage for another fifteen minutes. Dad and I have been practicing our timing ever since we moved to Wilmington.

Sarah turned onto a double-lane road and we were suddenly back to civilization. We drove by two gas stations, *Four Oaks Bank*, *Crispy Chix*, *Food Lion* and a string of tackle and bait shops. Lopsided banners and road signs sprung up in every direction, advertising *Fresh Bait*, *Boat Rentals*, *The Surf Zone*, *Salty's Dock Side Pub* and *Larry's Place*. An especially large and flashy billboard announced the arrival of *Casey's Casino Boats*, enticing tourists to test their luck on the next weekend sail.

In the midst of the clutter, right in front of the dazzling casino sign, a weathered local with knobby knees and cut-off shorts, wearing a straw cap and flip-flops, sat perched under a tattered awning reading a magazine. His feet were propped on a set of coolers advertising *Fresh Shrimp*.

Sarah honked the horn and rolled down a window, "Hey Sam!" She turned to me. "That's Shrimper Sam or Shrimp Man to most folks. He comes to Larry's just about every night for dinner. Always gets a well-done burger with mustard and onions, small fry and a vanilla shake. Oh, wait! Look! Right there! That's my grandmother's shop."

A narrow sign stood perched near the roadside. It was a painted woman designed to resemble a mermaid. The dark-skinned girlyfish shimmered a golden bronze with heavy lidded eyes and, as Sarah would say, voluptuous lips. Her mermaid scales, a blend of pinks, reds and gold, shimmered in the five o'clock sun. A fringe-vest covered well-endowed breasts and a red bandana slightly controlled a mass of bluish-Black curls. The mermaid held out a flipped thumb like she was hitch hiking, and in the other hand carried a cardboard sign that read *The Sea Queen*.

"That resembles one of your paintings."

"That's because it is my painting."

My eyes went wide. "Cool."

"Ah ha!" Sarah cut me off as she tapped her watch. "What did I tell you? Perfect timing."

We were close now, about five hundred yards from the metal causeway. I watched as the yellow blinking light tripped over to green. The ten cars in front of us started to roll and by the time we caught the line Sarah drove freely, not once dropping her speed.

Applauding her efforts, I gave my best friend a nudge. "Welcome home."

Chapter 5 (College)

As soon as my parents realized the apartment I'd be staying in was owned by the infamous Viola Fox, it was easy to sway their summer decision. That and the fact that Sarah had promised to keep me working.

"She'll have two jobs, Mrs. Mack. Every spring my grandmother takes a trip to the Caribbean and it's my responsibility to get the store cleaned up and ready for Memorial Day. That's when we officially open."

"What kind of store is it?" Mom had asked.

"A beach shop. We sell books, hats, little trinkets, a lot of fishing gear, surfboards, buckets and pails, Gran's prints and, of course, her mermaid books. Local artists sell stuff in the store too, including me."

"You?" My mom questioned. "Are you a writer too?"

Sarah blushed. "Painter. I love to paint."

***

From the height of the bridge I could see the island's coastline; maybe a half-mile separated the Atlantic Ocean from the intercoastal. We entered the small business district, a patch of scattered buildings that checkered the southern half of the island. The intercoastal side was cluttered with rows of docks and boats, just like Sarah had described. Salty's was in the midst of the congestion, a dock side pub advertising *Gas and Giblets*.

Sarah fingered a circle of seagulls that littered the sky. "Ever lost? Those dirty birds will lead you straight to Salty's. It's their home away from home."

She swung a quick right and gave me a tour. "This is the fishing sector. The boats have easy access to both the intercoastal and the ocean, and during surges, this parcel of land offers the best protection. Up ahead we have a designer surfboard shop, take-out pizza, Larry's Place, The Breakfast Shack, and Benjamin's Steak House. Everyone goes to Benjamin's on their first date 'cuz it's fancy. Gran says that's how you know who's sleeping together." Sarah pointed abruptly. "Her shop is in that little plaza."

"Can we go see it?"

"Sure. But first I want to show you the North Side." She took a sharp left just after the entrance to South Pier, completing the block, and we headed north into what Sarah deemed the residential section. Brightly colored homes, big and small, from three-tiered mini-mansions to tiny trailers, trimmed the main road and stacked the narrow side streets, many still boarded up for winter.

"The beaches," Sarah directed my attention east, "are not necessarily private but there's no public parking. This is where the ocean runs the calmest. If you like to swim you need to stay mid-island. Locals refer to North Beach as the Tipp. It's gorgeous but there's a horrible riptide. Nobody swims the Tipp unless they have a death wish. "

"But it's okay to surf?"

"Surfing's farther out, way past the current. Tragically, we lose at least one tourist every year."

"They must not be very good swimmers then."

"Idiots, far as I'm concerned. They visit from other places like California and New England, always one fool that doesn't pay attention to the warnings."

My brow furrowed. I was a life guard. I beat out hundreds to get my job. Sarah had to be exaggerating. "Do *you* swim at the Tipp?"

"Not really. It's more like cooling down at the edge. I do my bathing out on Gran's boat. There are so many cool lagoons and inlets up and down the waterway, if you know where to go. We pack coolers and head to the dog beaches, that's what they're called. Heaven on earth, sister. If we're lucky, maybe we'll spot a mermaid!"

Sarah skidded into a sandy parking lot. One very steep set of stairs ascended over the dunes and seemed to kiss the clouds. "Come on! This is what I do every time I come back to the island, first thing. It's totally incredible!"

She ran ahead excited to show me. It was close to sunset and my legs were cramped from sitting in the car for so long. I followed her up the never ending flight.

Automatically, I counted as I climbed. *Eleven, twelve, thirtee…* Winded in seconds I called out as she neared the top. "ARE YOU TRYING TO KILL ME?"

"JUST THE OPPOSITE! STAIRS PROMOTE HEALTH!"

"Health? I'm going into respiratory *distress*." I grumbled and pushed my fat ass into the sky, so out of shape it was ridiculous. While Sarah continued her daily ritual of jogging campus before breakfast, I was lucky to wake up in time for lunch. I slept in, scheduled all of my classes in the afternoon and ate way too many delivered pizzas. The first year I gained fifteen pounds and the second another ten. Sarah and I had already discussed it. This was my summer to get in shape. Huffing up the steep stairwell was just the beginning.

When I hit the top I was so dizzy and out of breath I tripped into the sand and dropped to my knees. The wind picked up and I could barely hear Sarah's voice shouting over the ocean's roar.

The sun tilted on the edge of the world, a ball of orange in a sky of purple and magenta casting a shimmery glow over the water. I fumbled through the sand feeling and tasting the salty breeze. But the time I reached her, Sarah had already lost her shoes and stood ankle deep in sea foam, arms stretched wide, regarding the ocean like an old friend.

My feet took comfort in molding with the dark wet sand as I stretched out my aching limbs. "Where are all the shells?"

"It's high tide! I'll bring you back in the morning. You'll see."

Sarah reminisced as we strolled, going on about the good old days, stories about her father and Gran. I suspect if I had spent my childhood on an island like this I'd have similar encounters. Watching her talk, so animated and lively, I could respect her nostalgia.

My stomach growled as we climbed in the car. "I'm starving."

"Choices are limited this time of year. We can go to Salty's or grab a burger at Larry's."

"Burger sounds good."

"Then Larry's it is. You might as well see where you'll be working?"

"Working?"

"Larry's Place," Sarah nodded enthusiastically. "Your second job."

Chapter 6 (College)

Larry's Place was a glorified hotdog stand that stood in a gravel parking lot right across from South Pier. The narrow unlevel building opened for business every morning by raising wooden shutters with a couple of hooked chains. There was no indoor seating, just a handful of umbrella-covered picnic tables scattered in the grass. A back dock descended to the waterway, planks of dilapidated wood that acted as a drive-thru for boaters and jet-skiers alike, in search of ice-cream and burger bliss. The meager establishment looked rundown to me, nothing more than an oversized beat-up double-wide.

"A slow night," Sarah commented as we stood crunched in a line that snaked around the building.

"This is slow?"

"Larry's Place is always busy. You'll see."

"Why?"

"It's legendary. Been on island since 1940. A fisherman from Mystic Seaport in Connecticut supposedly stole the concept, relocated, and started up a stand here. Gran told me about it and I thought she was embellishing to make my hotdog taste better. She does that, Gran. Everything in her store, the tea she drinks, the jewelry she wears, always comes with a little trivia.

"I Googled *Connecticut Burger Stands* and, sure enough, an identical building popped up mid-state. What surprised me about it was the location. Who would've thought a seasonal burger joint could do so well in such a beach-less town. Anyway..."

The order line moved swiftly. Sarah spent our wait time waving, chatting, shouting out salutations and offering a few formal introductions; each one followed by Sarah's muttering commentary of the individual's back story.

"That's Savanna Skip. Lived on the Tipp his whole life, except for a few short months that he spent in Georgia, and still they call him Savanna Skip. He can't stand it but that's how it goes with nick names. You don't get to pick. Skip's got twin boys. Identical. Butt ugly the both of 'em. Nicest guys you'd ever meet and perfectly smart. That's what they always say about ugly folks but in this case it's true.

"You've just met A-Dock Allison. She runs a snack barge that trolls the dog beaches selling ice-cream and beer. Whatever you do never order an Italian Ice. I say that because she also sells fishing bait, worms mostly, packaged in little Styrofoam cups. During a busy afternoon, it's not uncommon for her to retrieve the wrong container. I've seen one too many close calls. You'd think kids would know dirt when they taste it, but sometimes it takes a few gritty spoonfuls before figuring it out."

"Hey girl! Is this my newest recruit?"

"Ronnie Gallagher meet Maggie Mack. Maggie, meet your new boss, The Ice-Cream Man, owner of this fine establishment."

"*One* of the owners. The *working* one. Not as lucky as my silent partners who do nothing but reap the benefits." Gallagher grinned mischievously and flipped his feathery brown hair.

Sarah swore to me that Gallagher wore jeans or jean cut-offs with work boots all the time, no matter what the temperature, and a cotton t-shirt with a breast pocket so he could stuff it with gum on good days and cigarettes every other. He carried a red bandana in the seat of his pants and when the grill got too hot he'd tie it around his head like a hippie.

"What can I get you, Maggie?"

Bewildered, I turned to the item list. "I…uh…Sarah, what are you going to have?" The guy behind me huffed obnoxiously. *How could I possibly not know what to order after standing in line for so long?*

Sarah jumped to my rescue. "We'll have two medium-rare cheeseburgers with—do you like ketchup and mayo?"

I nodded.

"Both with ketchup and mayo. Oh, and grilled onions. Toast the bun, will ya? A large fry, not well done, you know, just golden."

"And onion rings." I blurted out. "I love a greasy ring."

*

"What do you think of our manager?" Sarah whispered as we waited on the food. "Kind of hot for an old guy."

I giggled. "I don't think thirty-something is old."

"It's kind of old. He's *married*." Sarah retorted. "And I hear she's a real bitch."

"Isn't that what you always hear when a guy's cute and married?"

Sarah considered my statement. "That may ring true if I was jealous but Gallagher's a friend and I still can't stand her. They live across the bridge in a hoity-toity little mansion. She spends all of her time shopping and getting her poodle pedicures. She may want Gallagher's money but never will she admit that he has to work for it. One of those high society types who thinks cash just spews from ATM machines."

"Ah... *true love!*"

"Gallagher can't see it. He's like putty in her manicured hands. Bet she doesn't even sleep with him even after all the hours he puts in. What she needs is a good bitch slap."

"Easy killer. He's your boss not your boyfriend."

"It burns me up..."

"Sarah Fox? Is that my little darlin'?"

An old man from two picnic tables away hollered in our direction. He looked familiar. The straw hat..."

"Shrimp Man! How's business?"

"It's going." He squeezed a burger between a weathered thumb and forefinger, a mustard splattered onion hung from the bun, fries piled high on the plate. By the milky white foam covering his upper lip, I was pretty sure he was downing a vanilla shake.

Sarah mumbled without moving her lips. "See his order? What'd I tell you? Shrimp Man runs like an ocean tide. Never waivers. How's your burger? I mean, how *was* your burger?"

"Awesome."

"You're going to love working here, Maggie. It's so fun! Wait 'til you see the ordering system. No tickets! All by memory and…you'll see. We're going to start your training tomorrow morning. Eleven a.m."

"I've never worked in a restaurant before."

"Just don't cry or use the "F" word. Can't be swearing at the fryolater."

"Why would I swear? It's just food."

Sarah's laugh sounded sinister. "That's right, Maggie. Just food."

Chapter 7 (College)

It was pitch dark by the time we lumbered off the picnic tables. I'd been introduced to over a dozen locals who rambled even more than Sarah. Already I felt at home.

"The apartment is that way." Sarah directed my gaze to a nearby plaza. "Parking's tight so I keep the car here at Larry's. Gallagher doesn't mind."

We tripped across the gravel to a dirt road that led down to the docks. It was lined with golf carts. Sarah climbed into one painted metallic green with a big mermaid swishing up the side. "This is our summer ride, Maggie. Get in."

She flipped the ignition and whipped it around, back to the Volvo, retrieving our suitcases. We then veered off road, down a grass path that ran adjacent to the waterway, and minutes later pulled up behind a small shopping complex plastered with billboards. Sarah tossed an arm at the intercoastal as if to explain. "We advertise a lot to the boaters."

Sarah led me up the steps of a two-story porch attached to a two-story dwelling. The first deck was furnished with an outdoor refrigerator, two painted rocking chairs and a brightly colored hammock rigged from the rafters. I fell in love with it instantly. Sarah unlocked the store with a simple turn style key. No bolt lock, no alarm. I had to comment.

"Break-ins don't happen around here. All we get is the occasional drunken sailor sleeping in the hammock."

"That's weird."

"They stumble down the strip, back from the pier, or veer the wrong way leaving Salty's, and spot the mermaid billboard. Every fisherman knows that mermaids represent a safe haven for the weary sea traveler. I'd come down to open the store in the morning and hear snoring. It would scare the crap out of me. No matter, Viola has a rule that we supply every guest, no matter how ragged, with a hammock, breakfast, and anything they want from this fridge, which reminds me that I probably need to get it stocked. What's funny is I've never seen the same person twice. In these parts, nobody abuses the Sea Queen."

"The store?"

"Technically, it's my grandmother. Everyone calls her Miss Viola but generally speaking she is the Sea Queen. My great grandmother died giving birth to her so Captain Marco, Viola's father, bundled her up and took her out to sea. They say it is bad luck to have a woman on board, but little Viola was a fisherman's daughter and that made her special. Even the crew could sense her magic…"

Viola spent endless days in the middle of the ocean listening to epic stories about pirates and sea monsters, legends of hundred-hour fish fights and hidden treasures. Beefy men with rotten teeth who sang the most agreeable lullabies rocked her to sleep under starry nights. Captain Marco taught her to read while other anglers lectured about history. Viola learned numbers and letters by using the deck as a chalkboard. By the age of seven, she could tie a proper knot, rig a sail, and read pretty much any kind of nautical map.

Every few weeks Captain Marco would port for provisions. Depending on the month, it could be St. Thomas or Key West, and sometimes Tippany Ridge. The Captain had been fishing for so long he had hundreds of friends up and down the eastern seaboard. Viola and her father were always welcome and would stay with a different family in each village. Strangers became mothers to the child. Mothers who loved her like a daughter, washing and mending her clothes, twisting and braiding her hair, teaching her local customs and the ways of a woman. Every night, as Viola nestled into bed with the biological children of the house, one of these many caregivers would tell a story. Oh, how Viola loved these adventures, especially when they involved mermaids!

For her fourteenth birthday, Viola's Key West mother presented her with a canvas, oil paints and an easel. Being an artist herself, she began teaching the young woman about mixing colors, textures and technique. Every visit thereafter, the two would paint side-by-side until the sun dipped behind the ocean.

At a very young age, Viola understood that she led an enchanted life. Instead of having no mother at all, which of course had been her initial fate, Viola was lucky enough to have twelve. Twelve separate women who loved and cherished her like a daughter. One day, just after her eighteenth birthday, Viola devised a way to thank these incredible ladies. Two years later she published 'The Mermaid Chronicles', a picture book filled with paintings and stories of each housemother's favorite mermaid.

Viola continued to fish with her father for many years. Although he loved their time together, the old captain was growing concerned. She had already reached her twenty-third birthday, which was considered over the hill in 1961, and yet no man could tickle Viola's fancy. The captain remained silent for he knew the ways of the ocean. No matter how it worked for the rest of the world, in the fishing community the woman always chose the man.

Right when Marco had given up on grandchildren and a son-in-law, something happened. And it went down right here on Tippany Ridge. After winning yet another tournament, Viola and the rest of the crew went into Salty's to celebrate. At the bar sat a very tall, handsome stranger, drunk as a skunk, chatting up the bartender and flirting with a flock of women at the same time.

Viola spotted him from a distance, marched straight over and asked for his hand. The band was playing Carolina Shag and the floor was mobbed with dancers swinging about in a fast rhythmic frenzy. As if hypnotized, Viola and the stranger strolled into the crowd, embraced, and rocked slowly in each other's arms.

His name was Andre Fox, a roguish Swede who loved his rum and adored his women. To the powerful Poseidon and the attending townspeople, Andre swore an oath to quit everything if Viola would take his hand in marriage. Of course she agreed and announced on that very spot that he didn't need to make such ridiculous promises. Captain Marco married the couple that very night on Salty's back deck.

Six months later, Viola walked onto her father's fishing boat *and for the first time in twenty-three years felt a tilt in the ocean. With a watery mouth and churning stomach, she rushed to the edge and promptly vomited over the side. Viola gasped. Impossible! How on earth could a fisherman's daughter be seasick?*

The doctor laughed when Viola spoke of her symptoms. With a tender hand, he softly patted her belly. "Dear child, you are not dying. You're pregnant!"

Andre ran out of the office screaming like a banshee. "WE'RE HAVING A BABY! MY BABY'S CARRYING MY BABY!"

For the first time in her sea-worthy career, Viola bowed out of the Tippany Ridge Fishing Tournament; a three-day event taking place twenty-five miles off the eastern seaboard. In want of a replacement partner, Captain Marco commissioned his new son-in-law.

Then something wicked happened. Twenty-four hours into the competition, the currents shifted. The weather reporters were clueless, droning on about eighty-five degrees and partly cloudy, but Viola knew better. She could feel it in the wind, taste a change in the salty breeze. Moreover, she wasn't alone. The whole town was on edge, everyone skittering about, continuously checking the coastline, praying for the fishermen's return before whatever was brewing tore loose.

The ocean engulfed the sky. Black clouds rolled in like waves, lightning flashed, and buckets of blinding rain poured from the stormy squall. Thankfully, anglers are born with common sense. As the great Atlantic gouged holes into the coastline, the ships began to port. Every boat made it back…

…except one.

"Since my grandmother refuses to talk about that fateful day, I got her best friend, Connie, to tell me the story one late night during a very similar storm." Sarah continued. "You meet her soon enough. She works part-time at the store. Anyway, Connie said the ocean took a piece of Viola's soul that day…and in return she received the gift of sight."

"What's that supposed to mean?"

Sarah shrugged. "I think it has to do with the

44

mermaids. She paints them, you know."

"Paints what?"

"Every so often someone shows up at the shop and claims to have spotted a girlyfish. It's really kind of wild. Some folks put on a heck of a show."

"Wait. Are we talking *real* mermaids?"

"Yep."

"That's ridiculous."

"Maybe, but how do you suppose legends originate? Every mermaid pictured in Viola's books, there are three editions by the way, are based on myths and personal accounts. You'd be surprised at how many girlyfish pop up on the North Carolina coastline alone. For every sighted mermaid, Viola creates a portrait."

"And she uses it for her children's books?"

"Most of the time. But not everyone gives permission."

"Permission to use her *own* painting?"

Sarah shrugged. "Viola's stubborn that way. The person who sights it, Viola claims that it's their mermaid. "

"Do they pay her to paint?"

"Do you really think my grandmother's strapped for cash? *Please.* She made a mint off the first storybook, and the next two...*forget about it.* They're in every library and kindergarten class across the country. She sells thousands of autographed copies to grammar school kids alone, who visit The Ridge on annual field trips. They all crowd around the reading circle and listen while Viola narrates the first set of legends. She lets them ask questions, anything they can conjure up. It's amazing to witness. They discuss pirate food, scurvy, and how mermaids wash their hair. Do girlyfish shed scales? How do they poop and does it entail toilet paper? I'm not kidding. As far as I know, Viola has never been stumped.

"And let's not forget about this store. It may look small but, trust me, does a whopping business. Besides, Viola would never take blood money."

"Blood money?"

"That's right." Sarah attempted a laugh but it sounded forced. Uneasy. "You *do know* what they say about mermaids?"

"No, actually, I don't."

"If you're sighted as a mermaid, well...then you're already dead."

***

"Careful not to bump anything." Sarah opened the door. "Wait here. Let me get the lights."

Even in the dark the shop looked cluttered. The aisles were narrow and dark looming shadows swallowed the walls. Sarah was complaining about the antique fuse box when she hit the lights.

I gasped. Literally. In awe.

Strings and strings of aquamarine bulbs flashed around the room, interlaced between paper lamps of various shapes and sizes. A large metallic disco ball hung center ceiling, reflecting rainbow prisms as it twisted in a slow spin. It felt like I was standing on the bottom of the ocean caught in a swirl of bubbles.

"Well?" Sarah asked. "What do you think?"

"It's awesome!"

"Last year, when Gran let me remodel the store, I changed all of the lighting. And, oh wait, wait! There's more..." Sarah plunged excitedly into the storage room as I found myself fingering through the shelves.

In what appeared to be the boys section were rows of reptile gear—glossy fish heads, crocodile puzzles, stuffed salamanders, and my favorite, an alligator backpack with a swinging tail. Big metal buckets painted with seashells crowded the aisles, some filled with shovels and water guns, others with fishing nets and crab traps.

I discovered a reading circle centrally located under the disco ball, the floor scattered with puzzles and books, Lego sets and plastic dinosaurs. "Gran does her book parties here, but more often it's used as a play station," Sarah added breathlessly as she hustled to my side, "so parents can shop."

The mermaid section was located at the very front of the store. Assorted diva dolls with shimmering tails, shell purses, sequined costumes, coral jewelry, key chains, magnets and rows of Viola's famous storybooks. Mesmerized by a bottle of swirly green *scale polish*, I stretched on my tippy toes and attempted to reach for it.

CRASH!

I yelped. *What the hell?* Rumbling followed and then a second booming crash. The sound was coming from wall speakers.

"It's beach music!" Sarah chimed. "We used to play straight rock-n-roll and reggae, you know, like Jimi Hendrix and Bob Marley, but that all changed one afternoon during a book reading. The sweetest kindergarten class was sitting innocently in the circle when the *Iron Loafers* boomed from the speakers. Have you ever heard the *Iron Loafers*? They're loud and cuss a lot. Everyone's a motherfucker — definitely not the best lyrical choice for the angels educating at South Central Christian.

"Gran had just started the story, but it was cut short, kind of like this... *Once upon an island there was a beautiful mermaid...pause...*AND A HAIRY MOTHER FUCKER...

"I howl every time it's mentioned. Gran apologized a hundred times over, the Christians got free books, and still she got stuck answering questions about *The Hairy Mother Fucker.* It's true! You can't make this shit up. We switched over to playing Yoga tapes after that, nature sounds like rainstorms, chirping birds, and my personal favorite — crashing waves."

"But the store is so close to the beach. Why not leave the doors open?"

"You can't hear the surf this far out unless it's high tide or dead of night. Besides, come June, air conditioning proves essential. As for Viola's music, we still play her rock-n-roll but not until sunset."

"I feel like I'm floating across the ocean floor."

"Cool right." Sarah yawned. "Let's hit it. I'm beat."

She led me up to the second floor, a two bedroom flat with a small kitchen/living room separated by a flashy checkered counter top and a couple of fuchsia painted bar stools. White wicker furniture with flamingo printed cushions dominated the living space. (Not totally comfortable but very cute.) In one corner, an easel, slightly tilted and splattered with paint, held a partially finished canvas of an octopus draped in jewels — Sarah's project no doubt. Star shaped lights, similar to those hanging in the store, lit up the room.

"I kind of over ordered on the lanterns." Sarah confessed.

The apartment floor was tiled completely white and strewn with brightly colored rope rugs, and the only wall without bedroom doors displayed a floor-to-ceiling entertainment center. Books and magazines filled the top half while the bottom shelves managed a very large old fashioned Boom Box and an extensive collection of CDs and tapes.

I picked up what looked like an enormous cassette and inspected it. "What is this?"

"That's ABBA."

"I know the group but what is *this*?"

"An eight-track."

"No shit? I've never seen one before."

"You think that's cool, check this out." Sarah opened up the console and in place of a television sat a very ancient record player. "I have stacks of vinyl," she gloated. "And hundreds of seventy-eights."

"Seventy-eights?"

"Little records. *Duh*! Where did you grow up, in a barn?"

"It was the nineties, *duh*, and the millennium, with CDs, MP3 players and, I don't know, *phones*. Old fashion to me is a *Walkman*."

The two bedrooms were practically identical. The

orange room, my new living space, was covered top to bottom with vintage rock posters— Zeppelin, KISS, Joplin, Lennon, Marley...

"This was Dad's room when he ran the store. Mom refused to let him bring the posters to Wilmington, said she had enough nightmares of the KISS boys with their painted faces and wild tongues."

I unclamped the window lock, pried it open and welcomed the most glorious breeze. I dropped back on the bed and found myself staring up at a Van Halen poster. "Eddie is kind of cute, you know, for an oldie."

Except for the excessive pink and poster content, Sarah's room wasn't much different.

"As you can see, I have a thing for pink."

"And Jim."

"You know it."

Jimmy Harrison was Sarah's Nirvana. Her dream guy, her on going quest and soon-to-be ex-husband, but I'm getting ahead of myself again. At the time, all I knew was that she met him at Larry's Place, five years before, at the ripe age of fifteen. He ordered a strawberry shake and when Sara passed it over, she got a shock from the static that was so intense she almost spilled the creamy mixture down the front of his shirt. Gallagher blamed it on the new slip-resistant floor mats, but Sarah knew better. When she learned that Jimmy was a Wilmington transplant, relocated to help run his father's boating business, Sarah marked him as her fisherman.

"Now all I have to do is ask him to dance, just like Gran did."

"Then what are you waiting for?"

"My parents said destiny would have to wait until my eighteenth birthday. For once, my grandmother agreed."

"But you're twenty!"

"Exactly right... and soon... very soon I'll find my courage!" Sarah announced triumphantly as we unpacked the suitcases.

The pink bedroom portrayed a perfect example of Sarah's devotion to Jimmy Harrison. She had posters, photographs, paper clippings, some framed and others autographed, all in mint condition, and all displaying a similar theme—they all showcased a famous musician named Jim. She had James Taylor, Jimi Hendrix, Jimmy Buffet, Jim Croce, James Rogowski, Jim Morrison, Rocket Jim, Jim Ciaglo, Jimmy Page, James Ellis…the list went on…

"Is this right?" Bewildered I pointed to a framed black and white photograph. "Is this Morrison's autograph?"

"It sure is. Gran's especially proud of that one. She met him at Salty's early in his career. He was just a kid touring the beach circuit with a couple of bands. Gran said he looked half-starved, purchased that photograph so he could get a bite to eat."

*

Eventually we went to bed. I climbed under the covers and snuggled into the pillow, exhausted. A hushing silence fell over the room and only then could hear the tide crashing in the distance.

"Night Maggie." Sarah's voice echoed in the darkness.

"Night."

"Goodnight Jim," we mumbled in unison and giggled ourselves to sleep.

Chapter 8 (College)

Sarah and I celebrated the majority of Memorial Day Weekend working at Larry's Place. I have to say it was *crazy* busy. She was running orders as usual, and I was still trying to master the fryolater.

"We don't use tickets in this restaurant." Sarah had explained that very first shift. "Each order is marked by a box." She held up a red and white paper boat. "You've got your onion rings, fries, clam rolls, chicken and whole bellies. They all get fried in one of these gazillion degree oil tubs. The first two vats are for cooking orders and the third is a blanching station, where you pre-cook fries so they don't take so long during a rush."

I held up a boat. "How is this supposed to mark an order?"

"When Gina yells *fry*, you place one on the counter. If she calls for a ring, it's flipped upside down. Put a hot dog bun in a box if it's a clam roll, bellies get a fork, and fried chicken gets a small container of coleslaw. Every box represents a different order."

"What if I miss something?"

"The counter girl, that's me, calls out *on deck* orders so if you're short, it gives you a chance to catch up."

"Sounds relatively simple."

"A few key points. Number one; try not to fall behind on pre-cooking the fries. It'll kill you during a rush. Two; don't overcook the clam strips or undercook the chicken. The strips take two minutes and the chicken takes seven. And let me just say it's a *long* seven minutes in front of a pissed off customer. Three. VERY important. Watch that wind. If you're not paying attention, the sea witch will sneak in and do her dance. Then it gets really fun."

The wind. Or should I say the fucking wind.

Don't get me wrong. I love a good breeze reading on the beach with my toes squished deep in the sand, or after a refreshing swim when it goose-pimples my flesh. But over the dunes, past the sticky tar road and ruddy gravel parking lot, standing in front of a hundred and fifty degree fryolater, the wind and I have more of a love-hate relationship.

By high noon on that particular Memorial Weekend Saturday, my face and arms were already slick with sweaty grease. My hair was balled up on top of my head like the rest of the crew. I tried wearing it down the first couple of shifts, well-defined curls pulled back with the cutest of clips. Sarah warned me as she twisted up her own locks. "You'll never make it, Maggie. It's too damn hot."

I didn't listen because, like I said before, my mother is a stylist. You just don't go to work with your hair a mess, especially on the first day. But after one hour of grease and heat (I'm talking holding-your-hand-over-a-broiler-scorching heat), I begged an elastic off a customer and joined the masses. Even make-up proved fruitless. My eye-liner leaked immediately. The amount of times I washed my face that first afternoon alone made the thought of re-caking foundation sound absolutely ridiculous. I sighed. So much for cute.

Sarah consoled me as I readied myself that second day, warning me against the eyeliner. "By two o'clock yesterday, you resembled a manic raccoon."

"A what?"

"A…never mind. Here. Wear these." She handed me a pair of big thick silver hoops. They were Sarah's signature earrings, the one accessory she never went without. I have to admit they made me feel sexy. For the rest of the summer, shoot, for the rest of my life, like Sarah Fox, I never went without a pair of big loopy hoops.

So there I was, Memorial Day Weekend, already fifteen boxes deep, beads of sweat crowding my upper lip, trying to concentrate on Gina's raspy cigarette voice as she shouted orders from the register.

"Storm's rolling in." I heard a customer say.

All heads turned to the sky as thick dark clouds shadowed the ninety-degree sun. A cool breeze swished into Larry's and kissed my scalded skin. I reached for a glass of water, turning away from the fryer for just an instant, when a second garrulous wind flushed against my back trailed by the trickling sound of rain drops.

Except it wasn't rain. It was the sound paper boxes make when they hit the floor.

I yelled over at Sarah who raced to my assistance. We both scrambled as Gina shouted for more orders.

"Hey darlin'," A voice dripping with amusement sang out from the food line.

Sarah perked up and responded in a similar tone. "Well, well, well... look what the cat dragged in."

"What's up, Sarah?"

"Hey, Jimmy..."

Could it be? My neck snapped as I craned to get a visual. Gina hollered for another order of rings but Sarah didn't notice. She had stopped dead in her tracks, and was leaning over the counter playfully whispering to some dude.

"NOW I'M SHORT A FRY *AND* A CLAM FRITTER!" Gina howled and I cringed when she said it, positive my fritters were nothing more than a bunch of overcooked shreds.

Slightly irritated that Sarah hadn't come to my rescue, I struggled to get my station in order and at the same time attempted a glimpse at Mr. Wonderful. The guy was tall, maybe six foot, with a slender yet muscular build. He wore sporty white frames with polarized lenses so I couldn't see his eyes, but his lips were full and sensual. He was totally smoking hot!

Sarah's back foot tilted slightly as they quietly conversed and giggled in the midst of the congested line. Was Sarah really *that* blind? A fool could see the boy was smitten.

Figures. Sarah's fisherman turned out to be my Mr. Perfect.

"TWO MORE FRIES, PLEASE!" Gina growled and the way she said *please* insinuated *asshole*. I rushed to the front with a clam fritter, fries and a ring.

Sarah stopped me on the way back, oblivious to Gina's rant, still in flirt mode. "Maggie! I want you to meet a friend of mine."

Friend. Yeah, right.

"This is John Kilian Walsh the *third*. His daddy is one of the silent partners Gallagher was telling you about. Technically, he's the boss."

"Oh, hush there girly-girl. I don't want your friend thinking I'm one of *those* types." Holding out a brawny hand, he grinned easily. "Call me J.K."

"Ladies! We're *working!*" Gallagher chortled from the grill.

"ICE CREAM MAN! What's doin?" J.K. hollered in a surly southern drawl, which prompted the short-order cook to casually flip him the bird.

Gina was on the verge of a nervous breakdown. It didn't help that she had a drinking problem. Alcohol continuously seeped from her pores and she smelled like a sweaty ash tray. "TWO CHICKEN DINNERS! TELL ME THEY'RE COOKING! BURGERS ARE GETTING COLD, LADIES!" *Ladies* insinuated *tramps*.

Still giddy from her boyfriend encounter, Sarah hustled over to help. "Did you see him? Oh my *God!* I thought I was going to *die* standing there. I wish my hair was down but you see how it is? Impossible to be cute in this grease trap."

I tossed a bag of frozen fries in the blancher. "I thought you were sweet on a guy named Jimmy?"

"I am! He's standing right next to J.K. with *Cherry*, the girl in the checkered shirt. Jimmy's been dating her for over a *year*. J.K. says they're always fighting but shoot, will they ever break up? Quick, bring these plates to Gina before she starts having chest pains. He's at the counter now. Oh, *why* didn't I wear lipstick!"

I strolled down the aisle causally searching the masses. I found Cherry first, sportin' a Dale Jr. baseball cap and mirrored sunglasses. A long silky strawberry-blond ponytail fell down her back, but her lips were shriveled up like dried raisins. She was tall and thin with milky white skin, not quite the complexion compatible for coastal living.

A stout little fellow, with freckled brawny arms and an enormous gut, stood to her left. He wore the same stretchy-fat-boy shorts my father donned when his active military life ended and he began "doing lunch" for a living. His shirt was too short for his bulging girth and although I loved his hair color, a deep reddish brown, it was cut less than stylish in a boxy mullet receding at the hairline. The only feature I found remotely attractive was his goatee and even that was lost when I realized he was sucking snuff and spitting juice into a disgusting see-thru plastic cup. If this was Jimmy Harrison, Sarah had a screw loose.

"RINGS! FRIES! CLAM FRICKEN, I MEAN FRITTERS!" Gina snarled in an escalating panic. I snapped out of it and rushed back to my station.

Sarah flashed hopeful eyes. "Did you see him?"

"I err...I'm not sure. Is he the red head with the goatee?"

"Isn't he *adorable?* I just want to squeeze him! And guess what? J.K. invited us out tonight on the casino boat. The best part, Cherry'll be working so I get Jimmy all to myself!"

"Cherry works on the casino boat?"

"Cherry *owns* the casino boat. Well, her daddy does. She doesn't know, you see..." Sarah flushed, "about my crush on Jimmy."

It sounded like a bitch move to me, but that's love for you.

"Can you do my hair?" Sarah begged. "You know with those curls and stuff? Oh, and the liquid liner for my eyes? I always mess it up! Maybe I'll wear my sequined t-shirt, unless you think it's too much?"

"Definitely not. Wear it. It brings out your tan. Shoot, we've been here, what? Two weeks and you already look like a Tropicana Super Model."

"Genetics, baby. You should wear my red shirt with the low collar."

I dumped together another order. "Don't you have to be twenty-one to go on a casino boat?"

"We'll be with Jimmy and J.K. so nobody's going to say shit. They go every weekend. I think J.K.'s got a bit of a gambling problem but that's just between us." Sarah chuckled. "He's been talking up my 21st birthday like it's already passed. Made up a huge fib how I puked in a potted plant at Denny's after a wild beer pong party. You know what else?" Sarah's eyes gleamed. "J.K. thinks you're cute."

***

The casino boat turned out to be a blast. J.K. flirted me up while Jimmy paraded Sarah around the craps table, where she played lucky charm and won him five hundred bucks. J.K. ran out of money in less than an hour and I refused to gamble at all until he egged me on to try the slots. With my first and only roll of quarters I hit for 200 bucks. We ventured into the bar to celebrate.

Sarah resurfaced a few hours later and the second she arrived I could feel J.K.'s energy physically shift. Sure he continued to flirt and maintain a certain charisma, but whether he was conscious of his actions or not, J.K. kept one eye on the prize. And that prize wasn't me.

One martini and three beers later, deep within my sloshy bubble, I watched the scene play out like a dysfunctional sitcom. There was me, Maggie Mack, the animated sloppy drunk, working J.K. like a seasoned stripper. J.K., the sweet talking rich kid, drooling off to one side as

Sarah slobbered over Jimmy like a hyperactive Labrador. And finally, we had Jimmy, Sarah's life-long quest, not paying attention at all, staring vacantly at a small television screen anchored high in the corner, whispering spit kisses into another disgusting plastic cup.

Love…what a freaking disaster…

Whatever the logistics, be it romance or convenience, for the better part of that summer the four of us rarely parted. Twice a week Jimmy disappeared into what J.K. referred to as *strawberry bliss*, but the other five nights he belonged to us. They would show up at Larry's just before closing with an offer for a late night boat trip or a golf cart ride to the beach. We'd build pit fires and tell stories. Jimmy'd be strumming his guitar as we roasted marshmallows and drank canned beer. Sometimes we'd break out flashlights and chase surf crabs, or spend hours camped out on South Pier discussing music and movies, waiting on the poles.

What started as a giggle frenzy, with Sarah and I forever batting our lashes, playfully flirting while pretending it meant nothing, eventually turned into a comfort zone. Our fake girly pitch laughter transformed into more of a belching comical moan as we continuously reinvented ourselves and discovered the real men behind the masks.

In a warm salty breeze, forever peppered with fry grease and seaweed, those silky summer nights slipped away. It seemed like I had just unpacked my things and it was already August with my mother phoning daily, haggling a departure date.

"Don't worry!" Sarah chortled. "Next summer we'll work like dogs and then, come mid-July, drive clear out to California! Oh, and I still need to take you blueberry picking. Shoot! We never got to do that. But there's time, Maggie! Lots and lots of time!"

But she was wrong about that. September, that very same year, Cherry and Jimmy dissolved their fragmented relationship and by Christmas, Sarah's dream of landing Mr.

Spit-chewin' Wonderful turned reality.

***

It is custom for all Tippany Ridge winter residents to congregate at Salty's for the Christmas Eve Misfit Dinner. What sounded like a depressing lonely affair was actually quite the opposite. (Fishermen, you see, understand the debilitating effects of unwanted solitude and remember the year, or years, that the Misfit Feast had been their own saving grace.) For whatever the reason, hunger or gratitude, a variety of good people, young and old, assembled on December 24th for music, food and holiday cheer.

A live band always played the Gala, ringing in the season with a mix of traditional country and holiday jazz, while locals sipped libations and caught up with old friends. The music eventually tripped into dance mode as the sweaty souls of Tippany Ridge got their groove on, gyrating and twisting to the sounds of, but not limited to, *ABBA, Motown, Barry White*, and *The Filipino Cowboy*.

On this specific Christmas Eve, the band was having a hard time rousting the crowd. At ten o'clock, J.K. waltzed across an empty dance floor and mumbled something to a frustrated lead singer, who nodded appreciatively and chortled into the microphone. "JIMMY! JIMMY HARRISION! YOU'RE WANTED ON STAGE!"

This seemed to peak the interest of the audience, a few people clapped, Big Mikey bird chirped and Sudsy started barking like a dog. Hoots of laughter and jeering followed as Jimmy surfaced from the darkest corner of the bar. He had chopped off his hair, everything but the goatee, and his freckled head made him appear pretty boy fresh. The crowd howled as he reached for the microphone. J.K., Sarah and her parents, Cherry, Viola, Lucky, Gina, Big Mikey, even Gallagher chanted. *Jimmy! Jimmy! Jimmy!* As if in a trance, they assembled in front of the stage. Jimmy did not disappoint. The audience went crazy as he belted out *Santa Claus Is Coming To Town* by Springsteen and followed it up with *Try A Little Tenderness*, Otis Redding style. By now the lead singer was dying to jump in, but the masses called for more, so Jimmy turned to the bass player and mumbled for one final chord.

The deep mystical vocals of Jim Morrison vibrated off the rickety walls as Jimmy Harrison sang an almost perfect rendition.

"*...You know that it would be untrue...*"

The women responded with shrill screams as they slapped at the stage, hamming it up like Jimmy really was a rock star and not just some runty fisherman with a sexy voice. Sarah stood frontline and center, shaking her head, laughing and squealing like a groupie.

Cherry, annoyed and a bit sloshed, needled her way up to the stage and squeezed in beside her, obviously put off by Sarah's behavior. She elbowed Sarah in the ribs and yelled, "BACK *OFF*, SWEETHEART!"

Sarah scowled and whipped around even more aggressively, flipping her hair as she knocked Cherry sideways with a swing of her hips. This bumping and pushing continued as Jimmy mesmerized the crowd.

At the end of the song, right before the roar of applause, Sarah cried out. "HEY, JIMMY!" She batted her lashes and blew him an exaggerated kiss. "MUUAWW!"

Cherry's eyes narrowed as she rammed Sarah, waving frantically at the man she'd been sleeping with for almost two years. But nobody noticed Cherry.

With eyes wide and mouths ajar, all movement ceased. The audience was shocked by Sarah's sudden display of affection. Folks of Tippany Ridge had been waiting a long time for this moment, wondering when the granddaughter of the Sea Queen would find her courage. A woman of fishing descent had to make the first move after all, and apparently screaming Jimmy's name and blowing him a kiss fit a perfect description.

Sarah didn't notice the paralyzed crowd, or a manic Cherry trying to pry off her shirt working the hooters for a cheap win. In one athletic swoop, Sarah jumped on stage and smoothed her fitted cashmere sweater. She had worn red for the occasion, a color that shouted *THAT'S RIGHT, BABY! I'M IN CHARGE NOW!* Sarah giggled as she took the microphone from Jimmy's hand and passed it over to the lead singer. Then, with a confidence unlike anything she'd ever felt before, Sarah gripped Jimmy's bald head with two hands and pulled him close for a very long and sensual kiss.

There was a pause and then, well, you can only imagine the cheering. Encore material like you've never heard. Jimmy wrapped his arms around Sarah's waist, planted his bald head just below her neckline and whispered, "Sarah Fox...what took you so long."

They danced right there, center stage, for the rest of the night. Even between sets as the party raged on they continued to sway in a circling seventh-grade style motion. Round and around they went, laughing, whispering, and smooching of course.

And that was it. Sarah Fox had chosen her fisherman.

Chapter 9 (College)

The following May, Jimmy surprised Sarah with two tickets to Europe. So instead of driving cross country with my best friend, I got a postcard from Italy (my birth place) and a promise for next year. By summer's end, Sarah was so far gone, so infatuated, she never mentioned any such future plans. Every spoken word, every conversation, we couldn't discuss tampons without Sarah redirecting to Jimmy. It was *Jimmy this* and *Jimmy that*, she even scheduled classes early in the week so she could be home by Thursday. If anything, she became more annoying after the winter holidays. The minute Sarah unpacked, I caught her blubbering into the phone like a puny shirt-clutching side kick, whimpering that four days away felt like eternity. *Give me a break!*

Sarah's grades began to suffer. She couldn't focus long enough to finish the simplest of projects. She was forever calling professors, making excuses, begging for extensions. As for painting, forget about it. Her easel got more use as a coat rack, piled high with scarves and hooded sweatshirts.

I returned from class one afternoon and found her sitting at the desk with her head down, crying like a second grader. The Filipino Cowboy blaring from the speakers.

"A flaming sunset and some sweet tea,
...on the porch just my baby and me..."

It was Jimmy and Sarah's favorite Cowboy tune, *Sweet Tea at Sunset*. Jimmy would sing it to her every weekend as they rocked on the sailor's hammock. Every time the song played on the radio, her eyes would light up. She'd run her mouth and tell me the story like I never heard it before. I used to think it was cute, the song, and even her lust for Jimmy. Not anymore. Now it seemed the relationship held her hostage.

"What happened?" I asked flatly, the first words we'd

spoken in days.

Sarah sat up, her eyes red and blotchy. "Cherry..." She whispered. "Jimmy and Cherry..."

I went rigid, angry at first, and then indescribably hopeful. I know that sounds selfish and pitiful, but Sarah and I had been inseparable. We had plans!

"He ran into her at Salty's and he... they..." Sarah shuddered and dropped her head back on the desk.

I put my arms around her and squeezed. Shit. "You do know that Cherry probably instigated it. Still bent about last Christmas, I suspect."

"He didn't even *try* to blame Cherry! The only reason he confessed was because half the town was in the bar." Sarah reached for a tissue and blew. "You know what this is? This is my fault. If I didn't go to this stupid school... He's lonely, Maggie. And I hate being so far away. I need to go home..." She heaved a great sigh. "...for good."

"He cheats on *you* and now you want to quit school? Are you *nuts*? You're not being rational, Sarah. Listen to yourself. It's time to get off the damn Jimmy train. See a movie, go to a party, get smashed for all I care but give that *relationship* a REST!"

Sarah didn't hear a word. "There's a community college just over the bridge. I could finish school, live with Jimmy and not worry about Cherry or...or any girl for that matter."

"STOP, Sarah. Just stop! Don't you get it? Real love doesn't have jealousy! This relationship is a fucking *lemon*! HE'S NO GOOD FOR YOU!"

"YOU'RE WRONG!" Sarah cried, suddenly defensive. "He LOVES me! Jimmy Harrison LOVES *ME*!" Sarah honked her nose and dabbed her nostrils like she was sniffing a rose. "I wasn't going to show you but..." She held out her left hand and flashed an enormous emerald cut diamond. "See? He wants to marry me!" Without thinking, she broke into a smile.

"HE *CHEATED* ON YOU!"

"A *MISTAKE*, Maggie." Her voice dropped to a murmur. "People make mistakes."

"Sarah... don't do it..." It was my turned to blubber. "I...I want you to be happy, really I do. But this relationship... it's too *much*."

"What do *you* know about relationships?" Sarah snapped. "All you know how to do is slut around and *fuck* people."

I froze...

...And then I thought about it. So what if I hooked up with a random dude here and there? So what if I hadn't found Mr. Wonderful. This was college, was it not? It wasn't like I slept with *everybody*, just the occasional cute guy. My mouth drew thin. If there was ever a moment to remind Sarah that Cherry had been first in line and she got what she deserved, now was that time. But I didn't say it. I left the room without another word.

For the next few weeks we avoided each other. I hated it, but our relationship had been deteriorating for months. Instead of being nice, trying to meet her for lunch, or just work things through, I bought the headphones and shut her out for good. (I was pretty pissed off about that slut remark.)

But I missed her! Oh, how I yearned for my sweet Sarah.

So we come back to that fateful February day, happy hour, when Drew begged me to get her on the line. I jumped to the wrong conclusion when he returned to the table in such an excitable state. Maybe Drew had talked some sense into her! Maybe she would come meet us. We could drink and flirt, hanging out with Drew was always good for the self-esteem; Sarah would be happy again.

But, as I've already explained, that's not how it went down. And I had a half empty dorm room to prove it.

Chapter 10 (Present Day)

I woke up with a hangover in an empty bed. Buddy didn't bother staying the night. *Prick.*

I met him at a gas station. (That should've been a red flag. Who picks up a dude at the Circle K?) I was ripping sugar packets into my coffee, trying to wake up for my newspaper scrub job. (I'd never been much of an early riser so coffee had become a crucial ingredient to my existence.) I built the same concoction every day, a large morning roast with four creamers and six sugars.

Like clockwork, Buddy and the rest of the Johnston County linemen marched into the store wearing loose jeans and form-fitting t-shirts, layered with fluorescent reflector vests. I zoned in on Buddy right away because he was my type — tall, muscular, and smoking hot. Sure he looked young, but what was the harm in fantasizing about a juvenile babe? For one thing, it made my coffee taste better. I'd flap my lashes and strut about the java station like a friggin' peacock. He'd wolf whistle and applaud my efforts.

I should've been offended, and yet the flirtation exhilarated me, especially when he'd yell, *Have a sparkling day Hot Newspaper Girl!* My reply, *Until we meet again, Road Dog!* He'd bark like a coon and I'd giggle off to work.

"Do you shoot pool?" He asked, one random morning, as I stood in line waiting to pay for my coffee.

I stuttered, taken aback by the off-handed invitation. "It's been awhile."

"Meet me at the Pavilion, Tuesday night. It'll be fun."

Of course I went. Ever since landing this rinky dink job ten miles outside of Dixon, I had limited friends. My father had been relocated again, this time to Tennessee, and Mom begged me to move. I could get a job in Nashville, she added, and meet some rich country western star. To tell the truth, any town sounded more enticing then where I was living but I needed to hunker down. Newspaper jobs were hard to come by and it was important that I hit the two year mark before making any drastic decisions. So far it had been twenty-one months of grunt work and biting back remarks. My inner soul was being sucked dry by tedious edits and a horribly exhausting director who did nothing but over promise and under deliver. Oh, how I hated being the peon.

The Pavilion proved a definite boost to the self-esteem. Being a newcomer had its advantages. Every dude in the place was checking me out as Buddy paraded me around like a custom-built Chevy. I was the hot newspaper girl latched on to the sexiest road dog in the bar. And Buddy was such a gentleman.

Those first few after hour encounters we acted like newlyweds, lounging on the rug with candles lit and sexy music coursing through the room. Sometimes we danced. I taught him the Cupid Shuffle and he returned the favor by demonstrating his favorite break-dance moves. I bought the Michael Jackson *Wii* game. We pushed back the furniture, smoked some Carolina bluegrass, then started *moon walking* and snapping our fingers like the inner city gang-bangers in *Beat It*. What a hoot!

Sarah was right about one thing—I was a bit of a tart. Summer vacation after high school I had sex for the first time with Ace, a boy from the neighborhood, who confessed that he just wanted to get his virginity out of the way. We did it that afternoon on a lumpy old couch in his basement while his mother shopped Harris Teeter with her triple coupons. Ace and I "practiced" a lot that summer. When he headed off to Syracuse I was sad to see him go.

After Ace, sex to me became old hat. Don't worry, I uses both condoms and birth control pills to guarantee I don't end up one of those tragic saps, stupid enough to believe empty promises coming from a dude with an erection. Not this slut. But on a handful of occasions, I have to admit, I got a little miffed when the relationship soured.

Sarah confided nonchalantly as she painted a shell necklace on a Marlin. "Hold off for a month, Maggie. Thirty days isn't forever. Guys like a challenge. "

Not long after Sarah quit school, off to her matrimonial demise, I tested the sex-free month theory. Nathan Tate was the first guy I tortured and in turn managed to keep him around for nineteen months. He moved north for educational purposes, off to one of those second-rate law schools with outrageous semester fees. Last I heard he was scrambling for jobs, pursuing bogus motor vehicle claims and life changing slip-and-falls at the local *Wal-Mart* to pay for it. Shawn Phillips came next (but not for thirty days, LOL), a twenty-five year old computer geek, born and raised in Raleigh, who could've been decent if he wasn't secretly lusting for his mother. Sixteen months in and I dumped him. The mommy thing just got too weird. I had a ridiculously long dry spell after that, forcing me to lower my standards and claim territory at the Circle K. That brings me to Buddy—the twenty-one year old road dog.

One month to the day, I ripped off his clothes on the way up the stairs to my apartment and we did it right there, on the kitchen floor, next to a bowl of sour milk I left out for my neighbor's cat, who, on occasion, stopped in for a visit. Now, here it was six weeks out, and Buddy avoided me like the plague. If we had sex at all it was in the front seat of his truck when he dropped me off from the Pavilion. He would shake his head when I begged him to stay, claiming he needed to catch a few winks before a six a.m. wake up call. *What twenty-one year old guy picks sleep over sex?* Shit.

Just last night we had an end-all screaming fight in front of the apartment. I told him go fuck himself, marched inside and cried myself to sleep. Imagine that? Over a kid! When the alarm went off, I smacked down the buzzer, picked up the phone and called in sick.

I needed a change.

I trudged to the bathroom, splashed water on my face and inspected my reflection. *It's this town, Maggie. Married people live in this town. Married fat people with runty children who go to ball games and the park, church on Sunday and bible study every Wednesday. Teetotalers, who work nine to five, eat dinner at six, schedule sex for Friday, and exist for sitcoms and season finales.* Lisa's words exactly, my last high school friend, who skipped town three months before, off to NYC in search of a real life.

My clothes reeked of cigarettes and stale booze so I stripped down, preparing to bathe. Gone was the freshman thirty I packed on in college. Out of sheer boredom I became a gym junkie, like Sarah, and spent numerous hours lifting and running my ass off. I was wearing a size 6 but maintained the self-esteem of a 14.

Pull back your shoulders. Straighten your spine. Remember, you're gorgeous! Sarah's voice called to me. Even in her chubby years, when her hair was wild and her arms flabby, she managed a positive attitude. I wondered suddenly where she had run off to.

Without thinking, I reached for the phone and dialed a number. It rang awhile but I didn't stop at the cordial six rings. I waited for twelve...fourteen...Viola never answered right away. If it was important, she said, they would wait for her to pick up...

Chapter 11 (College)

I met Viola Fox Memorial Monday. She was hosting a book signing for a women's club traveling in from Pender County. Sarah and I punched in early to tidy up the store after an extraordinarily busy weekend. This engagement proved to be the first in a succession of scheduled events. (Sarah wasn't kidding about every social network and second grade class, from Topsail to Myrtle Beach, booking an annual gathering.)

Viola Fox was famous around these parts for her dramatic story telling. Narrations so rich in detail, the audience gasped at the amazing, cowered over certain death, and cried out for True Love's kiss. Curious with anticipation, I willed the clock ahead and yet remained incredibly anxious about meeting Viola for the first time. What if she didn't like me?

Sarah ran out to buy napkins while I set up a beverage station with pitchers of sweet tea and hot coffee. I proceeded to straighten the shelves and refold pile after pile of rumpled t-shirts. The store had been open for less than a week, but with merchandise so unique, customers couldn't help but manhandle everything. I peered out the front window at a cluster of traffic congesting Main Street, bumper to bumper, waiting on the bridge. Summer had officially arrived.

Dusting a magazine rack, I stumbled upon a thin paperback that sparked my interest. It was one of those books you find in every town, a composite of old photographs mapping history of the area. I flipped through the pages and landed on a picture of the metal bridge during construction. There were several photos of Salty's including one before its enormous deck. A row of women waving from a pier. Three children buried in sand. Dozens of random nautical shots. There was a surfing section and a double-pager of Larry's Place with its forever twisting line. I paused, intrigued by a photograph of two anglers, arm in arm, posing next to a very large Tuna.

A bell jingled signifying customers and a group of tourists puttered through the door, laughing and sputtering, caught up in a flutter of conversation. I hollered out a greeting but remained captivated by the caption before me. It read: *The Good Captain and Andre Fox. 1961.*

I snagged a chair from the reading circle and had the book fanned on my lap, my gaze positioned ever so closely, sifting through details wondering if this was in fact Viola's late husband. This Fox was big and brawny, with bulging arms and a sharp jaw—pretty boy fresh next to the leathery captain. Even in black-and-white his skin looked translucent. I recalled he was of Norwegian descent.

"I remember dat fishing tournament. It was Foxy's first big win." I yelped, startled by a very deep penetrating voice.

Expecting a man, I was surprised to find two elderly women hovering over my shoulder. The first lady was New Jersey tan, creased and leathery, with silver hair cut like a page boy. Pink-studded cat glasses covered her eyes and matched perfectly with her fuchsia pantsuit and frosty smeared lipstick. The second woman was dark skinned dressed in a more formal African-style wrap that shimmered golden purple illuminating velvety eyes. Her braided hair was twisted up loosely in a high bun and jeweled bracelets decorated both arms.

The women laughed at my expense and Catty Glasses added, "Ooh, you're right! That was a great fish! And what a party!"

Catty's voice was squeaky and high-pitched so I assumed Miss Purple was the baritone. "Is this...this Mr. Andre, was it Viola Fox's late husband?"

Miss Purple nodded. "Yes it was. And dat dere is me fa'der." Her accent sounded Caribbean. I pointed at the photograph, confused. Even in black-and-white I was pretty certain the Good Captain was Caucasian.

"*This* guy?"

"Yes, dear." She sucked her teeth, clearly annoyed. "He married me mum, a fisherman's daughter from St. Thomas. And me mum's mum, whose fa'der was half West Indian and half West Palm Beach, had a Costa Rican mum and a Filipino papa. We are an ocean family, dear, as diverse as da sea."

Catty clucked and nudged her friend. "Don't let her fool you. Females in her family are *very* competitive. It's all about the biggest boat and the hottest fisherman."

"Oh, *hush* Connie. Dat is truly ugly. It wasn't like dat. True Love brought us together."

"True Love and a fishing trophy." Catty cackled and the two women tittered like schoolgirls.

I turned to the baritone. "Did you...did you ever meet Andre Fox?"

The woman in purple reached over and took the book out of my hands. She pulled it up to her weathered lips and softly kissed the photograph; her reaction beyond sentimental. "I should say so, child. Andre Fox was me husband."

Chapter 12 (Present Day)

On the twenty-second ring Viola picked up. There was a muffled *hello*, a rattling clang as the phone dropped, followed by a string of muttering curses. A holler...and then...

"Hello...good morning!" The voice, deep and ruminating, man-like. I suspected differently.

"Ms. Viola, is that you? It's me, Maggie Mack, Sarah's friend from college. It's been a few years."

"MAGGIE? IS DAT YOU, CHILD?"

Before I could respond she continued anxiously. "Have you heard from me granddaughter? Is dat why you're calling? Tell me you have news! Tell me you have spoken with me Sarah?"

"Uh...no ma'am."

An exhausted sigh.

"Jimmy called."

"Oooh...You know dey've split. He's so sad I can barely stand it. I found him you know, de ot'er night when I was changing da locks at de store, stone cold drunk on de back porch fiddling with his music. He was in such a state."

I almost forgot Jimmy played the guitar, my memory forever jaded by the disgusting wad of chew he harbored in the lower pocket of his right cheek. Jimmy hugged on to that spit cup like a desperate lover.

"Cops have been following him all over de island." Viola sucked at her teeth, aggravated. "Dey t'ink he has somet'ing to do widt Sarah's disappearance. It 'tis rumored she's run off widt a lover, but nobody can say for certain. Nonsense, I say. Sarah just needs a little time."

"Didn't Jimmy and Sarah break up?"

"Yes, but what does dat mean? Jimmy's been terribly

upset. When I found him mourning on de hammock, he wept like a child. Sarah found a new mon, he said. I told him dat his mind was playing tricks. Dat's how it is at de end of marriage. Confusing. Every mon seems a lover."

"Hmphf! We can only hope. Jimmy was nothing but a *control* freak. This is his fault. He drove Sarah away."

The old woman sighed. "Some t'ings, Maggie, are hard to understand."

I wanted to continue berating Mr. Wonderful but Viola changed the subject.

"I'm in a panic, dear child. Sarah has never been gone dis long. And now widt me trip coming up, I'm not sure what to do! How can I vacation widt her missing?"

Every year Viola returned to St. Thomas for Spring Carnival. She'd dress in rich traditional wraps, sing, dance, and reunite with old friends and culture. After the party, which lasted a full week, island hopping ensued. Viola scoured the Caribbean, seeking out local artists and craftsmen, in search of only the most extraordinary merchandise to buy for her Tippany Store.

Viola favored legend trinkets. Every mini-statue and piece of jewelry, every plastic doll and furry stuffed monkey, anything considered for purchase had to have a back story or differentiating selling point. Only the most original paraphernalia made the journey to North Carolina.

"...Take dis doll, for instance." Viola picked up a hand-crafted straw-filled baby with a head full of silver braids. "Dis doll was fabled to be adored by de t'ird tribal queen's daughter, a princess from the Znuga Village. She was kidnapped and t'rown from de cliffs by a neighboring War Lord attempting to stir up trouble. It was reported dat dis doll accompanied da young child as she tragically plummeted to her death.

"Hours later, da very same princess sauntered straight from de waves, her once brown curly tresses streaked silver, carrying de braided doll dat kept her safe in da crushing waters. De War Lord was so fearful of jumbies and water ghosts, he jumped off a very similar cliff never to return. De girl rushed back to her village, explained to her fa'der de mysterious tale, and just in time, for de tribe had already started preparation for mortal combat.

"A message of peace was sent to the newly designated King along with a similar doll gifted to his youngest daughter. From dat day forward de two tribes knew not'ing but peace and harmony for da better part of a hundred years.

"And dis bracelet," Viola continued, barely taking a breath. "If a wo-*mon* is torn with indecision, confused as to which lover will be her life long match, dis charm will deliver de righteous mon."

Viola held up a pair of big stoned turquoise earrings. "Deez earrings? Dey keep your breath minty at sea, a big hit with de lady pirates back in de day. Minty breath is very important."

I remember rolling my eyes at that one, and Viola patted me on the back. "People love a good story, dear."

"But is any of it true?" I inquired when the first of many parcels arrived from the Caribbean.

"Dat depends on who you ask."

"What do you mean?" (It was noticeably apparent that Viola liked to answer questions with more stories.)

"Two men run a race. A hundred bystanders are asked de same question. What brought success to de first mon? Based on their own perspectives and beliefs, dey all answer differently. Dat's kind of how legends are made."

When I didn't get the analogy she added, "To some, deez are earrings, to a fisherman's daughter dey are decorative tooth polish."

*

Viola's voice snapped me back to the present. "…Widt Sarah gone, I have nobody to watch de store. And, oh it's been horrible child. We've had break-ins. Houses, storefronts, even Larry's got hit. Poor Mr. Gallagher was found in a pool of blood, struck from behind. He walked in on a t'ief and paid dearly."

"*Ronnie?* Is he going to be okay?"

"Poor mon. Dey took him to Emergency. Done one of doze Dog Scans."

"You mean Cat Scan?"

The old woman clucked. "Stayed in de hospital a full week. Gina tells me he's on nerve pills."

"More the reason to go away! You should take your trip, Viola. You're not getting any..."

"Younger? Don't remind me."

"And you love Carnival!"

The old woman sighed. "Me art'ritis is paining so much, I t'ink dis may be da last year I can dance."

"So go! You know...maybe I could..."

"If only you, Miss Maggie...would come to de Ridge? You can stay in de apartment or me house if you'd like. Dat way I can be sure dat me store is in good hands."

My heart lifted as I screamed into the phone. "Viola, I'd LOVE to!"

"Well den," Viola's tone officially lighter. "I'm glad I picked up de phone! I will contact me St. Thomas friends and book a flight. I must hurry. Carnival starts in ten days. Don't worry, child. I will make it a short visit."

"Nonsense. Stay as long as you want."

"But what about de break-ins? Won't you be nervous?"

"My apartment complex has been robbed three times this past winter. I can't worry about that shit." I replied. "The way I see it, you're doing me the favor. I needed a reason to quit my job and now I have it. I can be on island in two weeks."

"Den I'll take my regular trip and be home by Memorial Day. You remember Lucky don't you?"

"Deputy Stacks? How could I forget?"

"Lucky made me load up on security. Everyt'ing is locked and rigged widt alarms. I t'ink he would pass out if he knew about me money box, so I kept dat part to me self."

I forgot about Viola's cigar box, an old humidor where she kept petty cash and bank deposits. It sat under a desk in the back room without a single lock. Sarah had been hounding her to get a safe for years. Apparently, that has yet to happen.

"What about the porch? The Sailor's Haven? Did you get rid of that too?"

"Of course not! De porch is always available for me lost boys. Does dat worry you, child?"

"Not in the least."

"Okay den. Call Lucky when you get to de bridge."

"Will do. And Viola?"

"Yes?"

"Have a good time."

Chapter 13 (College)

Deputy Sheriff Lucky Stacks made up twenty five percent of the Tippany Ridge police force. He was also Viola Fox's secret lover. At least that's what Sarah and J.K. suspected since the first grade. Sarah confided this information late in July, when we spotted Lucky's rusted Buick pulling out of Viola's driveway. I remember because it was a couple of nights after what Sarah referred to as the *Summer Sighting*.

It had been another blistering evening, one in a chain of five in a row. Viola, Sarah and I were attempting to cool down by sipping milkshakes purchased from Barry's Ice-Cream Parlor located right across Main Street. It was past seven so the beach music was tossed and AC/DC boomed in the background. Sarah sipped on a *Very-Barry* strawberry shake and Viola pruned over her creamy praline, both disgusted when I ordered good old fashioned vanilla.

"Vanilla?" Sarah frowned. That's so boring. It needs nuts or fruit..."

"Or chocolate fudge and caramel," Viola added.

I shook my head haughtily, "You do realize that out of all the flavors vanilla still ranks number one."

"That's baloney!" Sarah chimed.

"*Google* it if you don't believe me."

This was a common response that settled most of our disagreements. Sarah whipped out my laptop, a piece of technology she got awfully good at borrowing. Her search cut short when she was denied a connection. "But it's not even raining!"

The wind chimes twirled in a melodious frenzy as two women entered the store. Fatty and Skinny, I immediately named them, except Fatty wasn't short and Skinny wasn't tall. Fatty could've stepped in for the *Hulk*, pushing six feet with enormous flaps for arms and watermelon sized legs erupting from the bottom of her gem enhanced moo-moo. She had her hair teased in a bee-hive, a pound of facial make-up marking a ring around her wide features, sharp green eye shadow and two smudges of blush.

Skinny was small like a bird, maybe five feet, hair stringy and unshaped, wet and dangling about her pointy features. She wore no make up at all. Her lips creased and blanched from years of smoking, her eyes covered with big bug sunglasses even though it had been dark outside for over an hour. From her blotchy nose and swollen cheeks, it was obvious that she'd been crying.

Fatty hollered over in a sing song voice. "Ladies! Ms. Viola, good evening!"

"Good evening, Miss Faye." Viola returned the greeting. Later Sarah explained that Faye was a summer local residing ocean-side, three blocks north of her grandmother. Faye had married well, to a dentist named Clayton. They had a house in Chapel Hill. During the summer months, Faye stayed at the beach permanently and the dentist drove down for weekends. Faye hadn't always been big, she liked to repeat, but since the birth of her twin girls she was having a spell of a time losing the weight. If anything, Sarah reported, she had gotten bigger.

"Do you remember my cousin, Rita?" Faye said. "She hasn't been here for years. We used to frequent your store as children."

Viola's eyes narrowed as she searched the blotchy little face. "No sweet heart, I do not remember you. But I am very old. Sometimes dis happens. You are upset. What can I do to help?" Viola's voice was soft and soothing.

Bird Lady hugged herself and began to rock nervously. "I...I usually look better then this, tell her Faye. I used to wear make up and curl my hair and...dress; I have the nicest clothes. But since Minny went missing I can't seem to gather the energy to care much about anything."

Minny? For such an odd name, it sounded extremely familiar.

"Minny?" I spoke out loud before I realized. "Minny Justice?"

Sarah kicked me behind the counter. A warning. The small woman turned to me and nodded aggressively, tears welling up her eyes. "Yes. Yes, Minny Justice is my daughter."

For months on end you couldn't turn on a news channel in the state of North Carolina without hearing that name. So the story went, seventeen-year-old Minny Justice left home on a Friday night to sleep at a friend's house four blocks away. When she didn't return the following day, Rita telephoned to learn that no such plans ever existed. Police searched high and low, scouring a hundred miles in every direction, but the mission proved fruitless. Either Minny Justice had run away, or she'd been abducted. Gone. Without a trace.

Fatty Faye nudged her skinny cousin encouragingly, like a child. "Go ahead, Rita. Tell her! Miss Viola needs to *know*."

As if forgetting the circumstances of her visit, Rita stiffened and jerked out a nod. Faye passed a tissue to the feathery woman who blew her nose with a deafening *HONK*. She wiped her beak and before the tears had a chance to dry she began weeping again.

"My doctor prescribed me Valium, you see, to get through it, but all I was doing was sleeping. Crying and then sleeping. In my dreams I always see my baby, my little Minny. Sometimes she's really young, maybe five, riding the pink bicycle we bought her for Christmas. Another time she was dancing at a recital. Minny never took ballet but in the dream, I could practically touch her as she twirled about in a big purple tutu.

"What's really crazy is that we converse in the dreams, like we're sitting at the breakfast table and I ask her to pass the milk. Except in the dreams, we're flying over the house or standing in the clouds. She points down to the pool and says, *We need to clean that out, don't you think? It looks a bit mucky from up here.*

"The conversations feel so real but then a little part of my brain taps me on the shoulder and reminds me that it's just a dream. *I can't fly!* But it doesn't matter. Minny says something else and I reach out and touch her face, I can even smell her! Ooh, she smells so good, like cinnamon biscuits on a cold winter morning."

Rita sniffled and rubbed at her leaking nose but continued the story. "I would take the pills just to see her. In my dreams she was my baby girl and we were *together*! So close, so *alive!*"

The small woman paused and reached for her cousin's hand. "Faye came to visit two weeks ago. She immediately packed my bags and made me throw away the pills."

"I'm not much for doctoring," Faye remarked, "but poppin' sedatives and sleeping all day isn't what I call fixing a problem. I convinced her to come to the beach. We could walk together. Rita could get her wits back and who knows, maybe I'd drop a few pounds. Told her it was easier facing the rough stuff with a friend."

"I didn't want to come," Rita chewed at her bottom lip. "Sure, seeing the ocean and exercising sounded just fine, but…but the twins… Faye's little babes with their sweet pudgy faces and sassy sandals, they remind me so much of Minny. I was afraid I might be hateful. I didn't think I could manage."

"Rita forgets that for a southern bell I'm a tough old bird. When I set my mind to something that's how it's going to be. We walked one *whole* mile that very first morning!" Faye announced triumphantly.

"I have to say the fresh air is incredible and visiting with Faye a blessing. I haven't felt this good since…well, anyway."

The three of us stood frozen, our shakes perspiring in

the evening heat as we listened to the strange confession, confused as to where it was leading.

"I started taking two walks, one with Faye in the morning and a second late afternoon. Faye's not much of a night person."

The boisterous woman scoffed. "How much exercise can a gal manage in one day? Shoot! Yesterday morning she had me out there for a full *hour*. My legs are in knots! I want to lose weight and all but enough is enough. Besides, at some point I need to feed the twins and load 'em in the tub. It's amazing how dirty two five year old girls can get in a day."

Rita nudged her cousin lovingly. "So at sunset I go alone. I'm not sure that traipsing through sand for two hours is any better than napping for five but I think its helping and I'm sleeping better. I try not to think about Minny when I walk but it's impossible. I get into a rhythm and focus on the ocean or the sky; anything to free my mind. Sometimes it works, but eventually I come back to my baby and wonder what the hell *happened*? I mean, she was a happy kid! Did she really run away? I don't believe it for a second. But if it's not that…then it's *worse*!

"At times I get all tingly because I've hyperventilated without meaning to, so I've developed a few games to divert my attention. How many black shells can I find in five minutes? Count the surfers wearing red swim trunks. Trivial stuff, you know. Anything but… but *possibilities*."

Rita looked so weary and pitiful. Faye retrieved a chair and had her sit down. The woman accepted gratefully.

"Tonight I was counting blue houses and before I knew it I had covered a solid four miles. Practically to the tip of the Tipp I was! Tell me when I was sixteen that I'd be belting out four mile hikes in ninety degree weather at my age and I'd say you had a screw loose. Isn't that right, Faye?" Rita gulped out a frenzied query before halting suddenly. Faye touched a shoulder encouraging her to continue.

"With the sun setting to the west, pink and orange skies

against an ocean of blue made the water reflect gold. A golden yellow so bright that it blinded me! And yet, it was so beautiful I couldn't look away.

"I was moving at a brisk pace, my arms swinging ridiculously, hair wild, probably talking to myself. Ooh, what a sight!"

"And then?" Faye whispered.

Rita's lips trembled. "And then I saw it. Thousands of shimmering fish...and something else. *Huge*! I stopped dead in my tracks, watching it flip through the waves. I've never seen anything like it, a creature that magnificent swimming at such close range?

"I followed it best I could but it was quick. First it flashed hundred yards to my left and before I could adjust it popped up fifty feet to my right. I walked straight at it, into the ocean like a friggin' zombie...

"IT WAS *HER*! MY BABY!" Rita jumped up with newfound energy. "Shaken, I fell on my ass and got crushed by a wave. I coughed and sputtered, frantically wiping the salt and sand from my eyes, a squeezing pressure building in my chest. I tried to stand but got pummeled by a second wave. As I thrashed in the water, working to regain my footing, I figured I must be dreaming. You remember what I said about my dreams? They felt so real. So *flippin'* real I never wanted to wake up. I kept smacking at my face, tasting the salt, feeling the gritty cold of the great Atlantic.

"Finally, I got a hold of myself and turned back to the sea, so sure my eyes were deceiving me. But Minny was still there, head out of water, hair glistening wet against her young shoulders. She smiled and waved just like she used to when I picked her up at school." Rita's voice broke into a throaty whisper. "And then she said...*Hi Mom*."

I don't know when my eyes welled up. Shit, the whole room was weeping. Rita didn't notice. She was still on the beach.

"Minny dipped below the surface and I lunged after

her. Here was my baby! My Minny girl! MINNY!!! WHERE ARE YOU? I was screaming so LOUD, calling out to her like a crazy person.

"Eventually I came back to myself. What in the world was I doing knee deep in the surf? And in my new cross trainers no less? I must be mad! As I inspected my sneaker, plum certain I'd finally gone over the top, ready for the funny farm, Minny broke through the waves. My baby was GLOWING like a piece of GOLD! She shot straight up, about twenty feet in the air, arched her back and flipped into a dive.

"...SPLASH!

"The moment lasted less than a second but, like a photograph snapped in my memory, I can still see her. Minny...MY MINNY WAS A *MERMAID*!

Rita gazed off at the invisible image. "Do you know she was wearing a cape that I made for her when she was seven? Sure enough, she loved playing *Wonder Woman and Bat Girl* with her little neighborhood friend, Lynnie Lefebvre. She *begged* me for that cape. It cost five dollars for the material and ten minutes to sew. Why it took me twelve months to make it, I have no excuse. Shoot, if I had known a piece of material could create such happiness, now that I think about it, I should've sewn one in every color!

"Oh, but she was a glorious mermaid! Her jewelry matched her scales if that's even possible! The necklace was golden in color, twisting and swirly, covered with ruby red stones. It reflected off the water like a burst of sunshine. Absolutely stunning it was! And she had a bracelet to match. I've never seen anything so beautiful."

"So the jewelry was not your daughter's?" It was the first time Viola spoke and, truth be told, I was surprised by the inquiry.

"No, ma'am, but all I can say is that it was not from this world. Like god himself placed it around my child's neck." The room fell silent as we absorbed Rita's image. She plucked a tissue from Faye's meaty grip and blew another trumpeting *honk*! "What does it mean?"

I turned to Sarah remembering what she told me about mermaids. She threw me another warning glance as Viola embraced the small woman.

Rita repeated her question. "What...*tell* me!"

Viola hugged her tight and pinched her lips together, shaking her head. "It means your daughter has finally found peace."

Rita crumpled back into the chair, exhausted and tearful. As if on cue, James Taylor eased in through the surround sound with *Fire and Rain*—almost too appropriate.

Strange to think that only ten minutes before Faye and Rita were Fatty and Skinny, the brunt of my inner sarcasm. Maybe it was the song or bearing witness, I couldn't help it I began to sob. And I wasn't the only one. Sarah and I came around the counter gripped onto Cousin Faye and circled the tattered woman. The five of us rocked in a group, crying and hugging at the same time. We all understood what Viola meant by peace...

Minny Justice was dead.

Chapter 14 (College)

A few nights later, the incident was all but forgotten. J.K. and Jimmy dropped by Larry's just before closing time, announced that they were off to buy shrimp and beer, and would be camped at the end of South Pier come eleven thirty.

"We're going to eat shrimp?" I asked.

Jimmy glanced my way and spit, black juice spewing off in the grass. "Shrimp're for the fish."

I can't tell you the last time I went fishing, but I do remember it involved one slippery Bass and a lot of screaming. No matter. It wasn't about the sport for me. My intentions were purely physical. As long as I could flirt with John Kilian Walsh *The Third* I could pretend to appreciate anything. Sarah was just as anxious to rub on Jimmy so we were in a frenzy to finish our side-work and get to the pier. Sarah insisted on bringing her own pole so we first had to drive up to Viola's and retrieve fishing gear from the storage room. I scoffed when she asked if I wanted to use Viola's pole, and explained that it would be safer for everyone if I just sat back and supervised.

We took the golf cart or, as Sarah referred to it, the *mermaid mobile*. Long ago Viola made it road safe by installing seat belts and a speedometer. Speed limit on the Tipp was a standard twenty-five miles an hour and during the height of season, with traffic, you'd be lucky to hit ten. So technically, we could drive anywhere. Sarah floored the gas pedal and the golf cart jolted into action. She tossed an old Zeppelin tape into the cassette player (another one of her father's old systems) and we zipped down the road, music roaring from the speakers. *...I gotta woman stays drunk all the time...dere, nere...nere na nere nere...*

As we turned down Viola's street, Sarah hollered over

the tunes. "Check it out! Gran's getting her groove on."

She directed my attention to a beat-up Buick leaving the driveway. As it passed, I realized Deputy Stacks was in the driver's seat. He didn't see us in the glare of the lights and puttered on without a second glance.

"I heard Viola earlier on the phone inviting him over." Sarah winked and silenced the engine.

Viola's bright A-frame bungalow seemed puny next to the hulking structures built up around it. Sarah had once questioned her grandmother on why she never expanded. The old woman frowned. "Dis cottage is two t'ousand square feet. How much space do you t'ink an old lady needs?"

Being from a *Brat* family, we always lived in furnished government housing and moved so much that it was a waste of time to even consider renovations. If the new place didn't come with curtains, we went without. Dad didn't believe in such nonsense, arguing that food and clothes were far more important than wall covers. We had two family portraits that Mom propped up *wherever* and that was it for decorations. She'd point to the photographs and remind us that people, not possessions, made a house a home.

Maybe that's why I absolutely adored Viola's cottage. It stood on stilts above an open garage that connected to a small storage shed and outdoor shower. Oh, how I loved that shower! Sarah and I bathed in it every time we came off of the beach.

The stairs led up to a big wraparound porch and a single door that entered the kitchen. A rectangular wooden table swimming with exotic painted fish took center stage, surrounded by a clutter of mix-matched chairs. Above it hung a hand-crafted chandelier made of sea glass and crystal that absorbed and reflected the room's brilliant hues.

Nothing but a few beams divided the kitchen from the sitting area so you could visualize the eclectic furniture from the door. There was a soft yellow couch, a printed pink love seat, shelves of dark wood filled with nautical knick-knacks and photographs, and a narrow coffee table carved to resemble a mermaid. The walls were plastered with island art, a tribal painting of hunters cooking over a blazing fire, another of a ship plunging through a tropical storm with lightning flashing in the distance.

Similar to the apartment, the floors were tiled white and scattered with colorful rugs. A towering lighthouse lamp glowed in one corner. The windows were draped with sheer yellow spangled curtains and ceramic salamanders crawled up the walls. The room was nothing less than one big schizophrenic treasure.

Sarah pointed to an enormous half-moon window lit up on the top floor as we drove in. "The view from the studio is phenomenal. Viola's got a gymnasium sized mat up there where she *meditates.*" Sarah flinched her fingers to enunciate. "When I catch her she's usually snoring."

For the first time ever Viola wasn't sitting at the kitchen table as we entered. The main floor was empty and Sarah banged on the wall at the base of the stairs, calling out. "VIOLA? YOU UP THERE?" The bass kicked in and the ceiling shook. Viola had the music cranked. I could hear foot steps, something scraped across the floor, and then more harmonious bass. The Beastie Boys thudded through the ceiling...*NO...SLEEP...TIL BROOKLYN!*

Sarah moved to the fridge and fished out a couple of Diet Cokes. "VIOLA! I'M TAKING THE POLES!" She banged on the wall a second time, took a few steps, and then hesitated. Passing me one of the sodas she mumbled, suddenly tense. "We shouldn't have come here." Something about her tone paused my inspection of a narrow topical print decorating the hall. "We need to go, Maggie. NOW."

Then I heard it. A high pitched moaning sound like a siren, or...or a cat in heat. A death cry. A sense of foreboding crept up my spine. Alarmed, I followed the noise back to the stairs. "Oh my God, what *is* that? Is that *crying*?"

On impulse, I started to climb. Sarah stopped me.

"Don't."

"Don't what? VIOLA! ARE YOU *OKAY!?*" I screamed, but Sarah pinched a hand over my mouth.

"STOP!" She whispered in a loud hushed tone, like Viola could hear anything over the music.

"But...did you hear that *racket*? Sounds like dying cattle up there! Viola's hurt. Something's *wrong!*"

"No. no. no. We can't."

"What do you mean, *can't?*"

"We're not allowed in the studio. Not while she's painting."

I paused. "She's...Viola's *painting*? How can you tell?"

Sarah clamped onto my hand and dragged me outside, down to the shed where she retrieved the fishing gear. "Viola always paints after a sighting. I kind of forgot that. She moans a lot. The dead cow sound...that's her."

"You're *shitting* me? That...that guttural *hounding*? Are you *serious?*"

Sarah passed me the tackle box and grabbed a pole. "Probably should've left you in the golf cart. Viola gets weirdo scary when she picks up a brush.

"...The first time I heard her I was seven years old. Kind of the same shit happened, like with Rita and Faye, but that time it was a guy. He stumbled in from the beach in a state of shock. He was a sales man out of Massachusetts, I remember, in town for a conference...

The mermaid was his sister. Sue, or Slippery Sue, nicknamed during adolescence on account of her persuasive nature. He hadn't seen her since she went missing in college. She had taken a train down from the University of Maine, where she was finishing a Criminal Justice degree. (Surprise, surprise, she wanted to be a lawyer.) At the time, the brother was a junior studying at Boston University, his major undecided. They had dinner at an outdoor patio on Boylston Street and then, after hours of cocktails, things got a little wild.

They both got lucky in a basement bar on Newbury Street,

at a saloon called Daisy Buchanan's. The boy's last recollection (before jumping in a cab with a chick named Summer) was of big sister Sue, all grown up and sassy, swapping spit in the corner with some up-and-coming stockbroker named Ben. That was it...POOF!

"I was in the store with Gran when the man trembled through his narration. That same night Dad got nervous because Viola wouldn't answer her phone, not even on the thirtieth ring. We were living in the apartment at the time so Dad pretended he needed a specific album from his old music collection. We puttered over to Gran's in *The General Lee*."

"The who?"

"Dad's old golf cart. He named it after the roadster on *The Duke's of Hazzard*. It had the number and everything. Dad thought Beauregard Duke was the bomb."

"Who?"

"Bo, silly. Anyway, I remember Viola's music blasting. I could hear it from the street. It was that AC/DC song, Thunderstruck. You know...*THUNDER!* I followed Dad into the house and even through the torrential song I could hear that...that *sound*.

"What's going on, Dad?' I remember asking. My body was shaking so violently I could barely squeak out the words. He dropped on a knee and wrapped me in his arms. Then he tousled my hair and said, *'Grandma likes really loud music when she paints. Everything's fine.'* He never told me why she cried." Sarah flipped the ignition, "And I was too chicken shit to ask."

***

The following October, two months after my favorite summer with Sarah, a shallow grave was reportedly found in Pender County. Clothes ragged and torn over a body so decomposed and mutilated, it took experts several hours to identify the sex. The body was wrapped in what appeared to be a red and gold silk shroud. Already theorists were at work questioning the possibility of sacrifices and ritual killings.

I shivered when hearing the story. Before the forensics team acquired any genetic information, before every cult in the county had their fifteen minutes of fame, before they began interviewing students at the nearby college about suspected foul play, I knew two things for certain. One: It wasn't a shroud but a cape. And two: The unidentified corpse was no other than seventeen year old, Minny Justice.

Chapter 15 (Present Day)

Peace Train by Cat Stevens played on the radio as I maneuvered the North Carolina wilderness. I welcomed the fields of fresh-tilled soil and spiked cabbage, reminisced as I passed chicken coops, horse pastures, and a different church every five miles. My thoughts intermittently flashing images of fibrous Carolina snow, disappointed that cotton season was still months away. A spring breeze flipped at my hair, flicking it against my sunglasses. I wondered if Cat Stevens really was a spy. Possible, I guess. Anything was possible.

Like time hadn't slipped by in a frenzy of weekends and scheduled appointments, I found myself at that same country stop sign, mimicking Sarah, guesstimating my distance to the bridge. I turned onto the main strip, drove past the thicket of commercial stores, happy to see a new Dollar General squeezed in next to the Food Lion.

The mermaid sign stood faded and warped in front of a string of refurbished bait-n-tackle shops, followed by the enormous, not so new, casino billboard. Sure enough, parked right out front, under a very weathered *NC State* tailgating tent, with his feet propped on a cooler, lounged Shrimper Sam. *Medium-well cheese burger with mustard and onions, small fry and vanilla shake.*

"SHRIMP MAN!" I yelled from a crack in the window. He lifted a hand and offered a tepid wave.

As the metal bridge clicked into place, I rolled over the causeway as the yellow caution light switched over to green never once having to hit the brakes. Sarah would've been so proud.

The late afternoon sun dipped to the west as I drove a slow loop around the southern half of the island. The docks were busy with men hauling fish and hosing down decks.

Salty's parking lot was packed to the gills. The chef probably sizzling up the daily catch, while sailors saturated themselves on rum and beer telling and retelling sea adventures to the point of exhaustion.

I peeked in at the strip mall, home of Viola's store, and found the only place open for business was Pepperoni Charlie's. The pizza house delivered every night of the week except Tuesday. (Tuesday was bowling night and the whole staff played on *Team Charlie*. Island champs going on seven years.) A maintenance crew stood diligently painting the front of a new hair salon, *Prism's*, according to the sign, but otherwise the parking lot was deserted.

Larry's, on the other hand, had its shutters open and was bustling with business. Gallagher was working the grill with Gina behind the counter, her stubby hand holding up a ketchup bottle, mouth ajar and red in the face. I wondered if another fry girl was pissing her off.

I tried catching a glimpse of the ocean as I turned the corner but the dunes had been built up and newly planted beach grass obstructed my view. Continuing north, I passed ridiculously lavish houses and rusted-out trailers sprouting from different worlds and yet built for the same vacationing purpose. I followed the narrow road straight up to the Tipp and parked in the sand, taking the sky stairs two at a time, no longer the out-of-shape college girl I had once been. I flipped off my shoes and rushed to water's edge. The sky had turned an orange purple and the water shimmered silver-gray. I spread my arms wide embracing the wind as it whisked through my clothes, tickling my senses, whispering...*welcome back, Maggie...welcome home.*

I traipsed the beach for an hour, stretching my stiff legs, energized by the ocean's salty smell and rhythmic tides. Eventually, I turned back to the car. I needed to see Gallagher, maybe get a burger, and ask permission to park in Sarah's old spot. When I drove into Larry's my heart seized. Sarah's Volvo, not the first but the second, a twenty-first birthday gift from her parents, was parked in its usual spot. *Is Sarah here?* Flooded with panic, I hustled over to the car.

*

Sarah had contacted me a couple of months after the elopement. It was May again and she was helping Viola at the store. The conversation began tensely but after awhile we hit a comfort zone and chatted like old friends. She told me that Jimmy borrowed one of his father's mega yachts for their honeymoon. (Let me remind you that Jimmy's dad is pretty loaded. He owns the fishing business and part of a yachting company ported out of St. Thomas.)

"We flew down and got married on the beach, Maggie, just the two of us. We sailed around the islands, snorkeled, sought out the tiniest inlets with sand so white and water so clear, like one ginormous aquarium. At night we'd barbeque on the deck, Jimmy would play his guitar and together we'd watch the sun ripple into the Caribbean. It was so beautiful, Maggie! I just love him so much!"

Attempting optimism, I said, "I'm happy for you, Sarah, really."

"So…when do you think you can come down?"

Her inquiry surprised me. Sarah hadn't suggested visitation in two years. "I got my job back at the pool but most weekends I'm available."

"Ah, oh." Sarah's tone changed. "Okay, but not this weekend. Jimmy's taking me to Oak Island."

"How about next?"

"Any chance you can visit on Wednesday? Jimmy fishes now during the week. He'll be gone for three nights."

"They'll never let me take off Wednesday, Thursday *and* Friday. I can probably get out of Friday and leave Thursday night…I can stay until Monday."

"But Jimmy finishes Friday. I don't see him all week so, well…I don't want to bundle up the *whole* weekend with friends. What about the following Wednesday?"

I don't know why this irritated me so. Maybe Sarah did

want to spend time with me alone, just the two of us. But the way it translated...*Listen, I'm bored with Jimmy at sea. Why don't you come down and fill in for him?*

I almost hung up on her, but why bother? It wouldn't change anything. "Yeah, Sarah...we'll see. Hey, I gotta go."

That was our last real conversation. I never made it back to the island. After that phone call I was afraid any visit would turn into a drag-out cat fight. She wasn't my Sarah anymore. Her heart belonged to Jimmy Harrison.

*

Everything in the dusty Volvo reeked of Sarah. The stack of tapes and CDs jammed haphazardly under the dash, a strawberry peach scented Christmas tree hanging from the rearview mirror. Furry pink seat covers. Crushed Diet Coke cans. The jumble of dirty clothes piled in back. I ran a finger over the passenger window, my fingertip immediately blackened by gritty soot. Disturbed by my thoughts, I stumbled to the burger line. *How could Sarah leave the island without her car?*

"Well, well, well, if it isn't the fry queen..." The voice low and raspy from way too many rum and tonics, I turned to find Gina, mustard container at full tilt, squeezing out the number two on a couple of cheeseburgers. (Another way Larry's tracked orders without paper.)

Gina hadn't changed much, still ruddy and short with a protruding abdomen and chicken legs, knees buckling from extra leathery skin. Her short straight hair had been dyed a dark red and a strip of gray widened her part. As my mother would say, time for a touch up.

She grinned a crooked ornery smile and hollered back to the cook. "Hey, Gallagher! Look who it is. Sarah's old side kick! Maggie, right? Your hair looks cute like that."

I reached up and touched my locks. What started as a couple highlights in the front had progressed to a mop of streaked brilliance. It dropped just below my shoulders and carried a nice wave. For years I'd been keeping it in a bob, too short, my mother insisted, for having such a round face. I finally took her advice and let it grow. "Thanks Gina. Hey, Ronnie."

Gallagher's brow furrowed from delayed recognition. Not surprising. My hair wasn't balled up on the top of my head, my shirt was cute and fit, not grease stained and disheveled. He blanched slightly and then his cheeks flushed. It was the same flustered expression Buddy displayed when I sauntered into the Pavilion that first time, out of work clothes, wearing a strappy little dress and cute shoes. Funny to think Gallagher might find me attractive.

Ronnie, on the other hand, looked ridden hard and put up wet, and it had everything to do with the break-in. His hair had been shaved in a buzz cut and he wore his pocket bandana over the front of his head like a washer woman. A long jagged scar crisscrossed the back of his skull.

I pointed at the bulge in his breast pocket. "How's the smoking?" I grinned, keeping the conversation light.

The cook scoffed. "Five weeks of smooth sailing and then, well..." He repositioned his bandana stating the obvious. "I just re-quit yesterday." He flashed a pack of *Doublemint* from his pocket and said, "Back on the chew."

As Ronnie plated my burger he leaned over the counter, his tone serious. "We need to talk, Maggie."

"IS THIS ANOTHER ONE OF YOUR *SLUTS*?" A voice, whiney and tight, snarled in the distance. Everyone in line perked up wondering who was causing the ruckus. Personally, I wanted to check out the slut.

Gallagher tensed as the staff groaned in unison. I turned to Gina who heaved a great sigh and called for the next order. A white Mercedes squealed up to the side of the building, parking dangerously close. Through the passenger window I caught a glimpse of a woman; hair weaved in a tight French braid, lots of bracelets on her driving arm. Ronnie muttered something that sounded like *witch* and disappeared into the back.

"The bitch is here." Gina mumbled as she drew a number three on a roll with a ketchup squirter.

"Who's the bitch?"

"Not you. You're the slut." Gina cackled and tossed a thumb over her shoulder. "The Wicked Witch is the bitch."

"Who?"

"Gallagher's wife. They're getting divorced, thank God, but she's fighting for full custody. Between court and getting his skull cracked, the guy's a nervous wreck. Cassie is claiming that the island is too dangerous for her babes, like she gives two shits about anything but nail polish and getting her asshole waxed. She's got a nanny and doesn't even *work*. Who *does* that? Personally, I can't fucking stand her."

All fifteen people in line nodded in agreement. Nobody noticed or cared that Gina said the "F" word. They were all eavesdropping on Ronnie and the witch arguing in the back room.

It seemed like a good idea to change the subject. "Has J.K. been around?"

Gina rolled her eyes. "Who? Fancy pants? He's out on the boat with Jimmy."

"The gambling boat?"

"Fishing. He and Jimmy run charters for Mr. Harrison. They'll be gone a couple more days. But you're dead on about the casino boat. As I hear it J.K.'s been doing way too much gambling. Last night he took a big hit on the *Heat* game, lost another two grand to C.J. and Peko. (All fishermen have nicknames, by the way.) J.K.'s going to need a second job if his luck doesn't turn."

"When do you think they'll be back?"

"Check Salty's on Wednesday. He usually pops a few after an overnighter."

Forgetting my original intentions, I gathered my food and crunched through the gravel, down the back lot, past a clutter of golf carts and up to Viola's store. I climbed onto the Sailor's Haven, retrieved a can of Coke from the mini-fridge, and continued up to the second story. I sat at the patio table on a rusty metal chair that usually donned a cushion, and watched the sun drop completely behind the skyline. I didn't want to think about Sarah, her car, or Gallagher and the Wicked Witch. I sat in silence, the wind my music, and enjoyed the most delicious burger in the world.

Chapter 16 (Present Day continues…)

The next week was total chaos. Sheriff Lucky stopped by to open the store and bump the alarms. Then instructed me on which key turned what lock. He pointed out a small white button located underneath the register and said, "Silent alarm, Maggie. Just in case."

Lucky was kind of ancient for a cop, early sixties at best, and yet at least a decade younger than the Sea Queen. He had long silvery hair that he kept in a ponytail, a handlebar mustache, and a lean solid build. Figures. Viola would be dating a hippie cop.

Lucky explained that the store hadn't been opened since Labor Day, except recently to drop off the boxes Viola had shipped in from the Caribbean. "The woman must be in a frenzy," Lucky reported. "Called me a few nights ago to say she hit the jackpot in St. Bart's. Met a guy from Venezuela selling magic monkeys. They turn pink an hour before it rains and bright green when they sense danger." The hippie cop sighed. "How can a stuffed animal sense danger? Before I had a chance to ask, she started babbling about some kind of jelly bean that makes you feel sexy. Said she bought me a bag for Christmas." Lucky smiled. "I think they make this shit up just for her. Sucker for magic, that lady."

I purchased a large ice coffee and cheese danish at Kyle's Coffee Nook, a very narrow breakfast place new to the strip mall. Praying that Kyle was smoking hot and available, I sadly learned that the store was named after the owner's grandson. The real proprietor was Gigi, a fifty-some granola cruncher, with long braided hair and a horsey face. Three-year-old Kyle was cute in a peanut butter jelly sort of way, and resembled his father who disappointingly lived in Arkansas.

Wedging apart the double doors to let the room breathe after a long and lonely winter, I got busy preparing Viola's store for its *Annual Opening*. I started the morning overdressed in a sports bra, long-sleeved shirt and yoga pants, but two hours into it, drenched in sweat, I ripped off my shirt and changed into shorts. The day was relatively breezy so I propped open the back door and let physics create a windy funnel. As if in a trance, I selected Zeppelin II, a CD that I hadn't listened to from cover to cover since the last time I worked the store, and hit *play*.

I cleaned for three straight days. Seventy-two hours of mopping, scouring, dragging out shelves and sucking up dead roaches. After that, I stocked, dividing flip-flops and sandals into proper bins according to color and size. I lined rows of sun block and aloe, folded pink mermaid towels and hung dozens of skimpy two-piece bathing suits. Boxes of refrigerator magnets needed unpacking, designs ranging from flamingos to hoola girls, beer mugs and martini glasses, all marked with the *Tippany Ridge* insignia.

On Wednesday the monkeys arrived, fuzzy beige creatures with big googly eyes, small butts, long arms and sticky velcroed hands. Holding one up to the light, I inspected it for hues of pink and green questioning Viola's judgment. I was randomly hanging the stuffy beasts throughout the store when the soda guy showed up.

"Hydee Ho! How are ya', girly girl?" He shook my hand with practiced enthusiasm. "Name's Mike. Big Mikey 'round these parts. Swear I don't know where *that* came from. Believe it or not, back in the day they use to call me *Slim*."

Big Mikey was not what you'd call a chick magnet. Except for the tattered growth he kept sweeping to one side, the hair on his head had all but scattered, cropping up between his eyes and gnarling out of his over-sized nostrils. His shirt was slightly stained at the pits and his trousers were buckled far below his waistline, making room for his exceptional girth. Usually this kind of middle-aged guy with droopy drawers and thinning hair gave me the willies, but he was cheerful enough and nothing less than a chatter bug. I suspect it had something to do with being isolated for three days but conversation flowed easily.

"It's a barn burner out there."

"You ain't kidding. I'd love a beer right now."

"Good thinking, missy. Let's blow this clambake and hit Salty's for happy hour. What-da-ya-say?"

Completely off guard, I stuttered, silently cursing myself for opening *that* door. Taking care not to offend Viola's soda supplier I said, "As if! Way too much work 'round this place. Can't get fired my first week on the job. Shoot, I'll be lucky to finish by midnight." Returning my own practiced smile I added, "Maybe next time."

"Change your mind, Maggie, and you know where to find me!"

*

I was bagging the sexy jellies when the water guy showed up. Now this was my kind of dude. Tall, muscular, blues eyes and hair streaked blond from the sun. I found myself hanging out by the cooler, flirting, flipping my mane and babbling like an idiot. I could tell he was into me because it took him forty-five minutes to unload a single case of water. As I signed the receipt I turned to him with pouty lips. "When do you get off? We could meet at Salty's for happy hour. I'll buy you a beer."

Guys loved when you offered to pay. I gave my curls another aggressive flip and flashed a dazzling smile, my tactics smooth as silk.

The hottie flushed bright red and said, "Gosh..."

Gosh? What the fuck did gosh mean?

"Gosh...I wish I could. But don't you need an I. D. to get in that place?"

Appalled, I coughed out a weak giggle. "How old *are* you?"

"Nineteen."

"Well then...I uh, guess I'll catch you in a couple of years." Completely mortified, I marched into the storage room and shut the door. Oh my *God*! What was *wrong* with me? *Had I always been a cradle robber?*

*

Right after the incident with water boy, I called it quits for the day and locked up the building. Back in the apartment I cranked *Sugar Ray*, hit the shower, and relaxed on the patio while a salty breeze blow-dried my hair. I curled the frizzy top layer, slipped into some jeans, and pried on a cute baby-T advertizing *Larry's Place* in small pink crystals. (Ronnie finally took the advice of his female staff by adding shape and bling to the original boxy t-shirts. I purchased one immediately.)

Sucking in my non-existent gut, I splashed on bronzer and a touch of mascara, popped in a pair of hoops and marched out the door. In minutes I was stumbling through the gravel, peering in the side door at Larry's. "Is Gallagher around?"

A teenage girl with hair balled up in fryer fashion shook her head. "Nope. Just left."

"What about Gina?"

"She doesn't work Wednesdays. Try the docks."

I forgot that Gina balanced the books and ordered provisions for most of the local charter companies, the very reason she was always up on dock gossip. *Maybe I should check Salty's?* I needed to speak with Gallagher, hadn't I? *He's probably sitting at the bar right now!*

Pretending it had nothing to do with me dying to hit happy hour, I convinced myself that I was on some kind of mission, hopeful that I'd run into J.K. or Gallagher or *anyone* to drink with. Personally, I hated walking into pubs alone, but with my only other option being solitary confinement I hustled up the courage.

The deck was mobbed. Heads turned and conversation shifted as I squeezed through the crowded tables. Very few strangers show up at Salty's this time of year, so I guess that made me interesting. Surprised by the influx of familiar faces, I found myself internally reciting burger orders as I passed. That was weird. Not one person recognized me as Sarah's chubby side kick from years before.

The restaurant was dark and cool. It felt like the underbelly of a great ship. A massive fish tank divided the tables from a large monopoly-shaped bar already jam-packed with customers, pointing and cheering at a big flat-screen that hung from the ceiling. I kept close to the perimeter; walls cluttered with fish netting and boat paraphernalia, and ran smack into *The Fisherman's Wall of Fame*. Faded Kodaks and colored Polaroids, hundreds of photographs depicting a variety of people clumped together in groups, flashing smiles, holding up enormous fish and shiny trophies. Some kissing, others laughing, a few shooting the bird. Years of tradition all crammed together in one giant collage.

A single weather-beat female, strumming a guitar, stood on a rickety stage belting out a country western tune. Her bleached-out hair and freckled appearance was shoddy at best, but her voice was rough and lively, in a way cigarette angelic.

My search for even Gina proved fruitless. Besides the musician and the bartender, there were no other women in the room. I walked stiffly past the mob of men self-conscious of the fact that everyone was gawking at me. I decided to pee and hit the road, already perusing the idea of running the beach. There was no way I could sit here alone surrounded by a hundred horny strangers.

"Hydee ho, girly, girl!" A voice chortled from the crowd.

"Mikey, you know this little lady?"

"Wow! She's a cutey!"

"Hey darlin' come and have a drink with us!"

The big fat soda guy was flapping his gums in the midst of several very scrumptious dudes. He looked so happy to be the center of attention, I couldn't help but smile. Playing it cool I said, "This is your fault, Mikey. You put that beer in my head and that was it. I had to close up early."

"Good for you, girly! Maggie, right? These are my friends." We all shook hands and before I could say *boo*, I was planted on a barstool flirting with a dozen fishermen.

"Well, well, well...look what the cat dragged in!" Hollered yet another crusty voice as Gina came trotting through the side door on spindly legs.

"Gina girl!" Mikey chirped. "You know this little darlin'?"

"Keep it clean, boys. Maggie's our newest local. We don't want to scare her away." Gina gathered me up and paraded me around the bar, introducing me to anyone she knew (which happened to be everyone). We ended up back next to Mikey who was in the process of ordering an entourage of appetizers. He handed me a beer as I repositioned on the barstool.

"I've never had canned beer in a bar before," I stated

"Beer stays colder in cans." Mikey's friend replied. "We bring in a bucket of salt water every happy hour and Cindi dumps it in the cooler. Chill a canned beer in icy salt water and that's as cold as it gets without freezing the prize. Go on. Take a sip. You'll never taste a colder more delicious beverage. And that's coming from me."

"They don't call him Sudsy for nothing!" Gina explained.

A plate of oysters and clams arrived and Mikey took a turn lecturing on the proper way to eat raw shellfish. "First you crumble a saltine over the top and I'm not talking the *sodium-free* kind. What moron thought a sodium-free *saltine* was a good idea? Anyway, follow it up with a dollop of cocktail sauce..."

"*Dollop?*" Sudsy crooned.

"Yes, a *dollop*, you pain in my ass. A touch of lemon, one shake of Tabasco and..." Mikey opened wide and sucked in his masterpiece. "COME TO PAPA, BABY!"

Sudsy waved at the bartender. *"Houlihan!* Cindi, my sweet! Line us up for Red, will ya?!" He turned to me. "You want a woo-woo?"

I shook my head. "I know this is a dock bar and all, but I'm not much into eating fish with scales."

Sudsy pinched his lips together and turned to Mikey. They burst into tears. Even Gina doubled over, her blotchy face red and puffy as she bellowed out a raucous laugh.

Finally Mikey caught his breath. "He said *Woo-woo* not *Wa*-hoo. It's a shot, girly girl."

Cindi the bartender, a five foot eight beauty with silky brown hair and full lips, retrieved every shot glass she could muster and a couple extra highballs to cover the crowd. She whipped up a concoction, pink and frothy, and passed around the tumblers. With every patron clutching a drink, Sudsy held up his glass and in unison they all started shrieking… "WOO-HOO! BEAST MASTER! WOOO-HOOO! WOO-WOOOO!"

The room quieted long enough for Sudsy to holler out a toast. "TO RED! MAY HE BE FISHING ON THE GOLDEN SEAS OF PARADISE WITH A SWEET GAL IN ONE ARM AND A WOO-WOO IN THE OTHER!"

Gina winked at me and shouted. "TOWING A FORTY POUND WAHOO!"

Again, Sudsy and Mike busted into hysterics as the crowd funneled shots. Gina explained that Red was a deceased fisherman famous on the fishing circuit for his tournament wins and Howdy-Doody appearance.

"We were always picking on him for drinking chick shit and now look." Gina pointed at the empty shot glasses.

"Did he die at sea?"

"Nope. Had a great fishing day, went home to take a shower and keeled over in the tub."

Sudsy sighed. "Shit ain't right."

"A day makes no promises…" Mikey sang. "Treat it like your last."

"You snagged that quote from the bathroom wall."

"Shut the hell up, Sudsy!"

Gina chuckled. "These two are always arguing."

Sports Center hit the television screen and the conversation waned. The ex-sport-something-or-other News Guy gave a play-by-play report of the previous night's crushing. Miami apparently stomped Chicago in another semi-final game.

A leathery ancient smoking a cigar shouted from across the bar. "Where's J.K? Owes me two hundred big ones! Told him the Bulls couldn't beat the Heat, but once again the sorry bastard didn't listen."

"Oh, he *was* here." Sudsy yelled back. "Paid a bunch of us off but then I think he ran out of money. Dropped a grand on the bar and hauled ass. You're probably gonna have to wait until next pay day."

"What's J.K. gotten into?"

Gina slugged the end off her Miller Lite and waved it at the bartender. "Kid's gotta quit gambling like I said. I swear he works a hundred hours a week and then pisses it away paying off bets. J.K.'d be loaded if he stopped screwing with the bookie."

"That's one way to put it." Mikey guffawed.

"When he wins he's Mr. Bigshot. Comes in and buys a round, jeers the losers, drops the win in their face like he hasn't been down for the last ten games. And then he hits another bad streak." Gina gulped at her new beer. "Thank God for Jimmy. Lets him work extra time when he gets into trouble. But the kid's off his rocker. If it's not basketball it's football. Shit, baseball season opens today...pretty sure he's gonna try to beat them odds which is plain stupid. Nobody bets baseball. Nobody but J-fucking-K."

"I thought J.K. was at sea?"

"Well he's back," Mikey said. "Passed through 'bout ten minutes before you."

"Was Jimmy with him?"

"Nah. Jimmy's been AWOL ever since Sarah skipped

town."

Mikey started to say something but Gina kicked him under the bar flashing a warning. For all they knew I was still Sarah's best friend. I pretended not to notice and excused myself to the bathroom.

I washed my hands and re-glossed my lips, checking the time. Still early. J.K. was probably sitting at his house right now, and I could be there ripping off his clothes...

Determined to hunt down my destined lover, I marched out of the bathroom in a flutter of hand waves and departing gestures. I thanked Mikey for the invitation and offered money for the tab.

He pushed it away dramatically. "Don't disrespect me, girly girl."

"For Cindi, then." I dropped a twenty on the bar and added, "See you next week."

Chapter 17

Like a vampire, the sun blinded me as I exited the building. It was almost six-thirty but might as well have been lunch time, still bright and sunny, the temperature holding at a balmy eighty degrees. I stumbled through the grass down the back lot, my confidence disintegrating as I progressed. *What if J.K. doesn't remember me? What if he's already married? Or divorced?* I didn't think to ask. Really I knew nothing about the guy.

I marched straight to the fridge and chugged a bottle of water before pilfering the dresser in search of my newest purchase. It was a two piece bathing suit with a push up top and a little skirt bottom, caramel brown with pink polka dots. Finishing the ensemble with a golden beige coverlet, I moved into the bathroom and brushed my teeth pondering my next move. *Maybe I should just skip J.K. and go for a swim?* I stood there arguing with myself when I heard...was it music?

"A flaming sunset and some sweet tea,
...on the deck just my baby and me...
Stealing kisses ain't no greater thing,
...than sugar lovin' on the porch swing."

The soft sweet lyrics of *The Filipino Cowboy* drifted in through the window and I wondered if I'd forgotten to turn off the store speakers. I slid open the glass and moved onto the deck. There was a shift in the floor and I realized the sound was coming from the lower porch.

"Hello?" I called out.

The music stopped, followed by heavy clunking and jarring chords. Jimmy Harrison scrambled out from under the deck, eyes bright and hopeful, face bursting with joy. "Sarah?

Baby! You're back! I was so *worried*...I...I didn't know what to think!"

He reached the steps still babbling, jumping two at a time, but stopped short when he saw me. I had planned on being existentially rude to the man but he seemed so friggin' overjoyed all I could do was shrug. "Hey, Jimmy."

His eyes darkened. "Oh. Hey."

Jimmy's once bald head was now covered with long stringy hair twisted up in a gnarly tail. The bulging stomach had disappeared, his arms were more lean than muscular and yet, overall, he appeared malnourished to me. Too thin for Jimmy Harrison. The only resemblance of the man I remembered was the red goatee and even that was peppered gray.

When he realized I wasn't Sarah his shoulders sagged. He silently turned on a heel and stumbled away from the apartment, dragging his guitar like a wooden club. He looked so pathetic I almost felt sorry for him. *Almost.* And then I thought of Sarah and how he manipulated her life...never letting her stay at school for festival weekends, spoiling any and every event we tried to plan. *Ooh Maggie, this weekend's no good. I have to go with Jimmy to Wilmington. His mom wants me to help her pick out curtains and I totally promised to make Jimmy pancakes on Sunday...* Shit, even the excuses were pathetic.

"Yeah, Jimmy..." I muttered. "Keep walking."

*

The one good thing about running into Sarah's ex, it gave me courage to climb in the golf cart and seek out J.K. I puttered down and around the strip mall on a not-so-secret dirt path that ran adjacent to the waterway. J.K. lived a few blocks north of the metal bridge on the Intercoastal side of the island. The street was lined with townhouses, connected in consecutive sets of four, each unit painted a specific color. Yellow, lime, teal and cottage-blue....yellow, lime, teal, and cottage blue... Like a village of Caribbean Row Houses, they stood pointy and narrow on neatly trimmed patches of lawn with steep front steps and small, enclosed porches.

J.K. resided in the third cottage blue house on the left which was easy to spot because his mother was a garden junky. She had one of those little trestles covered in vines and flowers (something you'd pass under at a high school prom) showcased on the front walkway. It was laced with the most beautiful white Clematis that she said bloomed every year without much effort and, of course, an entourage of Purple Passions.

"My mother's a purple freak." J.K. explained. "She was pretty torn up when the Home Owner's Association decided against purple. Cottage-blue was the closest color she could get."

Parking was cramped on the narrow street so I rolled up next to the end unit, Mr. Walsh's instructions from back in the day, and flipped off the engine. Immediately I heard an argument erupting from the window. I recognized J.K.'s voice right away, but the girl...

"SCREW *OFF* J.K. I'M *OVER* IT." There was a slam as the front screen banged shut, foot steps on gravel and then the rev of a car engine.

I wanted to sneak a glimpse but felt an awful lot like a Peeping Tom. *Was this J.K.'s lover?* I smiled inwardly, taking advantage of the situation. My instincts told me to hit the back gate. I could pretend to have missed the battering altogether, play innocent and sweet, and have J.K. dusting the bitch in a matter of minutes.

The backyard was surrounded by a wooden privacy fence. I remember Mrs. Walsh talking about putting one up five years ago. Her lawn was nothing less than a botanical paradise, thick with nectar sweet plumage, weird shaped leafy shrubs, creeping vines, and loads of flowers. She even had a bird bath. Truthfully, you couldn't find a nicer patch of earth on Tippany Ridge. The neighbors, she complained, didn't share her love for foliage.

I followed the perimeter in search of an entrance. As I

neared the end of the enclosure, a rush of vicious growling sounds and jangling chains penetrated the silence. I screamed and stumbled on my ass, instinctively balling up in a fetal position protecting my face. The accosting continued but surprisingly nothing big and hairy latched onto my arm. I open one eye, and then the other, slowly relaxing my taut muscles.

I crept to the edge of the wood and was met by a set of beady-eyed Pit-bulls bearing sharp slobbering fangs through a battered chain-link fence. The neighboring yard was nothing less than a redneck disaster. Half-dead patchy yellow grass and heaps of fly-covered dog shit scattered the muddy ground. One scrawny tree held in place with spikes and kite string struggled to grow in the stifling heat, and a beat up dirt splattered dog house stood disheveled in one corner. I suddenly respected Mrs. Walsh's need for privacy.

Struggling to dislodge the latch, another barking marathon ensued. "Shut the hell up," I muttered and entered J.K.'s yard. I must say the transformation was absolutely spectacular. Roses bloomed everywhere; patches of Zinnias and budding Azaleas bushes, flower ripe vines and bell-shaped bulbs. Daisies, Daffodils, and perennials unnamed lined a winding stone path, with strings of white lights completing the ensemble. They even had a peach tree.

"A door banged open as the dogs continued their rant. "SHUT THE HAIR TRAPS, YOU MANGY MUTTS!"

"J.K.? Is that you?"

John Kilian yelped and crouched into attack position. "Who's there? WHO THE *HELL IS* OUT HERE?"

Surprised by his aggression, I was quickly reminded of his recent argument. "Uh, it's me." I emerged from the foliage.

"Cherry? You came back! I...I'm *sorry*. I didn't think it was that big of deal...I was just...OH MY *GOD!*" J.K.'s eyes went wide. "Lordy be-Jesus! Is that who I think it is? *Maggie?* Whatchoo doing back here, girl? Scared the heck out of me!"

"Thought I'd stop by and check out your mom's garden. Beautiful as ever, I see."

"*Shoot*...she shows up once a month to make sure I'm watering everything properly. What the heck...it's cheaper than paying for my own place especially 'round here. You like the Magnolias I'm putting in?" J.K. pointed to the far corner at a half-dug hole and two bucketed bushes waiting to be planted.

"Bought'em for Mother's Day...now I just need to gittem' in the ground before Mom's next visit. But enough about that. Let's get inside so we can shut those fuckers up." He hurled an irritated thumb at the neighbor's pets.

J.K. snatched a couple of beers from the fridge and we settled in at the kitchen table. "So what brings you to the Tipp, Maggie?"

"I'm working for Viola. Watching the store for the summer...seeing Sarah's gone and flown the coop."

"Oh, yeah... right. How'd you find out about that?"

"Jimmy. He contacted me all frantic and shit."

"Oh, did he now?" J.K. scoffed. "Couldn't wait to be rid of her and now he's upset cuz she's gone? Crazy business love is."

"Speaking of crazy, did you just call me Cherry? *Casino* Cherry, Jimmy's old flame? Are you *dating*?"

J.K. sighed. "I'm not sure what to label it. Convenience or ball and chain?"

I slapped at him playfully. "That's terrible John Kilian. You can't talk about your girlfriend like that."

"It's never been much of a relationship, Maggie, definitely not a healthy one." He leaned over and twirled a piece of my hair around his finger. "Forget about Cherry, let's talk about you! *Damn* you look good! Love the hair."

I smiled mischievously. "Wanna go for a ride?"

We jammed a six-pack in a travel cooler and I rode shotgun while J.K. made a beeline straight to the Tipp. For the better part of an hour we leisurely strolled the beach, flirting, searching for shark's teeth and catching up on lost time.

J.K. explained that he'd been working solely with Jimmy for approximately three years. Now a licensed captain he could run a fishing charter single handed, but for the overnighters it was usually the two of them. "Gotta sleep sometime, you know?"

Jimmy's fleet consisted of three regular-sized fishing boats and one upscale yacht. (He didn't actually say *regular*, but due to my limited nautical expertise boat categories for me ranged from *it's-so-freaking-puny-we're-gonna-die* to regular, to *holy-cow-that's-one sa-weeeet-vessel*.) The yacht, J.K. joked, was for rich people who pretended to fish but really just snapped a lot of pictures, drank too much, and wasted the experience texting friends bragging about stupid shit like the boat's killer air-conditioning.

"Jimmy won't let me take out *The Foxy Princess* alone." J.K. rolled his eyes when he said the name. "Besides, rich people like a *staff*."

"Why did you go full time with Jimmy? I thought you liked mixing it up?"

"I did. But when Sarah and Jimmy relocated to Wilmington he made me an offer too good to refuse. Now Jimmy's the big-wig pencil pushing administrator, a job he can keep, thank you very much, and I his worker-bee. He only fishes when *The Foxy* gets chartered or if one of us peons calls out sick."

"Why did they move to Wilmington? It makes no sense."

J.K. shrugged. "Nothing made sense with those two. One minute they'd be laughing having a good time, and five seconds later they'd be cussing up a storm. I swear Sarah could pick a fight *over* a fight. Jimmy hoped that a change of scenery might give the relationship a fresh start. At least that's how he explained it.

"When Cherry and I got together you'd think Sarah would've been relieved, but her anger only escalated. Said she no longer felt comfortable visiting her best friend. Still pissed, I suspect, about the incident at Salty's even though she stole Jimmy in the first place."

"That's ridiculous. Sarah didn't *steal* Jimmy!"

"Come *on*, Maggie! We both know that Sarah's been working Jimmy since the tenth grade. *Shoot*. She's been schmoozing him almost as long as I've been hustling her." Without warning, J.K. clenched his fists and hurled an empty container at the portable cooler. He stared at the can as if hypnotized, his tone measurably sullen. "Beer's out. Wanna to go for a ride?"

Unexpectedly miffed because J.K. actually admitted to what I've been suspecting for years, I wanted to *scream*! I checked myself, certain that a drastic response would abolish any chances of late night kissing. Instead, I twirled like a ballerina and searched the sky, attempting a demeanor that shouted easygoing and carefree. "You go. I'll wait here. Don't want to miss the sunset."

The serious moment passed and J.K. seemed to relax. Picking up the cooler, he added, "I need to make a quick call while I'm gone. Sure you want to stay?"

I pulled off my coverlet and winked. "It's too nice outside to wait by the phone while you slurp sweet nothings to *Cherry Girl*."

J.K. chuckled. "For the record, Boston's playing at Fenway tonight. Home game against the Brewers. A friggin' no brainer. I'd be a fool not to bet. Last chance. You coming or not?"

Already knee-deep in the surf, I shivered. "Meet you right here." I mustered a playful smile and splashed him with spray.

"Watch yourself, girl. Tide's coming in. The rip'll do a number on ya'. No deeper than your waist 'til I get back." He blew me a kiss and jogged to the golf cart.

I waited until the mermaid mobile was out of site before unlocking my syrupy expression and trudging moodily out of the water. I couldn't help but marvel at the golden sunset, how it flickered on the waves, and yet my mind was twisted in conflict. I caught sight of a buoy about fifty yards out, big and red, bobbing in the distance. It was the very same one I pointed out to Sarah that first summer. *Come on Fox…I'll race you! Dangerous? Oh, don't be silly…it's the ocean! I can swim two hundred yards in ninety seconds flat. We'll be back before you know it.*

Sarah had stopped me then with similar warnings about the riptide. Tonight I leered at the buoy, my mind forming an equally disgusted response. *It's not my fault that half the country can't swim a full lap in a wading pool. But I can. I can swim twenty!*

And J.K…I *knew* it! He was in love Sarah. *Prick.* Sarah had Jimmy *and* J.K. And here I stood drunk on a beach, waiting for her scraps like some kind of horn dog, while she philandered across the countryside with guy number three. *What a bitch.*

Without thinking, I sprinted at the sea.

Lifting my knees high to get past the bubbling surf, I dove into an oncoming wave, the cold rush jarring me awake. I shivered from pure exhilaration and…*man, is it chilly!* I tried not to think about it and set my sights on the buoy. My legs taut, strokes smooth, I shifted into race mode…*Mouth in and breathe…mouth in and breathe…mouth in and breathe.* Minutes later I reached my destination, slightly winded and yet not too tired to cry out, "Yeah baby!" I rolled onto my back and floated taking time to slow my respirations. I laughed as I stared up at the clouds, now a golden purple as the last blast of sunlight dipped over the sky line.

I calculated time as I floated. Maybe one minute. Sixty seconds of long silky strokes and…*damn am I out of breath!* It had to be age. What a horrifying thought! Could it be possible that twenty-five was the beginning of the end? *Oh, don't be so dramatic, Maggie! It's the beer. Swim it when you're sober.*

I transitioned into a treading position and was surprised to find that I had already drifted twenty feet from the buoy. I tumbled swiftly in an underwater summersault like I always did at the end of a race and moved into a simple side stroke. My breathing picked up and it suddenly occurred to me why my trip to the buoy had proved virtually effortless.

The current had been an ally.

It reminded me of my first kayaking experience with Sarah. We thought we were all bad ass and skillful, pumping in unison with the sun at our backs, taking on the intercoastal like Olympians. We were flying! After thirty minutes of smooth sailing we stopped in a random alcove, snacked on carrot sticks and bottled water, swam, and discussed future boating excursions. What a great way to exercise! By the time we repositioned the oars, preparing for the return trip, we were both awfully proud of ourselves. Kayaking turned out to be fun and easy, a sure way to lose flab and sculpt the triceps!

And then we kayaked home. Two words. Not pretty. Sarah and I learned a valuable lesson that day. Always begin water excursions against the current so the ride home doesn't kill you. Our thirty minute county-club float downstream transformed into two hours of grueling torture. By the time we reached our destination, both of us were irritable, shaky and absolutely famished. Sarah phoned the pizza guy on our way home, ordered an extra-large everything that we rifled down in ten minutes flat, not completely satisfied until the whole pie was gone. (So much for carrot sticks.)

My stomach bubbled with discontent. *The buoy swim had been way too easy...* At least I was only a fifty yards from shore. I pushed lurking images out of my mind and returned to race mode. Kicking hard, I pumped my arms and got into an oxygen rhythm. *Mouth in and breathe... mouth in and breathe... I can swim two hundred yards in ninety seconds flat...what's a mere fifty?*

I could feel it then, the power of the ocean. Like a gentle belly massage rubbing sideways, tugging back and forth like two toddlers fighting over a cookie. Dizzy from exertion, I flipped onto my back and tried to calm down. My hands were tingling and I knew it was from loss of carbon dioxide. I was breathing way too fast. Catching a glimpse of the coastline, now silhouette black, I was startled by movement in my periphery. I yelped thinking solely of Jaws and his monstrous teeth. Using the moon as my flashlight, I attempted a peek. *What the hell is that?*

...Oh my God.

Not twenty feet to my left was the buoy, the very same friggin' red bobber that lured me in. My efforts had not bettered my situation one bit. Even more terrifying was the fact that I had started on one side of the buoy and now treaded water twenty feet in the opposite direction. The rip was taking me north. *Shit.*

I got scared and dove under. With renewed determination I surfaced and set my sights on the next wave. I let the current suck me in and on its release pumped with all my might, using the ocean's force to drive me closer to shore. I rested between waves and continued the cycle again and again. The resting and pumping went on for so long my strides became sloppy from exhaustion. Desperately I searched the shoreline hoping to see headlights from the golf cart. Nothing. My heart dimmed as I visualized J.K. pacing his living room, ear stuck to the phone, spewing Red Sox statistics, rebutting his distorted rationale why the Brewers were going to take a beating.

I imagined Cherry waiting patiently on the couch, wearing a cute little skirt and strappy sandals, all dolled up for what was supposed to be a very hot and romantic evening, only to have it sucked dry by another seventh inning stretch. *How many times am I going to do this?* J.K. kisses her softly on the lips and offers a glass of wine. *Just a few minutes, babe...and then we'll go.* An hour later the wine is empty, Cherry's slumped over inspecting her toenail polish, and J.K.'s just warming up. Now he's talking three-shot madness and why the Lakers should've never let *The Shaq* go. The second game ends and Cherry stands. *Finally.* He rubs her arm effortlessly and says, "*A few more minutes, doll. Gotta catch the replays.*"

In the middle of the ocean, I envision myself planted in J.K.'s living room. But it's not me, it's Cherry. Cherry fed up. Cherry disgusted. Cherry inevitably concluding that she just can't fix this. I hear my voice coming out of Cherry's mouth as she slams the front door. "SCREW *OFF*, J.K. I'M *OVER* IT!"

My arms feel like lead as I transition into float mode. I'm gasping. I peer up at the now darkened sky, a blanket of stars and a flashlight moon. *Man, am I beat...*

A wave crashes over me and before I can manage I spiral downward. Down, down...so far down! How deep can it possibly be fifty yards from the coastline? Like the sea itself has its own agenda, it sucks at my ankles and flips me about like a rag doll. I struggle to resurface just as the second crash hits. This one rams me back under. Again, I've lost control and go thrashing off into the abyss.

Miraculously, my feet touch gravel. The rough sand shreds my knees as I climb up on all fours. A sand bar! *Yeah baby!* I cough and gag, desperate for oxygen! *Breathing feels fucking fantastic!* I sit on my knees and check the coastline. Dumbstruck, I can't see anything. *Am I even searching in the right direction?* Clouds look like sand and sand looks like clouds.

Confused, I stand on my tiny strip of salvation and try to figure out which way to swim. I squint and step forward forgetting myself... A wave crashes at the same time and I'm off again, struggling, flailing for a piece of rock or sand or any goddamned thing.

My body turns to Jell-O. I'm numb. Euphoria takes hold as the next crash pummels me deeper into the sea. A fuzzy sensation tickles my underbelly and I want to giggle. Maybe I'm not that excited to get to shore. Maybe I should just sit here under the ocean and relax for a bit. Shoot, I could take a nap!

Girl...what have you done? I told you swimming's not safe at the Tipp. Now look at you?

I try to speak but no oxygen makes it tricky.

Keep your mouth shut under water, lifeguard lesson number one.

I feel arms wrap around me. Strong arms. They pick me up like I'm nothing more than a minnow. You know in dreams when you want to run but can't? And speaking is useless? Telepathy always works so I give it a try. I do the mind speak and say my peace forgetting that it's bad form to berate a friend when they're saving your life. As I'm pushed onto shore I hear the response.

Yeah...I'm sorry too."

***

"Look Mommy! A mermaid! But she's...she's all sandy and...and *dirty*. I thought mermaids were pink and shiny with pretty hair. This one looks...dead."

A shriek. "Oh my *GOD*! Josie...quick honey...help me roll her over. PEGGY! PEGGY! HELLLPPP! IT'S A *WOMAN*!"

In the distance a second person responds but her voice is lost in the wind. "IS SHE B R e a t h i n g?"

"I CAN'T TELL!" The woman turns back to the body and slaps it. "Wake up! Breathe, damn it! PEEGGGGY!"

"No, NO, NO! LOOK, LISTEN AND *FEEL*. LOOK FOR CHEST RISE, LISTEN FOR AIR AND FEEL FOR BREATHING WITH YOUR EAR CLOSE TO HER LIPS!" The second woman is running. She's much closer now.

"But she's all sandy! Eww! Wait...I FEEL SOMETHING! YES! SHOULD I PUMP ON HER CHEST?"

"NO! Check for a pulse. YOU'LL JUST BREAK RIBS IF SHE'S ALREADY GOT A PULSE!"

"WELL, I DON'T *KNOW*! I'M NOT A NURSE!"

"Aunt Peggy, is...is the mermaid dead?"

The second woman dropped down next to the body. "No baby. See? Feel in her neck. Right here. She's got a pulse *and* she's breathing..."

"Then what's WRONG with her?"

"Smells like one too many beers to me. Maybe she fell asleep."

"We should call 911. Where's your phone?"

"At the mother ship."

"We'll need to move her."

"POWER RANGERS! Get the wagon! We need to take the mermaid to base camp."

"You get one leg, I'll get the other. Yes, like that. Secure the head. Black and Blue Ranger, let's get a move on. LIFT! Silver Ranger, enough with the marshmallows...no slacking! We need to *hustle*. Look! ...*HEADLIGHTS*! HEY! HEY! OVER HERE!"

***

I woke up staring at a ceiling poster of Van Halen. *Helloooo Eddie. Oh, how I've missed you!* Dazed from sleep and beer toxins, my head pounded and the blazing pink walls didn't help. I quickly realized that I made it home in one piece but fell asleep in the wrong bedroom. Hendrix and Page tossing heavy lidded gazes from their designated posters confirmed my theory, while Mr. Morrison rolled around in nothing but leather pants gripping at his barely hairy chest. I peered up at Eddie? *What the hell? Who put Eddie in the Jim room?*

Dropping my legs over the side, I struggled into a sitting position. Straining to patch together any recent activity, I inspected my clothes—a *Hot Chelle Rae* t-shirt and boxer shorts—normal sleep attire. Hair matted and grimy; my tongue felt like sandpaper and stuck to the roof of my mouth.

I padded to the kitchen in search of fluids. One Diet Coke stood alone in the fridge. I cracked it open and slugged it down. Suddenly gassy, I let out a rumbling burp.

"That's attractive."

My knees buckled and I yelped. "*JESUS!*"

J.K. stood in the doorway of my regular bedroom. In wrinkled duds from the night before, he swiped a hand through his silky hair. "How you feeling, girl? Gave us all quite a scare."

"What happened?"

"You fell asleep on the beach and the surf rolled in. How much did you actually drink at happy hour? Gonna have to rip Big Mikey a new asshole for that one."

Oh shit...the beach. The buoy. I cringed. "Sorry."

"No worries. But listen, I gotta hit it. Jimmy wants me down at the docks by nine. Got a big trip tomorrow on *The Foxy* and there's lots of preparation. Plus I need to collect." J.K. grinned. "Sox smoked the Brewers last night. Time to brag, baby!"

He leaned over the counter and kissed me on the cheek. "I'll give you a holler when I get back."

Chapter 18

I put the night at the Tipp behind me and got back to work. Viola arrived on schedule the Tuesday after Memorial Day. She swept into the store like her sea goddess self, all jazzed up in a two piece taffeta number, hair beaded and spangled pink and gold to match the outfit. Her skin shimmered bronze and her almost purple eyes lit up like firecrackers. Viola had always complained about horrible arthritis but now I could see it was taking a toll. She moved slower than before, a deliberate hitch in her gait as she pushed off with a cane. (Not just any cane, one bejeweled in studded leopard print fabric.)

"Maggie Mack!" She cried as wind chimes announced her arrival.

I hurried from the counter and met her half-way. She pulled me into a hug, a sturdy grip for a woman pushing eighty, and inspected my face. Her eyes watered. "Oh how I've *missed* you, sweetheart."

She sat down in the reading circle in her designated mermaid chair, painted and designed by teenager Sarah, and instructed me to do the same. "Take a squat, dear. Let's visit."

I raced out to the Sailor's fridge and filled two glasses with chopped ice and freshly made sweet tea. On my return Viola jumped immediately into conversation, rambling about old friends, travel delays and of course newly purchased merchandise.

"That's a cute necklace!"

Viola fingered the beaded piece around her neck. "Got dis beauty from a Pigmy working a craft show in Martinique. It's made of dyed beans and root berries, glazed in a special mixture dat keeps mosquitoes at bay. An easy summer sale, believe you me. I was getting chewed alive in de rainforest but as soon as I put dis jewel 'round me neck de jungle transformed into a bug-free paradise, which is a down right miracle dat close to de equator." She unlatched the necklace and handed it over for inspection.

I studied the bean and root menagerie amazed by the intricate detail. "You could make a mint on these if they really work. How much do they sell for?"

"Hey, Ma! Mom! *Look!* It's the Mermaid Lady."

While we sat catching up, a group of patrons entered the store and were browsing the aisles. A voice, high pitched and excitable, caused us both to turn.

Viola put on a show face and waved. A preschooler with unkempt curls and rosy cheeks squealed in delight. Both of her knees were smudged with dirt and chocolate ice-cream dribbled down the front of her floral dress. She gripped an original hard-covered mermaid book in one hand flashing an image of the Sea Queen on its back cover. In this particular photograph, Viola's long braided hair was flipped to one side, her full lips twisted in a smile. The be-jeweled outfit she donned presented colorless in the black and white portrait, but I suspected differently.

"She's over here Mom!" The girl skipped over and pushed the picture in Viola's face. "You *are* the Sea Queen!"

"Yes, my dear. Dat is me, long ago, when I was young like your Momma."

"But my mom says she's *old*." The girl replied frankly. "Forty-friggin'-five."

"Jocelyn Lane!" The woman flushed and rushed over to her daughter. "Mommy doesn't want you to use those words."

The little girl's brow furrowed. "But *you* do. You always say that."

Viola covered her mouth to conceal her amusement.

"I'm so *sorry!*" The woman cried. "Ever since I turned forty-five, last January, I've developed a habit of adding an extra syllable. I should be more careful. She absorbs everything, especially the bad stuff, like an enormous sponge."

Viola focused on the child. "Do you like mermaids?"

"Mmm *hmmm!*"

"Which one is your favorite?"

"I like the pirate mermaids!"

Viola's eyes lit up. "Ooh! I love de pirates. When I was a little girl..."

"*You* were a little girl?"

"Yes dear, way before you were born. Me fisher-mama's would tell me de stories because, guess what? We didn't have a television set."

The girl's eyes went wide. "Just DVDs?"

"No child, not even DVDs. We had de crash of da ocean, de light of da stars and adventures so magical you could feel de mermaid's silky tail as she flipped t'rew your imagination. I loved da stories so much I wrote dem in dese books for everyone to enjoy."

Jocelyn pointed to a specific page. "I like *her!*"

Viola gasped and nodded encouragingly. "Helen da Hook! She was one of de most beautiful women of her time. Men would literally drop gold at her feet, dangle jewels around her neck and beg for love."

"I want to be just like *her!* Ooh, what's *that?*" The curly girly pointed down an aisle and took off at a run, the mother calling out for her to slow down.

Viola watched the child race away and turned to me with twinkling eyes. "Helen da Hook was not only gorgeous but extremely dangerous. Formally known as Hooker Helen, she would sell her body for bury treasure to lonely pirates desperately horny after months at sea. Helen, dey say, had a way with herbs and developed a dissolving memory potion. She would target a sailor, drug him, steal his loot and be gone by morning. De drug worked so well many men forgot dey were even pirates and went on to lead honest lives. It was Hooker Helen who invented de date rape drug, for dat I am certain."

"Did you change her name for the book?"

Viola shook her head. "Eventually she got caught and dey chopped off her right hand for t'ievery. She had it replaced widt a sterling silver hook. Hooker Helen became Helen da Hook, but I t'ink it's best we keep dat version from Mom."

Our attention turned back to the little girl's mother who was scolding after Josie for yanking too many dolls off the shelf. "Let da child play, dear." Viola hollered. "Come and relax."

I pointed to the next page. "What about her? Rosie Anna?"

"Her real name was Smelly Anna. She needed a ride into Venezuela for her sister's wedding so she stowed away on a pirate ship dressed like a mon. She was getting away widt it too until Rufus de Rotten (named for his horribly mistreated teeth), got a whiff of her perfume. Stupid girl. No pirate wears fragrance! Anna begged to be spared, but Rotten wasn't de type to show leniency even to a wo-*mon* of such profound beauty.

"She promised to make him rich if he spared her life so the pirate gave her a week to prove it. On da seventh day, he vowed to chop off her head. Nobody really wanted to see de young wo-*mon* die since de open sea could get lonely for da average sailor, but even Rufus didn't mess widt curses. Women brought terrible luck to pirate ships. If Anna couldn't produce some t'ing incredible in seven days, which was going to be tricky since dey weren't scheduled to port for eight, she was in deep malarkey.

"With only hours to live, a British ship appeared in de distance. Anna had Rotten tie her to de mast in full makeup wearing her best silk dress, sprayed heavily with spices and fragrance. De wind shifted delivering a tainted breeze dat bewitched a mon's senses, luring da great ship. De scent was so intriguing de British Captain peered into his looking glass;

an action dat sealed his fate. When he discovered dere was a beautiful dame tied to da mast, instead of shifting course and avoiding de dangerous villains, he ordered a full on attack. By morning light, t'ree hours away from losing her head, Anna delivered on her promise.

"Rotten pulled Smelly Anna off de post and offered her a mate's position. Dey slept together right away which we soon discover pissed off her real lover, a mere second-in-command chef, who'd been making her perfume out of spices in da kitchen and secretly keeping her fed. Early de next morning, when da cook learned of Anna's betrayal, he stabbed her in de chest with a dirty butter knife and tossed her overboard before Rufus had a chance to yawn and brush his one tooth.

"Dat's how I heard it as a child, but de editor asked me to play down da sex and killin' and possibly sweetened da mermaid's name. Smelly became Rosie." Viola winked. "I should write an adult version but what da hell...dat's why old people visit for story time. Dey love da violent history of it all."

Jocelyn's mother eventually introduced herself as Betty Lane and as I handed her a glass of sweet tea she tensed. "*Oh...my...God!*"

My attention automatically shifted to Jocelyn, who was now playing with a stuffed mermaid doll swimming through an imaginary ocean. I turned to find Miss Forty-friggin'-five staring at me.

"You're the girl from the beach!"

"What girl, Mommy?"

"The mermaid, Josie. Remember? We found her."

"The dirty one?" Josie gripped the doll and marched over to me, her small hand pushing hair away from my forehead as she studied my face. "You don't look dirty now...or dead."

"*Hush*, baby girl! She was sleeping, remember? Sleeping on the sand."

"That's not what you said. You said...I'M NOT A NURSE!" Aware of her audience, Josie straddled the mermaid and mimicked her mother. "And then my mommy slapped her in the face. Whack! She kept yelling, WAKE UP! BREATHE! PEGGY! PEGGY!"

Betty cut her off. "Yes, well, I'm not good at the nursing stuff. But it was definitely *you* in the sand. PEGGY! Come over here! You're not going to believe it! It's the *girl!*"

Another woman surfaced from the fishing aisle. "What? Which girl?"

"The mermaid!" Josie chirped. "The dead one! She's alive. And...and she brushed her hair!"

Viola spoke for the first time. "What is dis all about?"

I sighed and cringed at the same time. "Not really the conversation I wanted to have at the start of summer."

"Lordy be, Maggie, what have you done?"

"I'm not really sure. I went to happy hour and then met up with J.K. We had a few drinks walking the Tipp, but I didn't think I was *that* drunk. Maybe I had five beers..."

"Five!" The old woman shook her head. "Dat's too much for a t'in little girl like you."

I didn't want Viola to think I was a lush so I agreed, happy I didn't mention the woo-woo shot. "J.K. went back to the house, said he needed to make a phone call. The sun was about to set and I didn't want to miss it. There was a buoy about fifty yards out and I kept thinking if this was high school I could swim the distance in sixty seconds flat. I must have fallen asleep." I shrugged. "Next thing you know it was morning."

Peggy, the second woman, whose features resembled Betty's in a sisterly way, cut me off. "We found you in the surf, dirty and soaked. Your hair was matted with seaweed. Betty thought you'd drowned."

Viola frowned. "Did you *swim* at the Tipp?"

I laughed nervously. "Shit. For a few minutes I thought maybe I did. I had the craziest dream. It was so vivid then, but now…" I pointed to Peggy who had much longer and curlier hair than her sister. "…your name." I turned to Betty. "You were screaming her name."

"What else do you remember?" Viola asked.

"Scattered images mostly. I dreamed of sitting on the bottom of the Atlantic, but it was bright like in a movie and my vision was crystal clear. I got sick of fighting the riptide, you see, and decided to take a break on the ocean floor. It felt kind of cozy down there even though my teeth were chattering."

"They say that about drowning," Peggy commented. "It's euphoric."

"I heard voices all around me like I was having some kind of out of body experience. Then, you're going to love this. The Power Rangers showed up and carried me to the Mother Ship." I laughed. "Remember that television series?"

Viola's concerned expression spread into a smile. "Sarah loved that show. She always wanted to be the pink one. Was there a Pink Ranger?"

Peggy cut in. "Not the Pink. Just the Black, Blue and Silver."

Confused, both Viola and I turned to her.

"I'm staying at Betty's beach house for the summer on account of a thirteen week travel assignment I contracted out of Jacksonville. June's in from Raleigh. Betty and I were watching June's boys so she could have date night with the hubby. We had the kids down at the beach flashlight crabbing. Ever try it?"

Viola nodded. "A hundred times."

"Josie found you," Betty continued. "I thought you were dead. I yelled for Peggy because she's a nurse."

Peggy scoffed. "I'm a *psych* nurse."

"Better than no nurse. I'm in *business*."

"What kind of business?" Viola asked.

"The business of not touching half-dead people for one. I freaked out. I don't know how Peggy does it. I could never wipe a person's ass."

Peggy sighed. "Betty thinks all nurses do is clean butts."

"Have you *heard* June's stories?"

"June is an ER nurse and believe it or not there's more to working an ER than emptying bedpans."

"*Anyway*," Betty cut her off irritably. "Peggy said to check your breathing."

"So she slapped you." Peggy laughed. "Betty also wanted to pump on your chest and crack a few ribs."

"I told you! I'm not medical!"

"We did agree on one thing, that you needed to get off the beach." Of course our cell phones were at the house and you were like dead weight."

"Not to mention waterlogged."

"So you called the Power Rangers?" I replied sarcastically.

"They were dragging you back in the wagon when your buddy in the golf cart showed up." Peggy turned and hollered down the fishing aisle. "Boys! Get over here!"

I heard rumbling in the fishing section and then around the corner scrambled three meaty boys. They were arguing over a fishing pole and Peggy had to raise her voice to get their attention. "This is Ethan, Carter, he thinks he's *The Terminator*, and Harry Ranger. Ladies…meet our version of the *Power Rangers*."

Chapter 19

Two nights later I was back in line at Larry's Place. Gallagher was cooking but when I waved, he brushed me off with a half-hearted smile and turned to the grill. Gina mumbled as she passed me a hotdog. "Don't think twice, Maggie. The Witch is pushing for full custody. She's hired a private investigator. If Ronnie even looks your way, some wanna-be cop sportin' a knock-off FBI shirt and an x-rated ass crack will be tailing you, snappin' pictures with his outdated camera. Talk about conspicuous. Son-of-a-bitch followed me to Salty's yesterday like me and the boss were gonna rendezvous and have a little party. I couldn't be so lucky."

"I need to speak with him."

Gina spoke without moving her lips. "I'll have him contact you on my cell. What's your number?" As Gina plugged in the digits, she asked another question. "Hear about Jimmy?"

"What about him?"

"Cops picked him up last night for questioning. They're getting worried. Sarah has never run off like this before and the way he's acting, it's like he's got a sign over his head announcing *I'm a fucking stalker.* They found finger prints all over Sarah's car and, get this, on the *outside* windows at Viola's place."

"They were married for almost five years."

"The very reason he's the prime suspect. It's always the husband, especially in *that* kind of relationship."

"How do you mean?"

"They were always either screaming or publically humping each other. Never went anywhere alone, gave up all their friends. One word: *fucking lunatics.*"

"Do you think Jimmy hurt her?"

Gina shrugged. "I don't know what to think anymore. Jimmy's been absolutely off his rocker since she's been gone, even worse than before. I don't want to believe it but prints on the *outside* of Viola's windows? We're talking second floor! The guy had to climb a friggin' tree to pull that off."

"Who's your source? Lucky?"

Gina scoffed. "When would I ever run into *that* guy?"

"I don't know, during the investigation. Surely he's been to the docks."

"The closest Lucky gets to the docks is Salty's and the man doesn't drink. His partner, Lou, on the other hand, is a bit of a lush and tells me everything." Gina winked. "I think he's got a crush on me."

"Why would Jimmy be creeping around Viola's place? I thought Sarah stayed over the store?"

"It wasn't until recently that she moved into the apartment, but I'm pretty sure it won't be long before Lucky swings by to check for prints."

"Oh, he'll find some. Jimmy showed up last week. Found him swinging in the sailor's hammock strumming that guitar of his. Thought I was Sarah and attempted to charm me with *The Filipino Cowboy*. He rushed the stairs shouting her name. When I stepped into the light I thought he was going to lose it. Ran off like a damn ape."

The line was building up and Gina had to get back to work. She shook the mustard container before squirting some dogs and replied. "I'll have Ronnie call you."

***

I finally slept with J.K. It was a Tuesday, no games to bet on, so I conned him into a night picnic at the beach. We cooked marshmallows over an open fire and drank red wine out of plastic cups. I brought Sarah's old cassette player and a couple of Van Morrison tapes. We laughed and joked as I told him about the twenty year old boy toy I picked up at the gas station and the newspaper grunt job that was supposed to change my life.

"I did something like that." J.K. retorted. "Thought I wanted to be *more* than just a fisherman. Got a job selling jet skis and speedboats. Figured I could make a bundle in commissions. Bought three ties and two business suits but never got to wear the third tie." J.K. rolled to his side. "Half-way through the second day I walked out, drove directly to Jimmy's house and begged for my job back. It took me less than forty-eight hours in an air conditioned cubicle to find myself. I'm a simple fisherman, Maggie, through and through."

I straddled him then and kissed his soft fleshy lips. He pulled me close and whispered, "Been fantasizing about you for five long years..."

And that was it. As he ripped off my skimpy top I momentarily reflected on Sarah's month rule. Sunday would make it thirty days. Screw it. I decided to go with Lisa's rule instead...*After you have sex once it's just an extension to kissing.*

That night J.K. stayed with me at the apartment but skedaddled right before dawn. Said he had to pick up a couple of rich folks flying into Myrtle Beach, and then cater their every need on *The Foxy* for three long days. He promised to treat me to a fancy dinner on the night of his return.

I lived for dinner dates. I loved dressing up, flirting over martinis, ordering one tasty appetizer at a time. We were booked at the only fine dining restaurant on island — Benjamin's Steak House. J.K. texted me from the boat reporting that we had eight o'clock reservations. I checked the time. Five-thirty. Only two and a half hours to go.

I was lining up our newest product, wind-up swimming mermaids, when Lucky sauntered into the shop. He was wearing a muscle shirt displaying buff arms tattooed from Vietnam. His long silver locks fell loosely over his shoulders and I was beginning to understand why Viola favored him.

"Miss Maggie? How's business?" He picked up a beige monkey. "Sell any weather pets yet?"

"I just ordered another two dozen. Had a grammar school class in last week and it began to rain. They all turned pink. Every girl in the group had to have one. I checked online and sure enough, they started making monkeys that turn blue specifically for boys."

"Perfect. My grandson'll be here the first of August and Viola thinks I should get him one to break the ice."

"What do you mean?"

Lucky shrugged. "Kid's all bent out of shape 'cause I won't take him deep sea fishing."

"Why not?"

"He's only four years old, for one. Besides, I don't *do* the open sea."

"Really? I thought everyone in this town fished."

"Everyone except me. Had a bad experience when I was a kid. But my grandson's relentless and I don't want to disappoint, so I'm bulking up on the action. I'll buy him a weather monkey, we'll go camping, have a cook out on the beach... I'll take him night fishing at the pier and then we'll spend a day in Wilmington at the water parks. That should keep him busy."

"I'm tired just hearing about it."

Crossing his arms, Lucky casually kicked at the flooring. "I stopped by to warn you. There have been five more break-ins since Larry's got hit. Two of the yachts had equipment stolen, radars and stuff worth close to ten grand. A bunch of cash and a couple of laptops were swiped from three different houses." Lucky sighed. "I feel like we're in Wilmington."

"Do you have any suspects?"

"Whoever it was knew the houses were rented. A house full of tourists usually means one thing—stashed money. As for the yachts, the owners were off island down at the Raleigh Boat Show. I don't want to admit it but the perp's probably local."

"I haven't noticed anyone strange except for the once in awhile drunk snoring on the porch."

"I begged Viola to quit that crap," Lucky grumbled. "Bringing it up just gets her angry."

"That's the Sea Queen for you."

Speaking of Viola..."

"She's not here."

"I know. She's wants you to stop by the house after work."

"Tonight's no good. I have dinner plans."

"You better go." Lucky warned. "Viola doesn't ask for much. If she wants to see you it must be important."

*

I immediately called J.K. "Viola wants to see me."

"Tell her you're busy."

"I live in her apartment for *free*, J.K. The woman needs something. I can't be a bitch about it. How about I meet you later at Salty's? We'll do dinner another night."

"The *Knicks* are on at ten," he snapped. "We'll have to sit at the bar."

I gripped the phone silently cursing my landlord/boss. *So much for a romantic evening.* "See you tonight then?"

"Fine."

Before I could say another word the line went dead.

*

Viola was positioned at the kitchen table drinking tea out of a big colorful mug when I knocked on the door. Surprisingly, she was playing ocean music and not her usual AC/DC, Def Leppard mix.

"Hello, child. Come sit widt an old wo-*mon*. I will make some tea."

"I can get it, V. You relax."

"*Tch-tch*" The old woman sucked her teeth. "You've been doing me bidding all day. Let me make you a special West Indian Blend."

She filled the kettle with water and I watched her work as we waited on the whistle. Viola loved creating her own tea blends. She had multiple canisters, some marked with words and symbols, others color coded. There were leaves that promoted health and harmony, one for memory, another for strong bones. Mixtures that promoted balance and created confidence; she had a lover's leaf and a blend for better skin. Viola's Voodoo Brew, Sarah liked to say.

The Sea Queen pinched and crumbled leaves from six or seven containers and dropped the mixture into a special parchment she ordered directly from India. She was folding up the tiny bag just as the whistle blew. Perfect timing.

We discussed store sales and brewing concoctions as I sipped the fabulous mixture. Thirty minutes into the visit and I still hadn't a clue as to why I'd been summoned.

"How is your tea, sweetheart?"

"Absolutely delicious. Love the lemon and pepper, and do I dare say I taste a hint of raspberry?"

She reached over and touched my hand. "I need to ask you some t'ing, Maggie. About dat night on de beach widt de little girl."

I cringed, apologetic. "Oh...*that*. I was stupid to even think about swimming."

"But did you? Did you go into de ocean?"

"I...like I said, I thought about it." Giggling nervously I added, "But then, well, I'd be dead right now. I must have fallen asleep."

"Tell me more about dis crazy dream of yours."

"Does it matter?"

"Maybe. Maybe not."

I tried not to sound irritated as I repeated the story, dreaming about a sirloin that I would never enjoy. Viola didn't notice. She just stared at my lips absorbing every word. I soon forgot about J.K., dinner and the dirty martini I had planned to order. When I got to the part about the bottom of the ocean Viola cut me off.

"You say dat it's bright. What do you see?"

"I...it's clear and vivid, but I...I can't remember."

"Take another sip, dear. Relax."

I followed Viola's instruction and shut my eyes.

"You were struggling, fighting de current. Den you felt warm, quiet...sedate. Sitting on da bottom of de ocean, odd don't you t'ink?"

"Yes. Very. But it is comfortable." I yawned, suddenly quite sleepy. "Man, the day got away from me."

"Come dear. Take a rest."

I stumbled over to the couch completely exhausted. I wanted to sleep. To dream. To nap for a hundred years.

Viola's voice sounded far away. "Can you see, Maggie? In your comfortable spot in da soft light of de ocean, what do you see?"

"Don't talk." I mumbled. *"Keep your mouth shut... Lifeguard lesson number one..."*

"Is someone widt you?"

"Yes." Euphoria takes hold and I'm back on the ocean floor. But this time I can breathe. And talk. "She's beautiful, Viola."

"Tell me about her."

"She has a wand. It's big and silver....she slapped me in the butt with it pushing me to shore. I...I'm pretty sure."

"What is she wearing?"

"A...it looks like a prom dress shimmering white...or yellow, hard to tell in the water. There's a sash swirling about, silky and bright...blue or...or purple..."

"What else do you see?"

"Water." I flipped on the couch and pushed my head deeper into the pillow, aggravated by the interrogation, too tired for silly chatter. The questions kept coming.

"Maggie...Maggie?"

"What?"

The voice whispered in my ear like an irritating mosquito. "Is it who I t'ink it is?"

What a stupid question. Leave me alone mosquito...
The voice changed. Firm. Abrupt. "MAGGIE!"
"YES!"
"Answer me!"

I sat up, wide eyed and anxious. I looked straight through the old woman, bleary eyed and defiant, punched my pillow angrily and turned to the wall. "Yes," I muttered. "The answer is yes."

Chapter 20

I woke up to the sound of bass. It thudded through the ceiling like a dull jack hammer. Disoriented, I checked my surroundings. I was lying on the yellow couch in Viola's living room. *How did I get here?* We were having tea and I got sleepy. I turned to my watch. *Shit! Two a.m. My date with J.K.!* I jumped up and raced for the door. I stopped shortly by the attic steps just as Marvin Gay's *Sexual Healing* rumbled from up above. I called out that I was leaving but didn't wait for a response. Shoot. The old woman was probably asleep.

When I climbed in the golf cart I discovered I wasn't Viola's only visitor. Peering up at the studio window I spotted Lucky. He had his arms wrapped tightly around Viola, her face buried deep in his chest.

"The old bird." I remarked out loud.

Inspired by Viola's eighty year old stamina I headed down Main. At the last second I veered off onto J.K.'s road. Figured I'd sneak in and surprise him, explain that I'd fallen asleep after a pot of Viola's voodoo brew. He'd understand, wouldn't he?

Half way up the street I hit the brakes. J.K.'s front screen flapped in the wind like he'd forgotten to close it. All the lights were on and the windows were open. I could hear music. *The Cars.* I held no great love for *The Cars.* Sure they had some good songs but as a child the lead singer freaked me out. His mannerisms made me picture a stalking Freddy Krueger sportin' high waters and bobby socks—my MTV nightmare.

That wasn't the worst of it.

What really yanked my chain from the middle of the road fifty yards away had nothing to do with the scary singer, the flapping door or the bright lights. My sole concern was with the shiny red mustang parked in the driveway. I crept forward to inspect the license plate — *ChariGrl*.

My first instinct was to march in the house and let J.K. have it. But who was I? Seducing him under a starry Tuesday night in the dunes didn't make me his girlfriend. I never considered the repercussions or Cherry for that matter. Maybe I was just another one night stand? I cringed thinking back to our conversation over plastic cup red wine and his jovial response when I spoke about Buddy the boy toy.

Shit.

Too damn tired to have it out with a guy and his girlfriend, I turned around and puttered home. I didn't know Cherry that well. How could I be sure she wouldn't pull a Rambo and jump on my back, pull my hair and scratch out my eyes? The last thing I needed was chick trouble on such a small island when I lived alone and had virtually no friends.

But what a piece of shit! *That's why you wait a month, Maggie, like I told you…*

I rumbled into Larry's lot and parked on the path, muttering curses all the way home. Not paying attention, I climbed the back steps to the Haven and froze. A sailor lay quietly rocking in the hammock. I don't know what Viola was thinking when she created this stupid Haven. Every time I met up with a stranger my knees buckled and I was lucky not to piss myself. Viola's response, *Dey're sailors, dear. Not pirates.*

I tiptoed past wondering why I bothered. If the guy was so hammered that he couldn't make it another five hundred yards to the docks then what was I worried about? Half-way up the second flight the sailor called out to me. The voice was low and steady. Sober.

"It wasn't like you think, Maggie."

Jimmy.

"Well, well, well…look what the cat dragged in."

Jimmy ignored my sarcasm. "Sarah never forgave me, you know, for kissing Cherry."

"Who? Cherry the *slut*?"

137

Again, he overlooked my comment. "We promised never to lie to each other, but if I could take it back..."

I opened the porch refrigerator and flipped open a Heineken. I told Viola that we should only keep it filled with hydrating fluids like water and Gatorade, but she insisted on a few beers. *In St. Thomas*, she said, *Heineken is water.* Under the circumstances I was happy she insisted. Still fired up about J.K. and Cherry, I chugged half a bottle and unleashed.

"I can understand why Sarah hit the road. If you weren't such a control freak then maybe she would've stuck around."

"You're so *clueless* Maggie."

"Am I? Have you forgotten about the dozen canceled visits? She wouldn't even commit to a day trip at the beach! Said that *you* got enough sun on the boats. I told her we could make it a girl's day. *I can't leave Jimmy at home*, she said. DON'T TRUST YOUR WIFE ENOUGH TO LET HER SPEND A DAY AT THE BEACH WITH HER BEST FUCKING FRIEND? FACE IT! YOU'RE A *PSYCHO!*"

Jimmy jumped out of the hammock and lunged at me. I thought he was going to swing or spit or something, but he gripped my arms in a less than angry squeeze and got directly in my face. "SARAH DIDN'T LEAVE ME, MAGGIE! I LEFT HER!" He stopped screaming suddenly, catching himself. "I left her."

I threw up my arms in disgust. "That's...THAT'S *BULLSHIT!*"

"It's not. I'm telling the truth." Jimmy gripped his hair and staggered back. "Sarah remained jealous even after I married her, long after Cherry and I kissed. That was it, you know. The *cheating.* We were never that serious, Cherry and I. That night a band was playing at Salty's and we were dancing in a big group to some Barry White mix. Cherry got all sentimental, wrapped her arms around my neck and laid one on me before I could do anything about it. The kiss lasted a couple of seconds but of course Gina was there and

Gallagher, Big Mikey; shit the whole town goes to Salty's when there's a band. I was afraid the kiss would transform into a bathroom blow job. You know how rumors spread. So I told her." Jimmy sighed. "It was the biggest mistake of my life."

"Telling the truth or cheating on her."

"Both. Sarah was devastated. I thought she was going to end it that's how bad she got. After hours of apologies and tears and drama she says to me, *the only thing that will save us now is marriage. If you truly love me, you'll marry me...soon.* So that's what I did."

Jimmy began to pace. (I felt very much like a therapist.) "For awhile it was cool. We did everything together. I *wanted* to do everything with her. We vacationed for five solid weeks! But eventually I needed to work. The boats don't pay for themselves, you know. My old man had been calling. Said if I didn't want to run the business then he'd hire someone who did. So I went back to A-Dock.

"Sarah offered to drive me in that first day. And then the second. It became habit. She drove me in, picked me up, texted me at least once an hour and phoned every four. At first, I thought it was sweet but then she asked about working the boats. Thankfully, my father stepped in and said he didn't think it was a good idea. People paid big bucks for The Foxy. They expected a captain and a first mate, not the owner's young wife lying out on the top deck ordering everybody around. He didn't use those exact words but you get the picture.

"My life went to pieces every time a woman boarded a boat, and if they were pretty forget about it! Sarah totally freaked one time, when a bunch of women rented the yacht for a bachelorette party. They were all young and cute; it was near the damned death of me. And when J.K. hooked up with Cherry, *holy* hell! Talk about drama. That's when we moved to Wilmington. If Cherry was a freaking *dot* in the distance, Sarah's eyes would narrow. She'd turn on me like a viper and accuse me of staring. SHE'S A THOUSAND FEET AWAY AND SCREWING MY BEST FRIEND, I'd scream! But Sarah was convinced that J.K.'s relationship was nothing more than a cover.

"She calmed down for about ten minutes in Wilmington. I let J.K. take the helm and picked up the sales end of the business. That way I only needed to go into the Tipp once a week which seemed to help. Sarah and I started hanging out with the neighbors, a nice couple. They were like fifty something. One night Georgia, the wife, smacked me on the butt and ordered me to get her a beer. I thought Sarah was going to fall off her chair. That was the last dinner date with those two.

"The final assault happened at Christmas. I bought Sarah a diamond and emerald tennis bracelet to match her ring. It was a little loose on her wrist so we went to the jeweler to get it sized. The sales girl came over, peered inside the box and said, *You are a lucky lady*. Then she winked at me.

"Sarah lost it. She told the clerk to keep the fucking bracelet and her lying cheatin' husband then marched out of the store. That was it." Jimmy stopped short in front of the fridge.

"But...but you never let her visit! And the beach day? What was that all about?"

Retrieving a bottled water, he said, "Every time I even insinuated that she visit you or take a day with the girls, she'd freak out and accuse me of trying to get rid of her. I love her, Maggie, I really do. But I'm so tired of the accusations.

"We separated after the holidays. I offered to leave but she packed her bags and was gone before morning. Went to live with Viola. I stayed in Wilmington until the house sold and then moved onto the yacht. I kept a low profile, didn't want Sarah to catch wind that I was back on island. I would see her now and again at Larry's Place and liked to watch her picking shells on the Tipp. I spied on her with binoculars crabbing in Viola's dingy, and one night caught her dancing on the beach without any music, pirouetting and kicking her way across the sand. She seemed so at peace, happy even...the Sarah I loved was beginning to resurface."

"You sound like a Peeping Tom," I muttered, still half stunned by Jimmy's monologue.

"I couldn't help it. I missed her! One time I actually brought a ladder and peered up into her grandmother's loft. Sarah and Viola were attempting yoga with Joan Jett vibrating through the walls it was so loud. Viola was pushing Sarah's legs over her head in some kind of stretch and they were both laughing their asses off. I wanted to bang on the window right then. I felt so lonely and lost. The separation had stripped my soul. But we were no *good* together! Sarah needed to find herself. And if it meant for me to stay away, well, that's what I did."

I slumped down in a nearby chair and digested the information. Reminded of Gina's comment about fingerprints I said, "This is all news to me."

"That's because you've been ignoring Sarah for years."

"She pissed me off! Every conversation was about you. It was Jimmy this and Jimmy that...friggin' irritating."

"A good friend you turned out to be."

"I had no idea!"

Jimmy hesitated, catching himself. "Like I said...Sarah was getting better. I started wondering, you know, if I was wrong about us. I never wanted to leave. I just so badly wanted the old Sarah, the one who trusted me, to remember what it was like before that stupid kiss.

"The night after the ladder I thought about asking her out. You know, like a date. I'd take her to Benjamin's for dinner and after that we could go to the beach. I'd build a fire and play my guitar just like old times. She loves it when I sing. In my head I had it planned out perfect.

"The next morning I had a fishing trip and didn't get back until after six. I showered quickly, bought some flowers, and hustled down to the apartment. I caught a glimpse of her through the window standing at the sink washing dishes. My baby had her hair tied up on the top of her head wearing those funny hoops she loves. It reminded me of the old days at Larry's Place when we both pretended not to notice each other.

"As I stood there I had a horrible premonition. What if Sarah flat out refused and slammed the door in my face. I couldn't bear it! Fearful of rejection, I chickened out and turned to Salty's for some Budweiser courage. Finally around ten-thirty, I plucked up the nerve. Figured I'd ask her out for the following night. I marched down the dirt path, determined. Before I reached the apartment, the door swung opened and Sarah came rushing down the steps. She had her hair twisted up in a ball cap and was wearing the pink and black windbreaker I got her for Christmas. I called out but not really, still worried about her reaction.

"The wind was strong that night. She couldn't hear me even if I screamed. I walked briskly attempting to close the gap without freaking her out. When she hit the golf carts near Larry's Place I lost sight of her. Then I thought about it and realized she was going night fishing. Sarah always wore ball caps on the water.

"I checked the dock behind Larry's and sure enough, my baby was already in a dingy motoring down the waterway." Jimmy paused. "She wasn't alone."

"Who was with her?"

"I couldn't tell. His back was turned to me and she was squeezed in between his legs. You know, like *not* friends."

"It's just fishing, Jimmy. Get a grip."

"That's what I've been telling myself but...but..." Jimmy crumbled into the hammock. "I'd never felt so afraid or nervous in my whole life. All this time I was waiting for Sarah to get her head straight and she falls for another guy."

"Oh, *please*. One fishing trip means *jack*. Besides, she probably noticed you were following her and positioned between the dude's legs on purpose. That's what chicks *do*.

They *play* you. Make you think about what you gave up. Sarah was teaching you a lesson."

"Well it worked." Defeated, Jimmy tumbled into the hammock. "I waited right here on this very swing, a complete mess, with nothing to do but check the time and think. Torturing myself with images of Sarah out on a romantic sand bar with Mr. Fucking Wonderful. I get to thinking, maybe breaking up wasn't such a good idea. Right then, swinging on this very porch, I decide that I'm gonna re-propose. We could go to counseling. I was willing to try anything even if it meant being isolated from my friends. Sarah was my baby and I wanted her *home*."

"I'm guessing *that* plan failed." I cracked sarcastically.

Jimmy heaved miserably. "That was the night, Maggie. Sarah never returned. I drifted off around six and when I woke up I raced upstairs and banged on the door. When she didn't answer I called the house. The machine picked up— Viola's voice claiming to be in Wilmington for the weekend. I checked the store. It wasn't open yet but Sarah had already started cataloging inventory. The doors were locked and the shop was empty."

"Maybe she slept at the dude's place..."

"I hope you're right, Maggie." Jimmy spoke softly. "In fact I pray that Sarah's cruising the countryside having the time of her life. I couldn't say that before. A month ago, I was so jealous visualizing my lady in the arms of that asshole. But now...I'm afraid, Maggie. She took *nothing*! No clothes, no music...every cassette is still in her car. Sarah can't live without her music."

"Maybe she was in a rush..."

"And the car? I mean *shit*, who leaves town without their wheels?" Jimmy trudged to the edge of the deck. It was close to four a.m. and the sky had lightened to a purple gray. He stared blankly at the horizon oblivious to its beauty. Without turning around, he spoke in a most unsettling tone. "I gotta real bad feeling, Maggie. Real bad. I'm not sure my baby's ever coming back."

He stumbled away. I watched him disappear before dropping onto the hammock, exhausted. There was an unusually cool breeze and it felt wonderful against my skin. Still foggy from Viola's voodoo tea, I drifted off...and found myself back again curled up on the yellow couch. Viola had gone upstairs and cranked the music. *QUEEN*. I could hear crying now, she wasn't holding anything back. Hysterical moaning and sobbing so obnoxious I shouted out for some PEACE AND *QUIET*!

It dawned on me as the sun burned away the morning mist—Viola Fox had started to paint.

Chapter 21

I woke up in blinding sunlight, my upper lip damp with perspiration. I checked the time. Damn! I had five minutes to open the store.

"Rise and shine sleepy head."

I yelped and fell off the hammock.

J.K. cackled as he leaned against the railing drinking a carton of juice from the Haven's fridge. "Got the day off, darlin'. Want to go to the beach?"

I brushed past him irritably. "Sorry, gotta work. Maybe *Cherry's* available."

"What's *that* supposed to mean?"

"You know."

"I don't. Really."

I stopped half-way up the steps but didn't turn to face him. "Can't keep it in your pants one day, J.K? *Really?* Viola lets me stay here for free. Blowing her off is *not* an option."

"And *that's* why I'm here, Maggie. We can go to the beach and then I'll spring for lunch. It'll be fun."

I twisted around and dropped on the step. "I stopped by your house last night."

"So? I was at Salty's, *remember*? Waiting for *you*."

"It was later than that. You were home. And you *weren't* alone."

"Is this about *Cherry*?" J.K. chuckled. "Shoot, you could've come in. You don't have to sneak around the bushes like Jimmy."

"Why would she be at your house at two in the morning? Do you really expect me to believe you were playing checkers?"

"Jesus, Maggie! You have no idea what you're *talking* about. For your information I can't *stand* Cherry. I *despise* the bitch. Hate her friggin' *GUTS!*"

"THEN WHY IS SHE ALWAYS AROUND?"

"BECAUSE SHE'S MY *BOOKIE!*" He practically snarled and then stopped short, running an anxious hand through his silky hair. "I...I thought you knew."

"What?

"Cherry's *connected.* Her dad owns the casino boats, remember? That's how it all started with Jimmy. Back in the day, he couldn't live without his Black Jack. Cherry'd be running cocktails, strutting around in a slinky black dress, dropping twenty-five dollar chips in his pockets every time she served him a drink. She eventually introduced him to the Boston boys. The Big Time. Jimmy thought he was all bad ass, bragging about his winnings, but soon enough his luck changed and he was down twenty grand. Jimmy's old man may be rich but he's a tough old bird when it comes to finances. He refused to assist his squandering son with a gambling debt.

"Jimmy admitted to me long ago that he'd been crushing on Fox since the day they met, but on account of him being twenty-two and her only fifteen he resisted the attraction. During the summer when you stayed with Sarah, Jimmy was dying to hook up with her. Problem was Cherry. He couldn't just walk away when he was in for twenty grand.

"The minute Jimmy paid off his debt he cut the cord with Cherry and stopped gambling altogether. Shoot, he even refused to tag along. So there I was gambling alone with Miss Slinky Black Dress. She started pushing chips into *my* pockets, rubbing on *my* leg. What the hell. Cherry introduced me to the big guns and I took over where Jimmy left off.

"Cherry loved gambling statistics. She was always giving me tips, easy hits on the line, secrets nobody knew about. Like which roulette tables were tilted, what horses were drugged and which boxers were on the take. I was cleaning up! The sex was by default. When I lost, she'd take my paycheck and, feeling guilty, would drag me into the bedroom for a round about. We were never a couple. I just hit a bad losing streak."

"Let me guess? You lost again last night?"

"Nope," he smirked. "I won. Four grand, baby! And it's about time! For awhile I thought I'd never catch a break."

"Four *grand*? Jesus, J.K., how much did you have to bet for that kind of return?"

"A thousand bucks. I bet the under and total points." He grinned. "That pays four to one."

"I have to open the store."

He reached over and pulled me close. "Can you meet me tonight? Come on, baby. Pretty please?"

I didn't like the way he squeezed my waist, desperately, like I was his last chance for a normal girlfriend. You'd think I'd be happy that Cherry meant nothing, but it kind of repulsed me. Weird, huh, coming from a sex junkie. And the gambling was concerning. Who bet their whole pay check on a basketball game?

As if reading my mind J.K. whispered softly in my ear. "Come on, Maggie. Cut me some slack."

"I can't tonight. Viola needs me."

"Again?"

"Yes. Again."

"Tomorrow then, I'll make it up to you."

"Fine."

Chapter 22

I lied about meeting Viola. I didn't want J.K. to think I was at his beck and call, so after work I went jogging, ordered take-out pizza, and vegged with a new book. I fell asleep early and woke up refreshed. I had a weird sex dream about John Kilian which caused me to deliberate all morning whether or not to give him another chance. At lunch time Lucky stopped in to forward another message. Again Viola was requesting my presence which was kind of good. It kept me from texting J.K. prematurely. I needed to let him miss me.

Under the old woman's direction, I closed up shop an hour early and drove the golf cart to her place. The June heat scorched my skin like dragon's breath as I crunched across Larry's crumbling gravel. Flipping on my sunglasses to avoid slow-moving bugs I twisted the key and hit the gas.

The stove light flickered in the kitchen as I simultaneously knocked and let myself in. "Viola! It's me, Maggie! *Heelllloooo!*"

I checked the living room and bathroom, peeked in the bedroom, but the first floor was empty. I propped one foot on the bottom of the attic steps and listened. *Is it raining?* Confused, I scrutinized the window. Still bright and stifling. Taking the stairs two at a time, I pushed open the studio door.

The West Indian Sea Queen lay flat on her back with arms spread wide, eyes glazed, fixed on the ceiling. She wore a black *DIVA* t-shirt, loose fitting shorts, and was splattered from head to toe with paint. A rainstorm tape similar to the ocean soundtrack was blaring from the speakers.

My stomach lurched as I raced over to the body. "VIOLA!" I shook her.

The sedate woman yelped and her eyes refocused.

"Lordy-be-jesus! Can't you see dat I'm meditating?"

I slumped on my rump, relieved. "*Shit*, Viola. Most people mediate like Gandhi, with legs crossed, sitting up. Not flat on their backs in a dead man's stare."

"I have art'ritis, child. It pains me to sit cross legged. Besides, since Andre died dis is how I do it." Viola's half-hearted smile deteriorated. Something was wrong. I helped her stand and led her to the stairs, thinking it was time for some tea. She shook her head and redirected me to an easel set up by the window.

"Holy Cow! Did you paint this? It's...she's absolutely *beautiful*." Before I had a chance to make any sense of it, I said, "It's Sarah! She was the girl...the voice in my dream! Sarah told me to keep my mouth shut. To try harder...it was *her*."

Painted Sarah shimmered golden in an ocean too bright for nighttime. Dark curly locks fanned out away from her face and seductive almond shaped eyes returned my gaze. Her lips curved slightly at the corners, in a knowing way, just like they did when she warned me to keep my mouth shut. She carried a long silver wand and her golden dress swished in ribbons reflecting shades of purple and blue. As for her feet, well...there weren't any.

Sarah Fox was a mermaid.

"It's *incredible*," I gasped. "Like you were in my head it's *exact*! Wow! That's unbelievable. What a *gift*."

The old woman's voice remained solemn. "A gift, you say. I feel it is a curse! It is...It is so *horrible*." Viola crumbled into a folding chair and covered her face.

I crouched in front of her and patted a knee. "Come on, V. Let's go downstairs. I'll make you some tea. I don't understand what this is supposed to mean, but it's apparent that you haven't slept. You need to rest."

Viola lifted her chin and nodded. "Tea sounds pleasant. If you could bring me canisters, Maggie, raspberry and citrus, together dey offer rejuvenating qualities. Maybe dat would help."

As I waited on a whistling kettle, I lugged up two mugs, lemon wedges, a plate of biscotti and the proper tea tins. Viola had set up one of her little paint tables and pulled out a second folding chair for me. She completed the tea bags just as I arrived with the boiling water.

In the distance boats were beginning to clog up the waterways, trolling against the tide on their way home. I cautiously sipped at my drink careful not to burn my tongue. Torrential rain was still pouring out of the radio accompanied by a howling wind. The air-conditioning tripped on and the cool air sent a shiver up my spine. Feeling relaxed and energized at the same time, I realized that Viola's brew was working its magic.

Eventually the old woman spoke.

"Do you remember Minny Justice and her mot'er, Rita, de skinny wo-*mon* who stopped by de store half-anorexic widt sorrow? She had a cousin, Faye, widt twin girls?"

"How could I forget? That day was absolutely crazy. They found the girl's body, you know, out near Blaire College that following October. Buried in the cape her mother described."

Viola reached beside her chair and retrieved a print she must have grabbed when I was heating up the water. She handed it to me. "I sent de original painting to Rita but I've learned to keep prints of me work."

The afternoon with Fatty and Skinny came crashing at me like an ice-cold wave. We were arguing about ice-cream flavors, the Fox girls refusing to believe that vanilla could be so popular. The memory so vivid I caught a whiff of Sarah's fruity perfume. Viola's print of Minny was just as the tiny bird mother described all the way down to her big intricate jewels and silky golden-red cape.

"When they found the body, reporters mistook Minny's cape for some kind of a shroud. All the freak cults were trying to get credit for the kill. It was disgusting really, but I couldn't help tracking the story. They picked up a bunch of college kids for questioning, but eventually charged some dude out in Arizona."

"Dat's right." Viola agreed. "Minny fancied an older boy dat she met at de community pool. He studied at Blaire College. She lied to de boy and her mot'er alike, told da boy she was eighteen and Rita he was seventeen. A senior, she claimed, from a neighboring high school.

"Trudt is he was twenty-two and she was sixteen, but widt a bit of makeup and de right clothes it was easy for girls like Minny, well-endowed and shapely, to lie about deir age. Nobody except Minny knew de real trudt. She even lied to her friends keeping a consistent theme so her mot'er wouldn't catch on. God knows de boy would've dumped her which was not'ing compared to if Rita caught wind.

"De boyfriend was a fraternity brother. For seven straight years de Kappa Gamma boys t'rew a secret Halloween party a mile off campus down a stray dirt road dat opened to a field. De land was University owned, initially zoned for an agricultural building, but lost its funding after de initial trees were chopped down. What was left was a nice level parcel of land, in a thicket of Carolina pines a mile from nowhere, de perfect place for a Halloween Festival. To ensure secrecy all guests were blindfolded on de ride in.

"Traditionally de party was a blast. Dere was always a D.J., beer kegs, power punch, bobbing for apples, and a costume contest. Rumors of dese legendary parties trickled about campus, but except for invited guests nobody could say for certain if de stories were true. Partygoers had deir costumes ready for weeks but were only given a days notice to de actual event.

"De night before da secret bash Minny gets a call. *Can I sleep at Karin's tomorrow night? Going to rent a bunch of movies...* She dresses up like Cat Wo-*mon*."

I inspected the print. "How do you get all that from this picture? All I see is an animated mermaid robed in a cape, wearing custom-made jewelry and cat ears. What am I missing?"

Viola sighed. "It was different, you know, before Andre passed."

"Andre?"

"Me husband."

"Oh...yeah."

"De night he died I was washing dishes in da kitchen. Andre had bought me a black-and-white television for a wedding gift, me first and last, and he set it up on de counter because for some reason da reception was better in dat room. I remember watching de news and staring out de window at da ghastly weat'er. Reporters were on island, down by de docks interviewing each boat as it ported. De fishing tournament was cut short because of de unexpected storm. Andre and Marco hadn't returned and I was desperate for a shred of news. I turned to da screen and who do I discover but little Louie, water-logged and puny, standing next to a big spongy microphone.

"De reporter wore an oversized slicker and was dramatically shielding himself against da wind during de interview. Louie, who wasn't a day older'n t'irteen, was a dock rat. He picked up work on all de boats, but was famous for wasting ocean time practicing his Morse Code on de radio. Louie answered so quietly dat de news guy had to repeat everyt'ing he said. I reached over to turn up de sound hoping he would report somet'ing about me Andre.

"Right at dat exact minute, as I twisted de dial widt me soapy wet hand, it was like Poseidon himself reached down and put a spear t'rough me heart. Everyt'ing went black. When I came around I was laying flat on me back, arms spread wide, staring at de ceiling."

"Like how you meditate?"

"Yes, dat's right. Oh, but I had a terrible dream. *Awful.* I could see me sweet husband struggling to swim t'rough de torrential rain and tilting surge. He's trying to reach Marco who's floating on shards of wooden planks, knocked out cold.

Dere are flames and boat wreckage everywhere. I actually sense Andre's relief as he clings to me Papa, comforted by de fact dat dey will face de final assault toget'er. Dey are only t'ree miles from shore but Andre knows de Coast Guard isn't going to make it. De boat is struck by lightning at de exact moment me television is hit. It sounds crazy, but for dis I am certain.

"As I lay dere, staring at de water-stained ceiling, a t'underous wave sucks dem under. Me sweet mon holds tight to de Captain and dey go down for da very last time. Dey swirl to de bottom arm and arm, and de ocean floor seems to flicker and flash. It is too bright for de depth, especially during a hazardous squall.

"Andre senses a change. He turns to Marco who is unexpectedly awake, eyes bright like he's just woken up from a restful nap. He points at a great white shark circling twenty feet above. Andre laughs out loud, he can't help it. Dey both double over in hysterics. *This is ridiculous!*" Andre says. "*I should be shitting my pants right now...*"

He quickly realizes what it all means, da warm fuzzy feeling in his tummy, de comfortable glow of de ocean floor. A little voice in his head tells him to FIGHT! It is my voice. I am crying out in da kitchen. But he's too far gone. Andre has already crossed over..."

Viola paused and reached out for my hand. Squeezing it, she said, "It is den dat de girlyfish show demselves."

"The *who*?"

"Mermaids, dear. Dey have come to take de fishermen home."

"*Mermaids?*"

"Oh, and dey are stunning!" Viola smiled sadly. "I'm not sure every wo-*mon* would share me appreciation for having such an attractive fish escort her husband to de Promise Land but it comforts me somehow.

"When I woke up I realized two t'ings. First, dat I'd been electrocuted. And second...Andre and me papa were gone for good."

Viola took another slow draw from her teacup. I struggled to stay quiet, so many questions I had! I held out for maybe a minute before blurting, "What does your husband's death have to do with Minny Justice?"

The old woman hesitated. "A story, Maggie, resides behind de birth of every mermaid. Ever since dat terrible storm I can see every t'ing, da whole trudt."

"What do you mean by truth?"

Rubbing her arthritic hip Viola limped to the storage closet and promptly returned hugging a medium-sized canvas. She pointed to Minny's print. "Dat is how Minny presented herself to Rita. And dis..." she tapped at the painting, "...dis is what I see. But before you inspect it, I ask dat you shut your eyes and merely touch de canvas."

"What?"

"Please, dear. It'll make t'ings a lot easier."

Reluctantly, I reached out... The sensation was hard to describe, like being swallowed whole by Minny Justice.

A hint of smoke and burning embers wrapped in a cool autumn breeze penetrates my senses. It takes a minute to focus but there are faces, distorted at first and then, suddenly...

...I'm standing next to a crackling fire in a crowd of costumed individuals...Prince Caspian, Fred and Wilma Flintstone, Velma and Shaggy, Darth Vader and a slutty Princess Leia. I am leaning against the Prince who has his hands wrapped tightly around my waist. He whispers in my hair, "Ooooh you smell like bubble gum." Being in his arms excites me, but I play it cool pretending not to care.

I am Cat Woman, sleek and sexy, envied by all. With velvety ears, black studded cat glasses and glossy red lipstick, my costume is absolutely adorable. I am garbed in a tight baby-T with "Meow" printed across the front in red crystals, black leggings and the golden red cape from my childhood. It matches perfectly with my rhinestone bedazzled converse sneakers. All the guys whistle when I pass.

I lick the back of my hand and hold it out to Fred who sprinkles it with salt from a kitchen shaker. "Lick, shoot and suck people! Get it right!" Vader shouts. We all raise our glasses and howl like creatures of the night. Man was I cool! At a fraternity party drinking Tequila shots with a hot guy! Tamara and gail are never going to believe this....

"Maggie. MAGGIE! Let go of de painting."

...I found myself lying on the exercise mat in Viola's studio, a pungent taste of gasoline and lime lingering in my mouth. Completely disoriented I asked, "Where the hell *am* I? What...what's happening?"

"You fell off de chair, dear." The old woman hovered, her expression creased with anxiety.

I sat up on my elbows. "That was weird."

Viola crumbled onto the mat next to me. "I wanted to stop you before de bad part. Don't touch da painting again, Maggie. It'll poison your soul."

The painting! I leered at the back of it greedily. How I wanted to disobey and continue my journey, but Viola's tone concerned me. "Can I at least *see* it?"

Slowly she turned the canvas.

My first reaction was that of complete shock. Horrified, my face drained of color and seemed to pool in the pit of my stomach. Churning acid shot up my esophagus and I promptly dry-heaved over a nearby trash bag, thankful that I had not yet eaten supper.

The creation before me was not that of a cute little vixen drinking too many shots at a party she didn't belong... It was dark. Extremely dark. Pure fucking evil was more like it, and yet I was fascinated to the brink of obsession.

"Dis," Viola whispered. "Dis is what I see."

Minny's body barely resembled a person, her face so beaten to a pulp that the eyes bulged like a beetle. The upper lip had been ripped up one side, all the way back to her left ear, and reminded me of that creepy Cheshire cat from Wonderland. I couldn't help but think it was the same ear receiving whispery flirtations only moments ago. *Ooooh you smell like bubble gum.* The *Meow* shirt was torn down the front exposing ghastly white skin streaked with dried blood and clumps of dirt. Remnants of a silky cape lay tattered and twisted over the swollen carcass.

I reached out before Viola could stop me and touched the red markings around her neck. Immediately my throat tightened and I began to wheeze. A pungent aroma of body odor, mint and Old Spice pierced my senses and a heavy weight pressed against my chest. There was music playing in the distance but it sounded far away. Too far! The lusty grip of enormous hands squeezed my airway. I tried to cry out but I...I couldn't *breathe!* I squirmed and twisted, momentarily breaking free. *HHEEELLLPPP!!!*

CRACK!

...SMACK!

Viola slapped me across the face. At the same time the intruder, a big sweaty man smelling of peppermint schnapps and cheap cologne, punched Minny Justice in the nose. *Shut the FUCK UP, Puss! This is a private party...just you and me.* The salty taste of blood trickled into my mouth. Automatically I reached up and touched my nose. It was bleeding. Alarmed, I turned to Viola who kicked the painting away and stood above me with hands on her hips.

"I told you, dear. Do NOT touch de painting."

I hugged myself and started to weep. "Oh my God! Minny....that *MAN!* He...he strangled her and...*CUT* her! Oh, and so much more! That...that DISGUSTING...*VILE* PIECE OF SHIT!"

Trembling, I peered over at the tortured dirty heap of a corpse and could feel the dysfunctional lust and anger and *hate*, a painting so emotionally charged that it *reeked*. Oh my God! I could actually *smell* sweat. Minny Justice had been beaten, ravished, and left to die alone in the darkness of a forest she would never escape.

Viola helped me into a chair, poured more hot water and ordered me to drink. She then cleared off the table and positioned the print and the canvas side by side for a visual comparison.

"The party gets started early widt a bottle of tequila and a dozen limes." Viola spoke quietly. "Minny has never consumed alcohol before so after t'ree shots and one juicy punch drink she begins to stagger. She's fallen at least a dozen times and it's not even nine o'clock. By ten even de girls are mocking her. Disgusted, da boy, Prince Caspian orders her to go lay in de truck.

"After a few minutes of spinning and severe nausea, Minny climbs out of de cab and stumbles off into de darkness. She is in da bushes vomiting when a costumed stranger approaches. He is dressed in scrubs and a white overcoat and introduces himself as Dr. Jekyll, but his real name is Drew or Don or somet'ing widt a D. He is kind and wipes her mouth with a handkerchief. He offers her a cigarette which she takes and pretends to enjoy before another round of barfing commences. Dey sit in da woods for a time, de good doctor pointing out stars until Minny falls asleep. He den picks her up and ventures away from de fest, deep into de Carolina Pines to be certain nobody will hear. While he walks he transforms. Dr. Jekyll is now Mr. Hyde...

"That's right! It was Darryl Donovan, wasn't it? He was a medical student!"

Viola changed direction. "Remember Rita going on about jewelry dat matched Minny's mermaid scales? Dat's a clue. Check da necklace in de print and den re-inspect da canvas, but please," she added warningly. "Do not touch it again."

The jewelry in the print was just as Rita mentioned — an intricate mix of gold leaf and sparkling rubies. I couldn't find anything remotely resembling a necklace on the canvas until

Viola directed my attention to a thin red string I initially mistook for dried blood. It dropped into Minny's neck line just above her right shoulder. One dirty silk rope connected to a shot glass.

"I had one of those cups. Picked it up on Spring Break, 2007. A bunch of liquor reps were passing them out on Ft. Lauderdale Beach."

"Look closely, dear. Do you see da symbol?"

I inspected the mini-beer mug and spied tiny golden script written in a swirly print that mimicked the necklace originally described by Minny's mother.

"Can you read it?"

"I reached for a piece of paper and scratched out the design." I shook my head. "It means nothing to me."

Viola grinned. "We sat here for hours scrutinizing it but den...check dis out. De shot glass is twisted. It's upside down and backwards. We need to turn it over and..."

"Look at it through a mirror."

"Dat's right, dear. To save time let me just show you." Viola took the pen and drew another picture. A symbol.

"It looks Greek."

"Dat's because it is Greek, *Kappa Gamma* to be exact."

"As in the fraternity?"

Viola nodded. "And let's not forget about Rita's elaborate golden bracelet. As you can see, it's not gold it's yellow. Yellow paper."

I searched out the paper bracelet now muddy and faded, and found a wrist band commonly used for drink specials or admission to events like water parks and haunted houses. In very small red lettering the inscription read...*BOO*.

"Red and gold," Viola stated. "Kappa Gamma colors."

"That...that *sounds* so ridiculous and yet appears to be obvious."

"Trust me, it wasn't easy. Lucky and I sat here for hours trying to figure it out."

"*Lucky*? Lucky knows?"

"You remember da kid, Louie, from de day of me husband's accident? Initially Louie was designated to work on me fa'der's boat for dat trip. Night before de Regatta, a fisher-*mon* from a neighboring crew had to bow out on account of gallstones. De captain asked Marco if he could spare a set of hands so he passed over da kid. It was Louie's lucky day. He quit fishing after dat, never stepped foot in de ocean again. Fearful dat death would be waiting. And Louie's been called Lucky every since."

"Louie is Lucky? That's crazy!"

"Lucky is my dearest and most trusted friend. Everyone t'inks we're lovers. Even me little Sarah was convinced."

I grinned. "She's not the only one."

"De lover story works well for our situation, gives us an alibi to be toget'er at weird hours of da night. It was Lucky who figured out de symbol. He whipped out his computer and how you say, *Googled* every possibility. We punched in de Greek alphabet, added red and gold, and finally searched local colleges dat had fraternities. Blaire College was only sixteen miles from Minny's house.

"Lucky contacted de Pender County Police Department. I don't know how he explained it, probably sounded like a nut job, but t'ankfully he's got a decent reputation. Early autumn dey sent in a number of undercover females to frequent de Kappa Gamma parties. One gal hit it off with a senior. After loads of drinks she asked about de *Boo Bash*. She winked as if she'd already been informed.

"We're just waiting to hear," he replied. *"They keep the date secret, you know, 'til the night before the party."*

"Dat was enough for a warrant. Cops hauled in de whole fraternity and questioned each of de members separately. Eventually dey found Prince Caspian."

"What did he have to say?"

"Not much. You have to remember dat Minny lied to everyone including de Prince. She said her name was Michelle

Jackson, pretended to be a student at de local community college. After he sent her to de truck for getting too smashed, da Prince t'ought she hooked up with someone else and never contacted her again. Da pictures Rita posted on television were over two years old depicting a younger, less endowed Minny, still in braces. De Prince never made a connection. Shoot. Kid said he never watched da news, only *Conan* and *Sports Center*!

"After police found de location of da party it was easy. Dey brought in de dogs..."

"But how did they catch the actual killer?"

"Every fraternity boy succumbed to DNA testing. I wasn't surprised. Da boyfriend's story mimicked me vision, how she got drunk, how he put her in de truck. Da killer had been invited to de party by his Kappa Gamma cousin, but never attended de school so slipped t'rough interrogation. When anot'er young girl was found dead in a desert outside of Phoenix widt a similar MO—de upper lip slashed to de ear, FBI computers made a connection. Long story short, Darryl Donovan was a t'ird year medical student at de same University as da second dead girl. He was one of de few enrolled students widt a North Carolina address and *surprise surprise* a Kappa Gamma cousin. Let me just say DNA is a wonderful t'ing."

Chapter 23

"This is…*lunacy*, Viola. I mean, who would believe it? *I believe you of course, but…well…is it…was it like this with *all* the mermaids? How long have you had this…uh…gift?"

Viola shrugged and sipped her tea. "Mermaids in me original book were based on legend. Stories I resurrected from childhood campfires. Me house mums claimed dat de girlyfish were at one time very real people who lived wild days full of great adventure. Dey were a mix of pirate's women and wo-*mon* pirates, dangerous females dat would fight for bury treasure and kill wi'tout cause. A tragic death was to be expected. Dey were burned, stabbed, shot, beheaded, some even walked de plank. If deir stories were true or fantastic I haven't a clue."

"Probably best to keep that part out of the kid's book."

"Exactly what me editor said," Viola chuckled. "Anyway, I didn't have any visions or crazy dreams back den. Remember me first picture book was written before de Regatta. I only noticed a change widt de next mermaid sighting, which was years later, way after Andre's death. It caused such a commotion… *Did you hear about the girlyfish? Surfers spotted her out by the reef! Who told me? Tony…I think. No wait…it was Jenny Sheppard or Jenny Jo, I can't remember! But I hear she skipped across the water like a string of diamonds…*

"I painted da mermaid on a whim like everyone described her, with shimmery scales and luminescent skin. I worked on it for twenty straight hours before stumbling off to bed completely exhausted. Next t'ing I remember is da sound of de radio, da volume cranked, and I'm standing in de kitchen in me nightgown swaying in front of da easel."

"The kitchen?"

"Yes, Maggie. Me son was barely ten years old and de

attic was his territory. I blamed me delirium on lack of sleep because I didn't know what to t'ink. Different shades of oils were squeezed onto a pallet, brushes were fanned out on de table, and a fresh new canvas sat on me easel. Without t'inking I picked up a brush and launched into me work.

"What I created slightly resembled a woman but widt crooked bones and distorted features. No matter how I tried I couldn't straighten me lines or fix de red splatters dat dropped on da canvas. I cried and wept, blaming me tears on da blunders as de second painting consumed me. I refused to eat and what little sleep I managed brought with it de most daunting nightmares. So horrific dey would wrench me awake and draw me back to de project. De finished piece both terrified and disgusted me, but I didn't know why. I never made a connection.

"A few years passed before de next fish goddess flashed her tail. Boaty-mon Bob gave me de scoop while I sat eating lunch at Salty's bar. As he relayed da details, I visualized a very young mermaid widt bright red hair and delicate features, flipping and twisting t'rough a school of lost porpoises. Without t'inking I hurried home and dragged out me easel, absolutely frantic to get started. Eighteen hours later I completed *Little Red* and I must say it was de best painting I'd ever done.

"But den," Viola heaved a weighted sigh. "As I recapped de oils I felt a vague sense of unease. Somet'ing was out of whack. Me apprehension escalated and anxiety had me chasin' me own wind. I couldn't breathe. Den me stomach was painin' so badly, de burning cut into me t'roat. It's hard to explain but I lost control of me faculties. Somet'ing from deep inside was poking at me innards. *Controlling* me."

"How do you mean?"

"Well, for one t'ing, instead of screwing on de cap I squeezed more color onto me pallet."

"You probably just spaced it."

"No, dear, I didn't *want* to paint anymore. I was

cleaning up and yet me hands refused to obey. I remember t'inking *stop! Stop squeezing dis damned tube.* But I couldn't. It freaked de jumbies out of me. I dropped da supplies and ran, literally sprinted down da street. Me mind kept visualizing red hair and black fish but after awhile de images transformed into not'ing more dan flashes of red and smears of black. De worst part was de screaming coming out me ears. A girl's voice drenched in terror begging...*Oh please, oh please, oh please...no, no, no, no, no, no, NOOOO!*

"De shrill made me run faster. I ran and ran, for so long I ran! Me legs began to cramp, paining me so much, but I kept moving away from de house and da kitchen...away from de canvas. Eventually I became aware of de wind and da sky and de warm sun as it baked me skin. I stopped suddenly, too t'irsty and tired to take another step.

"I found *me*-self standing on de front steps of *Abby's Arts and Crafts.* I bought a Coke and some art supplies, me hands knew exactly what to grab, and hurried back home. Da closer I got to de house da faster I went. I rushed up de steps, me hands already fingering me recent purchase. I pulled out a tube of paint." Viola paused dramatically. "*Red* paint."

"So? What does *that* mean?"

"De tube I had forcibly squeezed onto de pallet earlier lay empty on da floor. It was de red tube. I can't explain why or how, but right den, dat very *second*, I understood dat I hadn't run out to get away. I was on a quest to purchase more red paint!

"Again de act of creating consumed me. I screamed and cried and worked until da second painting was complete. Even den it meant nothing to me. Blobs of smeared blacks and browns covered in crisscrossed red lines—a first grader could've done better. Frustrated, I went to pick it up and toss it in de trash. But when I touched it...de canvas scorched me fingers. A disgusting foul smell crippled me senses. *Burning flesh.*

"Overwhelmed and terrified I phoned Lucky sobbing,

uttering gibberish so confusing that he arrived on me doorstep within minutes. I don't t'ink he believed me at first, until he sizzled a pinky on de crisscross canvas. His reaction was legendary!" Viola exclaimed. "He sat dere for awhile, dumbfounded, and finally asked did I t'ink dere was a connection? *Between what?* I questioned, fully perplexed when he pointed to little Red and de smoldering creation. For de life of me, I hadn't a clue. He fixed me a hot toddy and told me to get some sleep. When I awoke de two paintings were gone.

"We never spoke of de incident again until seven years later… Lucky determined it was different dis time because it wasn't a t'ird or fourdt account. It was Mr. Wickage who spotted de mermaid and Mr. Wickage relaying da details…

"I called her *Da Butterfly Girl* but her real name was Fiona Wickage. You can find her painting on page 14 of me second picture book. She was from Michigan.

"Fiona had been dead for nine years when her husband decided to take his two sons on vacation to de North Carolina coast. Mr. Wickage had business in Raleigh so figured he could knock out two birds with one stone. Lucky found Walter Wickage shaky and pale, hyperventilating, sitting on da roadside next to de phone booth dat used to be located in da Tipp's parking lot. He had called 911 t'inking he was having a heart attack or psychotic break or…*somet'ing.* Lucky was first on scene, and after hearing da mon's story brought him directly to me.

"I sat him down in me most comfortable chair and went straight for de Orange Lava tea blend. A bit spicy for most folks but really good for treating shock. And 'dis mon needed a fixin'. Walter stared off into space and gulped down da first mug oblivious to de scalding heat. For safety reasons I t'ought it best to pour his second glass over ice. Eventually he began his tale.

"*After our second son was born, Fiona decided to quit her job and stay home with the boys. To pick up the slack, I worked overtime which put me on the road two to three nights a week.*

Sales." He rolled his eyes. *"Should've known when she started in with those damn pep pills that Fiona was in trouble. Tried to take her on holiday a few times but bills were tight and nobody, she said, would be able to handle the babes. I didn't understand. She called them her sweet fat angels. They were always kissing on her and begging for stories, making her sing songs while they played in the tub. I thought she was happy..."*

Viola sighed. "Dat mon blamed himself for his wife's depression. And da wife blamed herself for feeling trapped by t'ree people who loved her dearly."

"She wrote a note and skipped town. Said she needed time. That's the last we heard from her. I lied to the boys. Told them God sent her on a special mission to care for a sick little boy who didn't have a mother. They were devastated of course, but what could I say? Mommy didn't have enough run-time in her twenties? She needs another decade of sleeping around and nightclubs before settling down?

"When the cops found her body battered to a pulp in a field by the interstate, I had a heart attack. Literally. Doc labeled it a stress-induced Myocardial Infarction. Fiona's autopsy concluded that she was hit by an automobile. I can't help but wonder. Why in the world was my baby traipsing the highway in the first place?"

Viola reached for a biscotti and dipped it in her tea. "Mr. Wickage wasn't far from de trudt. Holed up at De Motel Drifter four miles from home, a tearful Fiona lay in a pile of snotty tissues confused as to what she wanted in life. It had only been two days since her abrupt departure and already she missed de sweet fat angels. She yearned to kiss deir tummies and yet couldn't find de energy to return.

"Fiona washed up, fixed her hair and convinced herself dat a drink might be in order. She didn't make it far, just across de street to a roadside Honky Tonk. As she stared miserably into her Gin Fizz wondering what da hell she was t'inking, a strange man literally swept her off her feet. He was a sweet-talkin' truck driver in town for de night. One five-dollar bucket of beers and t'ree whirls around de dance floor was all the coaxing Fiona needed to climb aboard. *There's nuttin' better*, he exclaimed, *nuttin' better'n a wide open road!*

"Dey drove clear out to California. Fiona had never left Michigan and couldn't get over da vast countryside. She especially cherished early morning sunrises as dey passed t'rough da desert. At night dey'd lay on top of de cab and sip *Asti Spumante* as *Barney* (or as Fiona liked to call him—*Mr. Sexy Pants*), pointed out constellations he learned from an ex-girlfriend. A fifth grade astrology teacher, he said, who stripped part time at de Dusty Bucket just off Highway 62.

"On de fourth day Mr. Sexy Pants asked for a sizable loan. *Just until payday*. Being a trustworthy wife for ten solid years made Fiona a bit naïve and ridiculously foolish. She gave him de money, all of it, t'inking Barney was her new destiny. Not surprisingly, as de cash dwindled so did Mr. Sexy Pants' gentleman-like qualities. Fiona went from a sassy sweet darlin' with a generous smile, to a fat stupid road hog with gator teeth that were fucking up his blow jobs. No longer did dey lie on de cab searching stars sipping sparkling wine. Instead Fiona stared blankly out a bug splattered window while Barney gulped *Mad Dog* and listened to sports radio, intermittently spewing obscenities when da wrong team made a play.

"One night after an exceptionally long afternoon at de Dusty Bucket, (where Fiona got a chance to meet da ex-girlfriend, first hand, as she humped her cousin *Geraldine* on the stage in front of her), Fiona complained dat Barney was too drunk to drive. He pulled over, beat her senseless, and raped her in da back of de cab. Dat was de final straw.

"Fiona waited until Mr. Prick Face (Barney's transformed nickname) was out cold before crawling from de dirty blankets and hitting da pavement. Thankfully, Barney needed to pick up his paycheck and get de truck serviced, so Mrs. Wickage was less dan seventy miles from home. Close, and yet so far.

"De road ahead was pitch black and desolate, too

darned quiet to be labeled an Interstate. For hours Fiona trudged along, left thumb slightly extended, her weak attempt at hitch hiking. Few cars passed and nobody slowed. *Not surprising!* She grumbled. *The flippin' grass out here is up to my chest and who can see anything in this swallowing darkness? I need to get more aggressive!*

"Another set of headlights flashed in de distance. Dis time Fiona waved her arms frantically and jumped up and down suddenly desperate to get a ride. Any ride! Da long lonely walk got her day dreaming about Walt and de sweet fat angels, who loved her smile and gator teeth, who couldn't get enough of her terrible singing voice. *Why oh why did I leave?* She wondered, now quite baffled by her actions. After years of pep pills and a thousand tears, what finally cured Fiona Wickage was de wide open road and a lewd truck driver with a crushing right hook.

"As de lights approached, da vehicle slowed. Fiona leaped into view, practically to de center of da road, hopping and waving. Only den did she realize her fatal mistake. It was Mr. Prick Face, da evil truck driver, who woke up with a pounding headache screaming for de road hog to get him some aspirin, only to find de pill bottle empty and da cab deserted. Nobody left Mr. Sexy and got away widt it, especially not a buck-toothed housewife widt a big ass.

"De massive eighteen-wheeler slammed into Fiona full force. Da impact so treacherous, it t'rew her instantly dead corpse fifty feet in de air, clearing da highway guardrails and hurling it down a steep embankment into an open field of wild flowers—the WELCOME TO MICHIGAN sign clearly visible in de distance.

"When Mr. Wickage described da mermaid I could see his t'oughts and feel his every trembling emotion, everyt'ing from de racing heart to how his knees buckled when Fiona hollered out from de waves. De girlyfish was a more youthful version of de late Mrs. Wickage, a carefree energetic spirit spiraling t'rough de surf in a whirl of neon butterflies."

"...Fiona had her hair in pigtails, don't you know? That's how she liked to wear it when she puttered around the garden. I almost forgot about that! Can you imagine? After ten years of marriage forgetting something that significant? And by the love of Pete, you should've seen her tattoo! A metallic butterfly painted over her bellybutton in the most glorious design. Fiona always wanted ink and, by golly, she's finally puckered up!

"Clearly, de man was smitten widt da lovely creature. It broke me heart to unravel de trudt." Viola limped into the closet resurfacing moments later with another canvas and one of her storybooks; the same edition Sarah gifted Scarlett. The old West Indian flipped though the pages and said, "I didn't t'ink to keep prints back den but Mr. Wickage was ecstatic when I asked to use Fiona's image in me second picture book. See, Maggie? Isn't she beautiful?"

"Yes, very." I had flipped through Viola's book collection on numerous occasions at the store. "*The Butterfly Girl* is one of my favorites."

"Yes, well...prepare yourself, sweetheart. De second painting is very disturbing."

...The body of Fiona Wickage lay in a field of moth infested wheat grass, every facial bone dislodged with skin so swollen and discolored, a deep purple so bloody red, it was as if the Devil himself had taken her place.

"It pained me too much to tell dat mon de trudt, so I lied." Viola continued. "Did he really need to hear about da beatings or de relations or...or *any* of it? De Mermaid, I said, materialized in hopes dat it would help Mr. Wickage find peace in his heart and possibly forgive her. I explained as best I could dat Fiona was on her way home when de accident occurred. She missed him and da boys, and wished she had never left."

"But *was* it an accident?"

"Of course not." Viola said. "Remember, Maggie, what I told you about Minny's jewelry? It was her necklace dat led us to de fraternity. So we have to ask ourselves... What is different about Mermaid Fiona? What excited her husband? "

"Uhmm...The butterfly tattoo...*She's finally puckered up.*"

"Exactly." Viola turned to the canvas. "But as you can see, dere really isn't a tattoo."

I inspected the painting. "No...it's more of a bruise."

"Not just a bruise, dear." Viola traced a finger over Fiona's abdomen. "Look closely."

It took a second but, like an illusion, as soon as I spotted the imprint it was a wonder I ever missed it. Clearly visible on the corpse's battered abdomen in bluish purple coloring, I made out an H, K, 5, L, 6, and a 7. I shrugged. "Could be a tattoo...but it reads like...like a license plate?"

"Correct. But it's more dan dat, Maggie, much much more." The old woman pinched her lips together and shook her head. "De lettering on her belly was from impact."

"*What?*"

"When de truck hit," Viola's whispery voice trembled. "It struck Fiona's body so hard de license plate imprinted on her skin. And to t'ink...Mr. Wickage was so *happy* about dat butterfly." The old woman began to weep. I reached over and softly gripped her shoulder.

"It was Lucky who figured it out. He made some calls and systematically went t'rough each state beginning widt plates designed widt blue lettering. We weren't sure if de color meant anything other dan bruising but Michigan plates are blue and gold so we started dere.

"It took awhile but Lucky found de eighteen wheeler. Da driver, Mr. Prick Face, had died two years before from a massive blood clot to de lung. Dat's what happens when you drive for too long and don't stretch your legs. Anyway, since he was already napping with de crickets Lucky and I didn't pursue da case." Viola's voice resigned. "Some mysteries, Maggie, are better left on de side of da road."

Chapter 24

I helped Viola return the paintings to storage and caught a glimpse of her brilliant portfolio. "Holy Cripes, Viola! How many mermaids have you painted?"

"In da past fifty years, not counting de original t'irteen, dere have been t'irty seven mermaids. Ten of de sightings da women were dead for many years. I could only feel a vague essence. For example," Viola retrieved a canvas. "Dis mermaid died in June, and dis one some time in December. You can tell by de Christmas ornaments. Others were more vivid, too bloody graphic for me liking. Dis little girl, I remember, was tortured. I had to take sleeping pills for a month just to stop de screaming."

"That's fucking morbid."

"Who you t'ink you're telling, dear. It was in me own head."

Something occurred to me. "Viola? Does every mermaid have to die tragically?"

The old woman shrugged. "I can't say for certain but...well... T'ree may have been accidental--one car crash, an overdose and a boating accident, but I'm positive dat at least twenty one died by another's hand. In fact, Lucky and I have assisted de aut'orities in finding fourteen missing women, not excluding Minny Justice. Most of de time Lucky calls in anonymous tips or sends unidentified faxes to da closest law enforcement agency. I've been assisting de police without deir knowledge for many many years."

I let that sink in as Viola locked the closet. "That brings the count up to thirty-five. What about the other two?"

"What?"

"You said there were thirty seven mermaids?"

"Oh, yes. Dere was dat man fish."

"Like...a merman?"

"Stabbed to death at de kitchen table. He popped up in da surf years later and warned his only daughter to never criticize her mot'er's cooking, especially when she's holding a butcher knife. *Big* mistake!"

I laughed out loud. "That's not true!"

"It's what de daughter said. I'm not making it up."

"So that brings the count to thirty-six. What about the last one? Lucky number thirty-seven?

Viola tilted her head and walked over to the window. "You already know, Maggie."

"Know what?"

Viola *tched* and *clicked* making a sad sucking sound. "Dat's why I'm telling you 'dese stories, to help you better understand."

Dumbstruck, I walked over to easel. "Sarah?"

"Yes, Maggie." Viola's voice dropped to a whisper. "Sarah is number t'irty-seven."

"That's...you're *kidding*! That's absolutely *ridiculous*!"

"De paintings don't lie! Sarah showed herself to you as a mermaid. And if you're sighted as a mermaid..."

I finished her sentence. "...then you're already dead."

Viola began to weep. "I didn't want to scare you. I needed to be sure. Da tea you drank de ot'er night has special memory powers. Your dream, Maggie, was no dream."

"How can you be so certain when I can't remember shit?"

"Oh, I didn't want to believe! But when dose little boys showed up...Da Power Rangers! And den Josie...da way she described you rolling in de surf. Little girls don't lie sweetheart. When you drank de tea...I could see! Oh, my baby! My dear sweet Sarah..."

I crossed my arms defiantly and cut off her West Indian dramatics. "So you're saying that Sarah's a mermaid and we had a conversation at the bottom of the ocean?"

"I wouldn't call it a conversation. More like an

argument, if you asked me. You two really should stop fighting especially now dat she's...well... You seemed to be hell bent over some canceled road trip."

I attempted to laugh but my throat went dry and I started to cough. I never told a soul how miffed I was about California. "We were supposed to drive cross county when we graduated, but she married old fuck face. I...I never forgave her."

"But you'll go. Sarah said. Eventually you'll take the trip...with your future husband."

"What's *that* supposed to mean?"

"Beats me. It was your conversation."

"But this is so crazy, Viola? How? Is Sarah...*dead*? "

The old woman took another sip of tea, her voice husky and thick. "It's more dan dat, Maggie. Remember what you asked about de tragedy of it all? I'm not sure but I t'ink when people cross over to mermaids...somet'ing bad has happened. Somet'ing dark."

"Like what?" I ventured.

"Dere's part of de local legend dat I've kept secret for a half of century." Viola shivered and gripped herself in a hug. "I t'ink Sarah's been murdered."

Chapter 25

After absorbing the initial shock of the strange occurrence, Viola and I commenced dissecting Sarah's actions prior to her disappearance.

"She contacted me shortly after marrying Jimmy but I cut her off with some lame excuse and never phoned back. Seriously, V, I wouldn't know where to begin. When a person goes missing what do the cops do?"

"We pinpoint the most obvious perpetrator!" Lucky immerged from the attic steps, freshly showered, gripping a gas station coffee. "Which, in this case, would be the husband."

"Oh...uh, hey Lucky."

Viola limped over and gave the police officer a squeeze.

"Jimmy's been under surveillance for weeks, but ever since the sighting I've been working a full court press. We've matched Jimmy's prints at the apartment, the store, and even here." Lucky walked over and touched the expansive attic window. "Picked up a print on the *outside* of the glass. Sneaky bastard needed a ladder to get this high. Deviant behavior if you ask me. Sarah's golden boy is nervous for a reason."

Viola folded her arms with a *humph*. "Jimmy Harrison is Sarah's FISHERMON! He did not STALK and *KILL* de wo-mon he loves. I DON'T BELIEVE IT!"

"You *WON'T* believe it."

"WE ARE FISHERMEN'S *DAUGHTERS!* WE PICK DE MON! Sarah would not have chosen a MURDERER! You can't make me believe dat!"

"I hope not, Viola, but at least appreciate the evidence. Jimmy has motive, he has means..."

"STOP! JUST STOP!" I cried. "We don't even have a *body*! How can you talk murder without a corpse?"

Lucky mumbled to Viola. "I thought you were going to explain."

"I did."

"Then why are you so skeptical?"

"Why am I *skeptical*? We're talking about a *dream*! A girlyfish carrying a *wand*!"

"Crazy as it sounds; if Viola believes it then we need to pay attention."

Our focus turned to the easel. Sarah's mermaid grinned from the canvas and her golden scales shimmered in the twilight. Blue and purple ribbons flipped about as she swished a silver wand. The picture was exact. Viola hadn't missed a single detail.

"De ot'er night you babbled about de wand. How Sarah smacked you in da butt widt it as she pushed you to shore. My granddaughter has never owned a wand, not even as a child. She was more of a fishing pole and bucket kid. De wand," Viola claimed, "is important."

"The *wand*?" I remarked sarcastically. "How is *that* going to help?"

"It all depends on de second painting."

"Right. " Lucky headed for the stairs. "While you're working on that, V, I've got a meeting with the Coast Guard. As soon as the tide eases we're gonna start dredging the inlets. I've put together ten crews of police, retired military and volunteer fireman. If there's a body out there we're going to find it."

"Jimmy told me Sarah was seeing someone." I blurted.

Lucky stopped short. "You've been talking to Jimmy?"

"He was waiting for me, I don't know, a few nights ago. Said he spotted Sarah out on a boat with some dude."

"Who was it?"

"They were too far out. He couldn't see. You both know I hold no love for Jimmy Harrison but the guy seemed truly upset."

"For all practical purposes we have to assume Jimmy's

lying." Lucky sipped his coffee. "Pointing a finger at an imaginary boyfriend, a man he doesn't *recognize*, that's a stretch. Remember it was the off season. The island's too small in March to keep such secrets. It only proves that Jimmy's desperate."

"Do you have any other suspects?"

"Not really. We've interviewed fishermen, delivery people, Salty's wait staff, every kid that's ever plated a Larry's hotdog, and of course the usual suspects. Cherry was working the casino boats. J.K. was gambling on the same boat, probably losing his shirt—nothing new. Gina spent the majority of the weekend smashed at Salty's, Gallagher was in the hospital, and Viola was off island, shopping in Wilmington."

Viola's eyes went wide. "I'm a suspect?"

Lucky chuckled. "No leaf goes unturned, baby. Sorry."

"When did Sarah actually go missing?"

"There's a bit of confusion about that. At first we thought she just hauled ass so nobody paid much attention to the date. Sarah was back in the apartment by then so it was pretty common for a day or so to lapse without any communication." Lucky said.

"She always phoned on Mondays and T'ursdays." Viola cut in. "I t'ought I just missed her call on Monday. No big deal. I don't always make it to de phone on time. But when I didn't hear from her on T'ursday, I had Lucky check de apartment."

"Sarah's Friday mail was picked up but not Saturday's."

"So it was Friday?"

"Maybe." Lucky replied. "Or maybe she just didn't pick up Saturday's mail.

"I'll bet Jimmy knows the date."

"That's because he's our guy, Maggie."

"What NONSENSE!" Viola interjected.

"Sorry, babe, but your little fisherboy's a murderer."

"ENOUGH! Just *stop*! Do you two always argue like married people? It's no wonder the town thinks you're screwing!" Viola and Lucky shut their traps but continued to glare at one another. "Jimmy sounded pretty certain that Sarah disappeared the same night he spotted her fishing with the dude. He was so freaked out about being replaced he wanted to give the relationship another shot. He waited for her at the Sailor's Haven all night. Sarah never showed."

Viola growled at the police officer. "Hear dat, Mr. Asspain? Find de dude and maybe den you can find your killer."

***

I departed shortly thereafter and left Viola struggling with the second canvas. I drifted off while reading on the couch, but my dreams were ragged and clipped with bloody she-fish and manic truck drivers. I woke to the smell of searing flesh and horrific screams that were in fact my very own. I systematically grabbed at my skin in search of a source, and eventually jumped up to check the stove. *Just a dream.* Damn! I couldn't stop conjuring brutal possibilities. Was it true? Had my best friend been beaten or shot? Perhaps suffocated or buried alive, maybe even chopped up and tortured?

Even the breeze sounded cynical. Creepy and fucked up clanking sounds kept me wired and alert. I thought about Jimmy's fingerprints and wondered if he was out there stirring in the darkness, waiting to take out another victim. For sanity reasons I shut all the windows, (there were only three) and cranked the AC. In doing so I rechecked every latch and door lock, making sure the chain link was dually engaged. I got a visual of a burly monster with hairy pits and a flabby gut, wearing nothing but a *Speedo*, kicking in the door with a studded baseball bat. (*My imagination has a knack for getting a tad out of hand.*)

Placing a chair under the doorknob, I went to the fridge

and cracked a beer. Man, was I freaked! How could I be certain that Sarah hadn't been abducted from this very living room? Images haunted me to the point of heart palpitations driving me to dial the phone.

"Mom?"

"Maggie? Is that you?"

"Yeah, it's me."

"What's wrong, honey?" I could hear the panic rising in her voice.

"I...I couldn't sleep is all."

"Jiminy Crickets! It's two in the morning! Scared the heck out of me. Your father's down in Texas for the week so when the phone rings late all I can think is *oh shit, somebody's dead.*"

"Sorry. I had a bad dream. Kind of shook me up. But I'll let you go back to sleep. Didn't mean to scare you."

"What was the dream about? Oh, don't tell me...then I'll be stuck awake. Guess what, you'll never guess? I chopped my hair! Yes, by golly, I'm an official *old* person. It's all spiky and butch. Dad says I need to start wearing big hoops like yours to keep the lesbians away. Personally, with the chunky streaks I added to the front, I think it looks fabulous!"

"Who put you up to it? Susan?"

"Of course Susan, who else..."

Susan and my mom had been best friends since the six grade. Both married service men, both worked as beauticians, and both held very strong opinions about the how the other should style their hair. My mother continued chatting in her normal manic fashion. Every few minutes I'd comment but as Dad liked to say, mom could talk a hungry dog off a meat truck. I lay on the couch, positioned the phone on a pillow, and drank a second beer. Relieved to have my thoughts diverted, I temporarily forgot about mermaids, murder and my missing best friend.

Chapter 26

The following evening after locking the store, I climbed in the mermaid mobile and headed north, anxious to check Viola's progress. Instead of laying flat on her back in a deadman's stare, the old woman was pacing nervously slugging back a Red Bull.

"Jesus, V. I'm not too sure you should be drinking that."

"It's my fourth one."

"But you're like eighty years old!"

"Seventy four. Why do you young people always try and speed up time? I don't even live to eighty. I die four days before me birt'day."

I paused, shocked. "You...you know the date of your death?"

"Ain't dat a bitch?" She hissed. "Ooh! Dis has never happened before. Usually I finish de first painting and *WHAM*, de next one practically creates itself. Widt Sarah, I...I t'ink I'm too close. I can't see..." The Sea Queen pounced about like a manic Jack Russell Terrier.

"That's it, Miss Viola. You need some fresh air. Let's take a ride."

The sun descended to the west and offered a warm orange glow. It was much cooler than the tilting hundred it had been earlier, the thermostat leveling off at mere eighty-five degrees. We traveled up side streets, cut through back yards, circumcised bushes, and bounced down rutty dirt paths bringing us closer to water's edge. Viola waved at sunburned boaters, ogled trash birds maneuvering a changing wind, and prayed for a mammoth-size turtle taking a break roadside. Eventually dirt turned to sand and we found ourselves at the tip of Tippany Ridge. I shut down the engine and we sat quietly gazing at a dozen long boarders as they flipped and glided in a salty tide. I shivered thinking about it. Never again would I doubt the power of the rip.

We rode the State Ranger's path down the Atlantic coast and welcomed a temperate breeze. I couldn't tell if Viola was awake or napping behind bedazzled shades, her expression vague, mouth curved slightly and hands resting loosely on her lap. I remained silent and let her relax.

Exiting the beach at South Pier I pointed over at Larry's. The food line snaked around the building and I noticed two sets of team colors intermingled with the regular dinner crowd. Baseball season always brought with it an entourage of ice-cream lovers.

"How about something frozen, Viola?"

"Dat would be nice. Maybe a Rocky Road Coke Float"

"Disgusting."

"Have you ever tried it?"

"No."

"Den hush."

As we entered the lot, Viola gripped her seat and produced her *I'm irritated* sucking sound. Her eyes narrowed and I turned to examine the cause of her angst. Sarah's dusty car that for many months sat untouched in the corner parking lot was now package-wrapped in yellow police tape.

"When did that happen?"

"Lucky did it, I guess." Viola mumbled. "Pull up next to it and let me take a peek." I tried to say something but she cut me off. "Get da ice-cream, dear."

The counter girl was young, maybe sixteen, hair twisted up in a scrunchy, sporting a *Lady Gaga* t-shirt with the neck cut out. She scooped recklessly, smashing and cramming together cones and hot fudge sundaes, frazzled by the twenty something ball players shouting out orders. I couldn't stop visualizing Jimmy in the hammock, sadly plucking his guitar, waiting on a girl that would never return.

"What can I get you?"

Lost in a daze my turn arrived faster than expected. As usual, I hadn't picked a flavor. The line groaned as I stumbled through the selections. Flustered, I reverted back to the national favorite.

"Vanilla?" The frenzied counter girl frowned. "*Really?* With all the choices that's what you're going to pick?"

"Oh, and a Rocky Road Coke Float."

"That's more like it."

I recognized Gallagher's posterior as he stood in grilling position. He wore a light green t-shirt advertising over-priced tequila and a sweaty bandana. Systematically he flipped a row of burgers, loaded three with cheese, scrambled and seasoned a pile of fried onions and rolled a string of hot dogs that sizzled and spit in unison. Using the spatula he scooped up two meat patties and slid them on a couple of toasted buns.

Ronnie's eyes went wide when he spotted me. "Well, well, well...look what the cat dragged in." He attempted to sound friendly, but his tone carried a nervous edge that immediately caught my attention. He pointed a silent finger to the back so I stepped out of line and met him at the side door.

"Hey, Ronnie. What's up?"

"I just wanted to apologize, Maggie, for being such an ass. My ex...she's a complete lunatic." He gripped my shoulders lightly and offered a soft squeeze. "Can you come by later tonight? We still need to talk."

"Tonight's no good. I'm here with Miss Viola. She's in a tizzy about...*something*. I'm not sure I'll be able to get away."

Gallagher's neck whipped towards the crowd. "Viola's here? That's a surprise. Where is she?"

"She's over at Sarah's car."

Gallagher blanched slightly. "Oh shit, that's right. Can...uh, you come by tomorrow?"

"I'll try."

"We close at ten don't forget."

Gina emerged from the side door carrying my order. She elbowed Gallagher playfully. "Back to work, Ice Cream Man. Chop. Chop."

I stumbled over the gravel and found Viola sitting in the golf cart hugging a small leather case.

"What's that?"

"Sarah's music."

"You just took it from the car? Wasn't it locked? "

Viola rolled her eyes. "Sarah didn't believe in locks."

"Can't you get in trouble for crossing police tape?"

"Maybe."

"I forgot about that case. Funny, Sarah was so big on music and still used cassettes."

"My son gave her this box when she was ten. Almost every tape in it she mixed herself."

"You don't have to tell me. She played them incessantly. I held no love for Zeppelin back in the day, so Sarah forced me to listen to their second album until I couldn't get it out of my head. This one is good too—a mix of *The Big Chill*, *Clash* and *The Commitments*. Old stuff but good."

"Not *dat* old." Viola sighed.

"Kinda old, V. Oh shit, I forgot about the disco tape... *Dancing Queen*, *Sexy Thing*, and *Freak Out*."

"What in the world is this?" Viola frowned and held up a *Duran Duran* tape.

"Oh that. That's Jimmy's."

Annoyed, Viola whipped it back in the case. "For such a great vocalist, you'd t'ink he'd pick a better idol." Viola placed the box at her feet and reached for the Rocky Road Coke float. "What did you get?"

"A vanilla shake."

"Boring!" My spry little friend sucked her teeth. "You need to expand, Maggie. Now dis..." Viola stirred her chocolaty mixture that resembled dirty lake water and lumpy bird turds. "...dis is what I'm talking about."

We finished our ice cream in a most leisurely fashion

before motoring back to the house. As we hit the driveway, I had an epiphany. I snapped open the case and searched for a specific tape, a bright pink cartridge labeled in Sarah's loopy handwriting now faded from time.

We made the tape together one Tuesday night during the best summer of my life. Sarah had pilfered a joint from one of the Larry's crew. We lit candles and chilled on the deck smoking grass and eating Ritz Crackers with jelly, the only edible food in the apartment. I made up a stoner game that Sarah deemed super brilliant. First she had to list her top twenty musicians or bands or whatever, and then pick one song from each group. I kicked back and listened as Sarah not only deliberated, but played and replayed her options. For Sarah picking a single favorite proved to be a daunting task.

The crackers, I recall, were stale but tasted so fucking good. Sarah kept repeating herself, wondering why we didn't eat crackers and jam more often. I agreed and smeared another dollop of grape jelly.

Hours into it we got to Sarah's fourteenth favorite group, U2, and hit a wall. She had two favorites by the band, both for very good reasons. BAD reminded her of J.K. who introduced her to U2's music in the first place. ONE reminded her of Jimmy for obvious reasons. Sarah kept skipping over it, moving on to an easier choice. By three a.m. we were back for the last song. The final cut.

"Why can't I just pick two? This is so hard!"

"Because that's the rule." I said. "You only get one."

Sarah paused, put a finger to her head and pretended to pull the trigger. "One song...duh!" She giggled wearily. "Then ONE it is."

Completely exhausted and sick to our stomachs, we called it a night. What started as a quick little stoner game turned into a four hour event. I lay flat on my back and hollered so Sarah could hear me from the other room.

"YOU KNOW WHAT, FOX?"

"What?"

"I freakin' HATE jelly crackers."

*

"Play this one, Viola." I handed her the pink tape. "It's your best shot."

Chapter 27

Viola kicked me out so she could concentrate. Fearful of another sleepless night I found myself on J.K.'s doorstep. The screen door was slightly ajar, banging systematically in a not so stagnant wind. I knocked and rang the bell before twisting the inner knob. It was locked. *Hmm.* I marched around back.

As I approached the latched door, I got a whiff of some seriously foul smelling dog carnage. I followed the odor over to the neighbor's backyard and found the same shabby Pit bulls lounging in a heap of flies under the one shade tree. My arrival initiated a kerfuffle of rants. J.K.'s voice boomed through the wooden barricade.

"SILENCE YOU MANGY MUTTS!"

The evening heat seemed to suck the fun out of barking. The dogs coughed out a few more disgruntled yelps before giving up and lumbering back to their patch of shady dirt. I pushed open the gate and found my friend with his back to me, hose in hand, watering his mother's precious garden. An MP3 player strapped to his upper arm, J.K. was singing the girl part to an Eminem song.

I never held much love for rap music but couldn't help appreciate the singer's knack for nailing dysfunction. J.K.'s voice pitched soprano as he swung his hips and sprayed the garden in perfect rhythm. It would appear that Jimmy wasn't the only island guy who could carry a tune.

J.K. practically convulsed when I touched his arm. In his contorted hysteria the hose sprayed me full on. "Hey!"

"JEEZE, Maggie! What's *WRONG* with you? You don't sneak up on a man like that."

I coughed and wiped my drenched face. "Like what? I tapped you lightly on the shoulder. Who were you expecting? Frankenstein?"

J.K. chuckled and redirected the hose. "Neighbor's got it out for me. Ever since I threw a couple of open peanut butter jars over at the mutts, he wants me dead. Said they had diarrhea for a week. I laughed and said, *yeah, at least they were quiet for a change.* Those son's of bitches never stop barking and *Dickweed*," J.K. flung an arm at the adjacent yard, "won't take 'em for a walk. Shit's piling up back there and the smell is making me nauseous.

"To get me back for the peanut butter he called the county. Tattled that I was watering my mother's garden. Damn if the inspector didn't come by this afternoon and give me a speech about the water shortage. You just missed him. I figure now would be the best time to spray, right after the dude's hauled ass. If these plants die my mother's gonna have a fit. Besides, the flowers are the only thing countering the stench from those dirty maggots next door.

"What really pisses me off is the neighbor couldn't give a rat's ass about them dogs. Who you think puts water in their bowls? Me! I've had half a mind to call the SPCA myself, but then today…well, I got a better idea." J.K. marched over to the steps and held up a box of mothballs. He smiled maliciously and shook it.

"Something tells me you're not storing winter sweaters?"

"No, ma'am." J.K. chirped. "Found a family of copperheads under Momma's new magnolia bushes. About gave me a heart attack when I tried laying mulch."

"What? *Snakes?*"

J.K. cackled as I hurdled through the grass and leaped onto the steps.

Composing myself I asked, "What are the mothballs for?"

"The snakes, of course. They can't stand 'em. Figure I'll put 'em everywhere except the eastern wall. Let the slimy bastards slither over to the neighbor's yard. Shoot, if I wasn't such a pansy I'd stick a few in the prick's mailbox.

---

*Anyway...*what's *up* baby girl?"

I wiped a damp arm on my already drenched shirt. "I thought I'd let you take me out."

He gave me a once over. My hair had frizzed, my shorts were soaked and splatters of vanilla shake stained my left boob.

"Uh, sure, darlin'. High society here we come." J.K. swiped a muddy hand through his sweaty hair.

"I wouldn't talk if I were you."

"Why don't we meet at your place in about an hour? I'm going to finish up and take a shower."

I peered warily at the walkway, unsure. J.K. grinned. "Maybe you wanna cut through the house?"

Mrs. Walsh's impeccable garden was by no means reflected in the condo. Clothes were strewn everywhere, dirty dishes piled up in the sink and empty delivery containers overflowed the garbage. I veered off for a quick bathroom break before heading home. Washing my hands in the sink, I caught a glimpse of the mirror. *What the heck?*

Written in magic marker all the way down the right side of the glass was a list of numbers and symbols. It took me a minute but I figured it out. They were sports statistics — rows and rows of point spreads, dollar amounts, plus marks and minus signs, two and three letter team abbreviations, dates and scheduled game times. As I made my way out of the house I couldn't help but wonder, did J.K. really care about sports...*that much?*

*

Capping my hair, I slipped into the shower for a quick body cleanse. I re-curled my locks and added grease to combat the frizz. My outfit was easy, a simple A-line t-shirt dress and *Feet Candy*. (Feet Candy are beaded sandals that Viola picked up in St. Croix. Sprayed with a secret fragrance, they supposedly lure lusty men.) Splashing on bronzer, eyeliner and upper lid mascara, I finished the ensemble with big silver hoops. (The old pretend-to-dress-down-but-not-really kind of style.)

"Wow!" J.K. let out a wild wolf whistle when he drove over and picked me up. "You look smoking hot!"

Nudging him playfully, I said, "Not too bad yourself." J.K. was sporting a pale yellow golf shirt and plaid shorts. (Yuppie sweet, in my personal opinion.)

We meandered over to Salty's and scored a corner table on the deck. It was only Wednesday and yet the place was mobbed.

"Nobody on the Ridge fishes during a full moon." J.K. informed me. "Shoot, this is quiet! Saturday was the big shindig. A real hoot! If you hadn't blown me off for the Sea Queen," he playfully jabbed my ribs. "You could've witnessed the debauchery first hand. In forty-eight hours the winds'll change as the moon tilts. Come Friday we'll all be back tossing nets."

"Why doesn't anyone fish during a full moon?"

"Something about polarity and the gravitational pull. Fish don't bite, the wind stops, ocean gets so calm it's like one big swimming pool."

"Do you actually buy into all that?"

J.K. shrugged. "I used to think it was nonsense. Then I set out to disprove the theory."

"What happened?"

"Alternator blew on the boat when I flipped the ignition. Never made it out of the marina and it cost me two grand to fix the son-of-a-bitch. Deckman Joe, he's like ninety, swore it was 'cuz I tempted Big Blue. He got all weird and mystical and shit. Kind of freaked me out."

"What is it then that fishermen do during a full moon?"

"Fix stuff, eat home cooked meals, sleep with their wives, catch up on gossip…and drink. A lot of cocktails are poured this time of the month."

J.K. ordered white wine for me, a dark beer for him, and continued to babble. We shared steamers and nachos while I giggled and flipped my hair, now and again interjecting what I considered a witty comment. For one solid hour, it was just the two of us lost in conversation, flirting under an enchanted moon.

The waitress arrived and dropped a couple of shots on the table. "Boys are requesting your presence at the bar for the salute."

"They do this every full moon." J.K. said as we headed inside. I tried to explain that it wasn't my first woo-woo encounter, but the bar was so noisy it was easier to keep quiet and go with the flow.

The night festivities were in full swing. At least fifty or so fishermen and a group of retired ancients, still cloaked in golf gear, held shot glasses high over their heads. The room erupted into a state of hysteria, everyone yodeling and *woo*-hooing, banging chairs and counter tops. The crowd went completely insane before slugging back the one-ounce concoction in memory of a fisherman known to his colleagues as Beast Master Russ.

Big Mikey waved us over and grabbed onto J.K. They were screaming scores at each other as I stood close by chatting up Peko and Sudsy.

Flailing arms at a nearby table caught my attention and a young voice yelled, "Mommy, Mommy! *LOOK!* IT'S THE DIRTY MERMAID!"

Conversation halted and then J.K., Sudsy and Big Mikey roared. My face flushed as I walked over to little Josie and gave her a hug. Betty, Peggy, and a third female, were sitting at a long cluttered table finishing up a bottle of red wine. Betty introduced me to sister number four, Mary, who had similar features and the same low guttural voice.

"Where are the Rangers?" I asked.

"Back in Raleigh. We've got Mary now. Just flew in from California."

"How many sisters do you have?"

"One more, Charlotte. She lives in Massachusetts." Betty said.

"And let's not forget brother Nick, up in Ohio." Mary chimed.

"Here Maggie," Betty offered. "Have some wine."

"Yes, come and sit." Mary poured cabernet into a glass and slid it across the table.

"You got here just in time. Betty was re-telling the story of her past life regressions." Peggy gave me a wink. "She was a Jew, you know, in World War II."

"And before that she was a fisherman," Mary taunted. "That's why she bought a beach house here on the Ridge. Internal forces must have played a key role in the purchase."

The sisters cracked up and Betty frowned. "It's true! Maggie will believe me. Guess who she works for Mary? The Mermaid Lady." Betty turned to me. "If you can believe in girlyfish, then how can you *not* believe in past life regressions?"

Mary butt in, clearly more interested in hearing about my boss than Betty's reincarnation. "Is it true? *Can* Viola Fox see mermaids?"

"Technically...uh, no." I stuttered. "Mermaids surface for relatives and...and friends. The witnesses, they seek her out."

"But why?"

"Because she's the mermaid expert, I suspect. Viola spent the first part of her life on the open sea. You do realize that most of the book mermaids are centuries old, legends and myths passed onto her as a child."

I fell into story telling mode, repeating one of the many monologues Viola saved for her Wednesday afternoon book club. "My favorite legend is that of the Katz twins."

"Twins?" Peggy asked.

"Lisbet and Grace Katz, wild rich girls famous in the early fourteen hundreds for tag teaming pirates. Some called them water nymphs and others treasure whores. Shoot, they were no worse than downtown Raleigh chicks after a wild Saturday night. Anyway…every pirate and deck hand fantasized of a session with the sisters, especially after an extra long sea voyage. A poor man would beg and a rich man would brag, adorning the girls in their finest jewels. The twins received these bounties casually, but no gift, be it spoken or wrapped, meant the man would be chosen-fare for the sexually starved duo. It was said that the sisters held no love for one man, and therefore honored the wishes of many.

"One evening, while the twins were dining in one of the more elegant brothels in town, they heard the most beautiful sound. Pausing with wine glasses pressed to satiated lips, they locked eyes with a soft-featured pirate swinging in a nearby hammock. He was strumming a tune on his tiny guitar. Sorry, I forget what they call those little guitars. Do you know?"

Peggy and Betty argued for a solid minute trying to figure out the word. Again, Mary cut in. (I could see a pattern with these three.) "Forget it. Go with tiny guitar…it's good enough."

I took another sip of wine and continued. "His voice, deep and commanding, lured the young nymphs to his swaying lair where they sandwiched him in a bodacious cuddle. Clearly smitten by his exquisite voice, they tickled his ears while the young sailor belted out a series of moaning and melodious renditions.

"When the festivities came to an end, the duo propositioned the young man. Pretty Joe (that's what they called him) flat out refused to seduce both women at the same time. One, he said, would have the privilege of priority while the other slipped around for sloppy seconds.

For the first time in their very extensive career, the sisters scrutinized one another. A verbal argument broke out, then claws, and eventually hardware. Nobody could say for sure which knife made the first slash. Many argued that they drew simultaneously. Identical twins, after all, harbor comparable reflexes. Whatever the chain of events, one thing was certain. Before the barkeep could finish wiping the counter, the Katz twins lay dead on the floor saturated in a pool of sisterly sanguine.

"Based on the name, *Katz*, legend has it that this was considered the first true cat fight."

"*That's* a children's story?" Mary asked as she re-filled the glasses. (During my tale, Betty had ordered another bottle of wine and her husband resurfaced to retrieve Josie and carry her off to bed.)

"The Katz Twins," Betty slurred. "I remember them but I thought they died for true love. It didn't say anything about *stabbing* each other."

"There's a kicker to the story," I continued. "According to Viola, Pretty Joe resided in a nearby village historians like to compare to modern day Queens, if that's even possible. Pretty Joe's real name was Gloria Hodges. She was a lesbian. For the record, ladies, the Katz sisters dueled over a dyke."

*

Like the Katz twins, we stayed until closing time. Before leaving the bar I stumbled into the bathroom, bleary-eyed drunk, for one last piss before staggering home. I ran smack into Cherry.

"Hey, Maggie."

"Hey."

Thankfully, there was an open toilet so I rushed past her pretending to be in a hurry. Having no desire to play nicey-nice with J.K.'s ex-girlfriend or fuck friend, or what ever you wanted to call her, I stayed in the stall for what seemed an eternity. My efforts proved futile. Cherry was still waiting, leaning against the far wall quiet as a mouse.

"So..." she leered. "What's up?"

"Not much." I moved to the sink and washed my hands, fumbling in my purse for a lipstick.

"You here with J.K.?"

"Yeah…so?"

"So how's he doing? Frankly, I'm *concerned*."

Irritated by her tone, I flipped my hair and preened my lips. "Well *don't* be. He's with me now so you can just step back."

"'Fraid I can't do that, country girl."

"*Me*? Country girl!" I pointed a bewildered finger at her outfit. "I'm not the one sporting a NASCAR hat wearing a fucking *Hee-Haw* checkered blouse."

"Think what you want, Maggie, but J.K.'s not getting out of this one. He's got until Friday."

"What're you yapping about?"

She eyed me coolly. "Friday, country girl, tell him to meet me at our special place." She turned on a flip flop, red to match her stupid checkered shirt, and marched out.

*

J.K. and I were having such a good time that I didn't want to spoil it with Cherry's warning. Fuck *her*! I knew what she was trying to do—make us fight right before the good part. That wasn't going to happen. Not tonight.

I lit candles and loaded the C.D. player with seducing sex songs. J.K. ogled me from the couch and I danced over, giggling as I straddled his lap. We rolled around for hours performing our own version of a *Moondance*, harmonious and in perfect rhythm with Mr. Morrison's infamous melody.

In the early morning light, J.K. lifted me off the rug and carried me to bed, whispering something about six a.m. and getting an early start. He had business in Wilmington and wanted to beat the traffic. Without thinking, I mumbled Cherry's message. "Friday, she said."

I'm pretty sure he responded. Went on a bit about whatever Cherry was dramatizing. But the wine had taken its toll and I was caught naked in a dream—prancing about a sandy beach under a neon moon. Lugging a flashlight and a glass of wine, I was searching for crabs, dirty mermaids and my missing checkered dress.

Chapter 28

I woke up to a buzzing alarm with a pounding headache. Nine forty-five. Fifteen minutes to beautify before opening the store. With great effort, I trudged butt naked to the fridge, chugged two glasses of water and downed a couple of Tylenol. I read a scribbled note left on the counter. *Call you later, sleepyhead.* Smiling, even though it hurt, I lumbered off to the shower.

I opened the store twelve minutes late for an already irritated group of tourists and groaned inwardly when the second woman tapped at her watch as she marched past. *Man, this is going to be a loonnngg day.*

Gallagher stopped by around two o'clock. He smirked at my shattered appearance. I didn't have time to curl my hair so it frizzed every which way, and the bit of mascara I managed had already smudged from sweat and alcohol.

"Have a little fun last night, Maggie?"

"Something like that." I was wading through the daunting task of re-racking a pile of bathing suits. Three southern bells had me scrambling for the better part of two hours in their search for a perfect fit. Worse part, they were friends of Viola so I had to serve sweet tea and laugh at their stupid jokes.

"I was hoping to catch you alone but maybe not. Are we still on for tonight? Say ten thirty?"

Right then, a frazzled young mother waved me over. Her chubby sons were leaping like two hyped-up poodles, frustrated because they couldn't reach a pair of weather monkeys. Without thinking I agreed to a meeting. What a nightmare! Already exhausted, I climbed a stepstool and snatched at the pricey stuffed animals wondering how in the world I was ever going to make it.

At five p.m. the central air died. I didn't notice at first blaming excessive perspiration on woo-woos and red wine. When Big Mikey showed up to restock the coolers he commented. "Are you trying to save money or what? It's like a sauna in here."

"Really? I thought it was just me."

Mikey hustled to the storeroom and hollered out from the fuse box. "Sorry lady, but something's screwed up. You better call Marty."

"Marty?"

"Shrimp Man's brother. He's the island electrician."

I rang Viola to get Marty's number and as I hung up the phone she said, "Can you stop by later, Maggie?"

"The painting's finished?"

"No, but Lucky has information. He wants to keep you in the loop."

Mentally calculating time for a mini-nap I replied, "Will nine o'clock be too late? I wouldn't mind a shower." Stealing Mikey's line I added. "It's like a sauna in here."

*

Marty arrived at six thirty. He was older than Shrimp Man and puttered about at a geriatric pace. At seven on the nose I locked the front door, hanging a sign...*Sorry! Electrical Problems.* I asked Marty to stop by the apartment when he finished. The old man grunted so I raced out the back door taking the deck steps two at a time and dove onto the sofa.

Bang. Bang. Bang.

Dazed, I checked the clock. Eight thirty. Damn. Naptime flew.

Marty lingered at the door, arms crossed, staring off in the distance. He wiped a hairy forearm across his sweaty brow. "Breeze feels good, you know?"

"Better than that sauna."

The leathery man grunted. "Got a big problem, ma'am."

"What do you mean?"

"S'been rigged."

"What?"

"The wires. They're screwed up." Marty paused. "After all them break-ins, Lucky made Mrs. Fox get an alarm. I was off island for a month visiting my daughter in Sarasota on account she's bellied another youngin'. I promised to fix it when I got home but little Louie," Marty rolled his eyes, "Mr. *Deputy Sheriff*, told her not to wait. She musta hired some fool out of Wilmington to do the wirin'. Shit's so rigged it's a wonder the place hasn't burnt to the ground. The added voltage overloaded an already ancient cooling system and knocked out a bunch of gadgets. Your central air's toast, the outdoor fridge is melting and you can kiss that fancy alarm good-bye. The fuse box is nothing but a jumble o'wires. One big rigaroo."

"Can you fix it?"

"Sure can, but it'll take awhile. Need some special parts."

"Okay, then."

"And it's not going to be cheap." Marty glowered irritably. "Damn those Wilmington amateurs. Ms. Viola is not going to be pleased."

***

I shivered through an extremely frigid shower and towel dried so carelessly that my t-shirt rolled up under itself as I struggled to pry it on. Brushing through tangled locks, I was easily frustrated and twisted my hair in a ponytail. Very much resembling a drowned rat, I threw on a ball cap, popped two more Tylenol and headed for the golf cart.

Blackened storm clouds rumbled in the distance. How I yearned to be back on the couch, windows open, relaxing through a summer squall. Rounding the corner near Larry's, I scowled. *My meeting with Gallagher is tonight. Damn!*

I made it to Viola's shortly after nine-thirty, but Lucky's car was nowhere in sight. *Figures.* A couple of mugs laced with damp tea bags cluttered the sink, the only evidence of human activity. I called out. As if on cue, *Last Night,* by *The Traveling Wilbury's,* vibrated through the ceiling boards.

The music shifted my thoughts to more encouraging times, back when Sarah and I ruled the pool table at *Felci's,* a basement bar just off campus. Sarah was known to load the juke box right before game time so she could twirl around the table, dance with a pool stick, and work her magic. During the best summer of my life she would bring me to Salty's to practice, usually early afternoon so we could monopolize the table before getting booted for happy hour. To say our skills were comparable was a flat out lie. I never could master Sarah's level of expertise.

I swung open the studio door and found Viola sprawled flat on her back with eyes closed, arms spread wide, splattered in color. I silently cursed the trip. I could've skipped it and nobody would've been the wiser.

In front of the window on a tilted easel stood Viola's death piece, no doubt, covered in a sheet. Warily, I peered at the mat. The old woman let out a rumbling snore and rolled to one side. She was out cold. Before losing my nerve I tip-toed past and held up a smidgeon of fabric, disappointed and yet slightly relieved to find the lower half of the canvas relatively unfinished. *Do you really want to see it, Maggie? No, you don't. Leave it alone.* But when I let go of the sheet the silky material shifted and slipped silently to the floor.

I leaned in for a closer inspection. Viola hadn't gotten very far. She had dabbed part of the ocean, sketched the top of Sarah's head and part of her bare shoulders. They were painted an ebony-bronze but it was only a first layer, the skin tone definitely needed more depth. One slender hand unconnected by paint held a shiny instrument. But it wasn't a wand...

Horrified, I tripped back. Oh my *GOD!* What was it that Viola said...*pay attention to the wand, Maggie? It's going to mean something.* The wand had transformed...taking on the shape of a shiny silver cooking spatula.

I tried shaking Viola awake but she kicked me away and threw an arm across her skull, covering it like a pillow. I scratched out a quick note, raced to the golf cart and headed south. *No wonder Ronnie wants to see me. He knows! Or maybe it's more than that? What if he...what if Ronnie...?*

I willed the mermaid mobile faster but 30 miles an hour was its maximum speed. I felt like the *Six Million Dollar Man* moving in slow motion except without the cool bionic sounds. *This is crazy!* I veered onto J.K.'s street, parked in front of his condo and sprinted up the walk.

Last night's date lay sleeping on the couch, left arm dangling, and right hand clutching a television remote that rested on his chest.

"J.K." I didn't bother to whisper. "Get up."

His eyes shot open and in one swoop he was sitting straight up. He stared at me through foggy eyes and wiped drool from his chin. Grinning, he said, "What's going on, baby girl?"

"I need to meet Gallagher."

"And?"

"And you have to come with me. He's involved in Sarah's disappearance somehow and...it's bad."

J.K. frowned. "What are you babbling about Maggie?"

"I have to talk to him but I need you to be close. Uh...just in case."

"Just in case, *what?*"

"I...I'm not sure but..." My cell phone rang. "Hello?"

It was Lucky. "Marty called me."

"Oh yeah, right. I can't get into that now. I've got to meet Gallagher."

The line went quiet. "Don't do anything stupid, Maggie. The painting...it's not finished." *Lucky has seen the painting.* "You need to wait."

"I promised to meet him. He's been asking. I can't blow him off. Not *now*. Phone me in an hour."

*

J.K. blocked the front door. "Before we go anywhere, Maggie, you need to fess up."

With Lucky informed, involving J.K. felt almost negligent. I didn't have time to explain. He'd never believe it, anyway. Not unless I started from the beginning. Squeezing his arm I said, "You know what? I changed my mind. Let me go and we'll talk when I get back."

"Hold up, girly-girl," J.K. snapped. "You can't just waltz in here freaking out like a manic chicken, squawk about trouble and then leave me sitting here like a sack o' spuds." J.K.'s dramatics caught me off guard.

"When you say it like that..." I smirked. "Fine. Come. But there's no time for an explanation. I'm late as it is."

Chapter 29

I ordered J.K. to wait at the apartment for twenty minutes before heading over to the restaurant. Then directed him to park the golf cart next to Larry's side door so he had a proper excuse for stopping in. If Ronnie was exacting my demise, a witness was only moments away.

Gallagher was cleaning the grill when I found him. He poured seltzer onto the searing hot surface and used an enormous flat blade to scrape and scour. The fluid bubbled and hissed, turning to steam as he worked. *Van Halen* bellowed from an ancient radio/tape player crammed on a tiny shelf just above his head. Ronnie hummed along oblivious to my presence.

Once again it occurred to me how much Gallagher had aged. My first visit to the island, when was it? Five years ago? He seemed unstoppable. Always bouncing around during rush hour, telling jokes, boosting morale, his soft feathered seventies hair whipping in the wind. Never quite buff, Ronnie was more lean than muscular, but his wiry figure suited him well and somehow kept him looking young.

Now Gallagher was just plain skinny. Boney even. His stick legs shot out of cut off jeans, white as a sheet, like he hadn't seen the beach all summer even though he worked ten paces away. His hair was butch, still growing in after the accident, a red scar prevalent at certain angles. Gone was the spirited sweet seventies hippie I adored, replaced by a man beaten down by life. Ronnie Gallagher sadly reminded me of a middle-aged POW.

I gave the wall a hard knock. "Hey, Ronnie."

Gallagher yelped. The brillo pad flew from his hand as he twisted around like a petrified rabbit. "Jeeze, Maggie! Give me a heart attack, why don't you? Call out next time. Ever since the robbery I've picked up a bit of a nervous condition."

"Post Traumatic Stress Disorder, that's the professional term."

"Whatever you want to label it, it's kicking my ass." Gallagher laughed in spite of the topic and offered me a Coke from the soda fountain.

I pointed to the radio. "Still in love with *Van Halen* I see."

"You got that right, sister. This is my song."

"Sounds like a bunch of noise."

"Hey, hey, hey! No disrespectin' the music! This is *Ice Cream Man*, my favorite tune."

"*Ice Cream Man* is a song? Really? And I thought your nickname was a play on the job."

"That's exactly what Sarah said...when I told her!"

Maybe it was the nostalgic smile or the way Ronnie blinked sheepishly when he said her name, but suddenly...it all made sense.

"How long were you and Sarah sleeping together?"

Gallagher's body locked up. He reached over and clicked off the radio. "I never slept with her."

"You're *LYING!*"

Stunned, he turned to me. "I...we never did *anything*. I...we kissed a few times but nobody knows about that. How did you figure it out?"

"For starters, every time I lined up for a burger you ignored me. And don't tell me it's because of your ex. I only met her that one time. You were screwin' Sarah."

"NEVER! We kissed. So *what*. We're friends." He reached into his shirt pocket and pulled out a cigarette.

"Doublemint's not cutting it these days, huh Gallagher? I suppose if I was wanted for murder I'd be smoking too."

"*Murder?* Maggie, *please*. Take a chill. I didn't *kill* Sarah. For *chrissakes...*" He hesitated. "I'm not sure what happened." Taking an anxious drag, Ronnie began blabbing before exhaling, releasing smoke with each word. "I didn't ask you here to lie to you. I need to talk to…to *someone*. I'm so dag confused. My mind's a jumble.

"The witch is fighting for full custody and my kids phone everyday crying. You have no idea what that's like! I've constantly got the shits and my doctor put me on Zantac. I want to quit smoking but every time I do I have another *fucking* panic attack. And this mess with Sarah? I'm afraid to go to the police because my wife will hold it against me. And then you show up, someone I think I can *trust*, and get all *tough* when I just wanna figure things out! I don't need this, Maggie. I'm a basket case the way it is."

Gallagher stopped short and took another quick drag. He looked so friggin' pathetic I changed my tone. "What happened then? Tell me."

Ronnie pinched at his brow and engaged. "I ran into Sarah a month after her split from Jimmy. She was living at Viola's by then and not coping well. I dragged her to Salty's for Rib Night and we slugged back a few. She bitched about Jimmy and I went off on Cassie. Misery loves company, I guess. Cassie had been cheating on me for months. My private investigator, yeah I hired one too, caught her wrestling naked with one of the PTA dads. Not a pretty photo shoot that's for sure. Cassie still doesn't know about the pictures; thinks she's going to get me for abandonment." Ronnie paused. "Sad part, what's really pathetic, I keep hoping we can work shit out. Crazy stupid, I know. But that's love for you…

"I don't have to tell you about Sarah. She was torn up when Jimmy left. That very night we ended up wasted down on the beach and Sarah devised this ridiculous plan."

"What kind of plan?"

"To get Jimmy and Cassie back," Ronnie impressed. "Sounds stupid now, but back then we were both so desperate. Couldn't see past our noses."

"What was her big idea?"

"We were supposed to flirt with each other. Sarah

convinced me that if we completely ignored Cassie and Jimmy, and acted really happy, they'd freak out and come running. She made up rules."

"For instance?"

"No phone calls to the ex's, for one. We were supposed to act pleasant and sincere. Never get angry or jealous. Pretend to be having the time of our lives whenever they were near. It sounds easy but it's pretty friggin' hard."

I was quickly reminded of a stressed out Jimmy, lingering deep in the shadows of the Sailor's Haven, anxiously strategizing his comeback. Sarah was a genius.

Gallagher continued. "That's how it started between us. A game. But after a couple of weeks, I gotta admit, I was having a pretty good time. Since it wasn't *real* I didn't feel that usual freak-out date pressure, know what I'm sayin'? It felt kinda' good to be just plain old Ronnie.

"Sarah had me doing stupid stuff like playing bingo at the firehouse on Tuesday nights. You should see all the Baptists tanked up on sweet tea fighting to win black-out bingo. I hadn't been to church in years, but Sarah said rubbin' elbows with religious folks might be just the thing to lift my spirits. I actually won a toaster. Can you believe it? Nothing special, of course, just some five-n-dime number...

"Sarah would send me crazy text messages that made no sense at all. One night we climbed onto the roof of the old middle school, drank can beer, and she beat me in a head stand contest. A real hoot that was! We fished, of course, and crabbed. She talked a lot about school, stories about you and the dorms."

"I'm sure that was pleasant."

"You'd be surprised, Maggie, how much she misses you."

I nodded slightly and sipped my Coke.

"Some nights Sarah ordered take-out subs and would meet me at the picnic tables. Other times, we'd grill off her back deck. One evening, she lit candles and told me how the two of you made a special tape. She played it for me as we lounged under the stars." Ronnie sighed. "That was the night. I could feel it, a definite shift in our relationship. It wasn't just a bitch game anymore. Not for me. And I don't know…but I think Sarah…well, I couldn't get a read on her."

"She liked you."

Ronnie frowned. "How would you know? The two of you hadn't spoken in years. You never returned her calls."

I shrugged. "Sarah had a way of making me feel second rate, a replacement for when Jimmy wasn't available."

"Yeah, she said that too." Ronnie coughed. "Anyway, I had planned on confessing that I wanted more than just a pretend relationship. I was so *nervous*. It had been years since I was attracted to anyone other than my wife.

"There's this little grassy inlet about a mile up the coast that I used to frequent in high school. The old *Senior Make-out Spot*, we named it, where you'd bring your best gal after a big pizza date. The night I decided to take Sarah the moon wasn't perfectly full but almost, which made the trip easy on account of the lazy current. I figured we'd drop a blanket in the sand, build a fire and then I'd fess up." Gallagher paused and lit another cigarette.

"Five minutes into the trip I realize that I'd forgotten the music. I freaked. How could I get romantic without my favorite tunes? Sarah, of course, completely understood so we doubled back and I hustled into the restaurant to fetch Van Halen *1984*. I played the darn thing so often I was positive that it was right here, on this very shelf." Ronnie pointed to the radio/tape player.

"That explains the Van Halen poster."

"The what?"

"Sarah has a poster of Eddie on the ceiling above her bed." I added. "In the Jimmy room."

"What's the Jimmy room?"

"Long story, but I suspect she positioned it there because of you. Sarah was *Hot For Teacher*."

Ronnie's eyes flashed in a mix of delight and horror. He gripped at his butched head and squeezed. "If I had just kept my fucking mouth shut about the tape none of this would've happened."

"What *did* happen?"

"Like I was sayin', I ran into the building and made a beeline for the shelf. Not ten seconds later I hear Sarah in the prep room. She must've followed me in. But I wasn't really paying attention because the safe, you know, it was built into the floor right in front of the grill. I discovered it wide open with money piled everywhere."

"So wait..." I said. "The trip on the dingy was the same night Larry's got robbed?"

Ronnie nodded.

Perplexed, I added. "Somebody *opened* your safe?"

"Safe's been broken going on sixteen years. It looks locked but it isn't. That's common knowledge 'round here. Shoot...you worked with me what? Three months? Tell me you weren't privy to that information?"

"I guess I was."

"That's what makes it tricky. The thief coulda been just about anyone."

"Why not fix it?"

Gallagher scoffed. "This here's the safest island in the country or at least it used to be. Getting back to Sarah...I hear her holler as I'm kneeling down to check the safe, thinking it was just me in too much of a daggone hurry. And then WHAM!

"Next thing I remember is the hospital. Doctor said I got clocked something good. Cracked my skull wide open and caused bleeding in the brain. A Subdural Hematoma. I was lucky to be alive.

"The hospital cut me loose a week later but my memory was pure shit. Except for the forty-six stitches in the back of my skull, I had no recollection of the robbery. Shoot, I even called Cassie to pick me up! So far gone I done forgot about the divorce. Course she laughed and hung up the phone. Gina come by and explained things."

"What happened to Sarah?"

"Gina was clueless about Sarah and I had completely blanked out about our little flirt game. Nobody suspected that she was involved."

"What jarred your memory?"

"That first night when you came up to the grill, seeing you reminded me of Sarah. I had flashes of drinking with her at Salty's. Then the beach and the plan...but the whole relationship thing was hazy. I wanted to ask you about it, see if you could shed some light. Then my wife showed up and the moment was lost. That's when I discovered the bitch was actually going though with it, filing for full custody. After the robbery and my cracked skull, she didn't think it was safe for *her* children to be on island. I was so torn up about the kids I couldn't concentrate on anything but the divorce. You don't know how hard it is for a father in the court system. It's eating me alive."

"What about the robbery? When did it finally hit you?"

Gallagher's eyes filled. "Three days ago. I returned from another terrifying day at court and it didn't go well. I was angry and sick to my daggone stomach, petrified that I might lose. I kept thinking about Cassie and how much I fucking hated her. While I stood there watching her lie in court, I kept visualizing the two of us having sex. But right at the climax I'd pull out an ice pick and jab it in her chest over and over, you know, like in that movie where the chick shows her goodies? Sick shit but that's how disturbed I am. My head's all wound up and it's because of the witch. I packed a few beers, grabbed my pole, thought maybe fishing might settle the nerves. When I tried to find my favorite music...I...I...Oh my God, I *remembered*!

"Sarah on the boat, the fishing trip, the *1984* tape... What the fuck *happened*? I tried convincing myself that is was just the brain injury playing tricks, jumbling stuff, but I couldn't say for certain. Rumor has it that Sarah's run off, but that night at the restaurant, right before losing consciousness...I heard screaming."

My face went tight. "Jimmy!"

"Jimmy? What does Jimmy have to do with anything?"

"Jimmy was here that night. He watched the two of you gettin' all lovey dovey in the dingy. It practically killed him. Jimmy told me he waited for Sarah at the Haven. He planned to reconcile but she never made it back to the apartment."

"I don't get it."

"Come *on*, Gallagher, don't be so thick. You said it yourself. One minute you're having sex with your wife and the next you're stabbing her in the chest with an ice pick. Love makes people do fucked up shit."

"So...Sarah hauled ass because of Jimmy? That doesn't make sense."

"*No*, Gallagher. Sarah's *dead*."

Ronnie's knees buckled and he staggered into the counter. "What?" His brow furrowed. "No...no! That's ridiculous."

Before I had a chance to explain there was movement in the back room. "J.K.? Is that you?"

"J.K.?" Gallagher growled. "Why would *he* be here?" Bewildered he said, "*You*...you don't *trust* me? You think I had something to do with this? That I would *hurt* one of my best friends! ARE YOU *MAD*!?"

Lucky materialized in the doorway. "Easy, Ronnie. Let's take this one step at a time."

"What the MESS, Maggie?" Gallagher gasped. "You called the *SHERIFF*?"

Lucky turned to me. "I warned you not to jump to any conclusions."

"But a *spatula*?" I cried. "Sarah was here on the night of the robbery. Did you know that? Go ahead, Ronnie...tell him."

Gallagher scowled as Lucky muttered. "Shoot! Maybe it was Sarah's blood..."

Ronnie and I froze.

"The investigators found two different blood types at the crime scene. B positive and O negative. You, Mr. Gallagher, are O negative, which led us to believe the perpetrator has B blood. But if Sarah was present..." Lucky paused. "I'll have to make some calls. Hopefully Viola knows her blood type. I don't want to contact Sarah's parents until it's absolutely necessary."

"Ronnie heard screaming, Lucky. It happened here, in this very room."

"*WHAT* HAPPENED HERE?" Ronnie bellowed. "DAGGONE IT, MAGGIE! WHAT ARE YOU KEEPING FROM ME?"

Again, I tried to explain but Lucky cut me off. "Sorry, Mr. Gallagher, we have our reasons. Now tell me everything you can remember about that night. "

Ronnie heaved a great sigh and repeated his story. "I walked in on the robbery. Money was stacked all over the floor, right here near the safe. The spring breakers were in town, you know, and there was a surfing tournament. Larry's always makes a killing that time of year."

"The perp opened your safe?"

Gallagher rolled his eyes. "Tell me you don't know about the safe? It's been broken since 1996 when Bubba come in for the July (sounding like *Jew-lie*) fourth holiday. You remember Bubba, don'tcha sheriff?"

Responding in a serious tone, Lucky replied. "The same Bubba who spray painted *Bubba is bubbalicious* on the water tower?"

"Yeah, uh..."

"The same Bubba that dressed up like an old lady so he could get served at Salty's underage?"

"That's righ..."

"The same Bubba who streaked down the beach at high

noon during the New Years Eve Regatta while Channel 2 was interviewing the governor? *That* same Bubba?"

"Yep..." Gallagher coughed uneasily. "In his defense, sir, it's always been on account of the slippery nipples."

"The slippery who?"

"Nipples, sir. Every time Bubba drinks 'em he gets in trouble, like the time with the safe. We were drinking beer just fine and then, sure enough, Bubba's got to bring out the schnapps and Bailey's. Next thing you know it's three in the mornin', we've snuck into Larry's to fry up some clam rolls and Bubba's begging me to experiment with the safe. He wants to see if his homemade M-80 can blow the top off.

"I responded by saying that this here safe is a Civil War relic, older'n molasses and heavier than a constipated hippo. They just don't make'em the way they used to. I tell Bubba he's full of pigeon shit. No way is one of his flour-stuffed bottle rockets going to destroy my Civil War safe.

"He bets me fifty bucks and a steak dinner. Course I went for it. That's what slippery nipples'll do to your brain. Anyway, I didn't expect the little butt-brain to light up four of those sons'o bitches. Sure as sheet metal, they obliterated the inside lock mechanism. Bubba lost the bet because the top didn't blow off, but in the end it was me who got screwed. Now you just have to turn the combination dial to number 16 and this sucker opens."

Lucky chuckled. "What did you expect, son, making that kind of bet?"

"Been planning to get a new one, but never had any reason to worry before."

I turned to the sheriff. "Jimmy was here that night."

"In the building?"

"He followed Sarah to the docks. Apparently, Gallagher's the lover he's been whining about."

Ronnie blushed slightly. "Now wait a minute, Maggie. We only kissed..."

Lucky cut him off. "Jimmy told me he was at Salty's

that night, never mentioned anything about the docks."

"And why do you think that is, Lucky?" J.K. was the next man to emerge from the back room. By the sounds of it he'd been listening for some time. Ronnie threw me the evil eye, but I pretended not to notice and focused on J.K., who continued his rant.

"Why would Jimmy want Viola's *boyfriend*, the beloved *sheriff*, to know that he's been spying on his wife? You'd call it stalking and he'd be nailed to the wall like a virgin in a whore house. Whatever this is Jimmy didn't do it."

"Are you sure about that, J.K.?" I snapped. "You really think Jimmy had enough control to saunter away after finding his wife snuggled up with another man?"

"What do you believe, Maggie?" J.K. scoffed. "That Jimmy attempted to *murder* Ronnie Gallagher?"

"I...uh..."

"And staged a robbery to cover it up?"

"*Maybe*! But ..."

"...but *obviously*," Lucky shut us down. "We're missing a big piece of the puzzle. This evidence is very concerning. It proves one thing. Jimmy Harrison had motive."

"A motive for *what*?" Gallagher asked.

"For the abduction of Sarah Fox."

J.K. blanched. "*What*? But...but Sarah's gone! Off island somewhere getting her head straight."

"I hope you're right, Mr. Walsh." Lucky paused. "Sorry guys but this conversation is closed." He turned to me. "Maggie, maybe you should stay at Viola's for awhile. Until we figure this out I think it'd be best if you weren't alone."

J.K. wrapped an arm around my shoulder. "I got Maggie, Sheriff."

It was my turn to blush. Nobody noticed. Lucky was already half way out the door."

I called after him. "What are you going to do?"

"Get a search warrant. Sounds like Mr. Harrison left out a few details."

Chapter 30

Completely exhausted, I dropped like dead weight on J.K.'s couch. He skittered about picking up clothes and dishes, tidying up the man home.

"Are you hungry, Maggie? I could pick us up some Chinese?"

I remembered mumbling something about vegetable lo mein and that was it. J.K. spread an afghan over my shoulders and I drifted off to the sound of a running vacuum. The longest day of my life had come to a crashing end.

***

The aroma of delicious sustenance aroused me from sleep. My stomach growled and I immediately sat up. Bleary eyed and confused, I peered around the living space, now squeaky spotless, and spent the next sixty seconds puzzling back the pieces to my current situation.

"Hey, sleepy head. You want me to make you a plate?"

"A plate of what?"

"Food, silly? Remember? You ordered vegetable lo mien."

"What time is it?"

"Almost three o'clock."

"Naps are a wonderful thing."

"*Nap*?" J.K. laughed. "That was more like hibernation."

"What do you mean?"

"It's three p.m., Maggie. You've been out for almost fifteen hours."

"*Shoot*! The store!"

"Slow down, sister. Lucky phoned earlier. Said the shop was going to stay closed for the day so Marty could get in there and fix wiring screwed up by, and I quote, *some Wilmington amateur*. Marty brought in his buddy Dave, a Pender County Fire Marshall, who unofficially declared the building a very expensive bonfire waiting on a cheap match. Told Viola she needed to shut it down until a bunch of frayed coils were replaced. I left a note on the counter, but well, you'd have to be awake to read it.

"I feel so refreshed."

"Sleeping the day away will do that for you, darlin'." J.K. grinned and passed me a bowl of re-heated noodles. "Not to worry," he said. "Chinese food always tastes better as leftovers."

*

After breakfast, or should I say lunch, J.K. drove me back to the apartment where I showered, changed, and packed a bag. I stopped in the store to check on Marty who continued his bitch rant against the under-trained Wilmington city slickers.

"I got the central air working, thank you Jesus, but that's it so far. Still waiting on a special delivery part from Raleigh. Good news is Dave gave the okay for Viola to reopen come mornin'." Marty smirked. "Feeling a bit better today, ma'am?"

"Yes, much."

"Well you smell sweeter that's for sure. Much better'n that moonshine mess you were seepin' yesterday." The electrician cackled like a hyena.

"Thanks, Marty...I think."

*

J.K. grabbed my overnight bag and wrenched it into the back of his work truck, a rugged stated-of-the-art Ford F-150. (One of the perks, he said, working for your best friend.) Unlike the condo, J.K. kept his truck spit-shined and turtle-waxed.

"Jeeze, Maggie, whatchoo got in this here bag, a bowling ball?

211

"Girl stuff."

"Like what?"

"Make-up, blow dryer, anti-bitch cream and hairy wart removal."

"Oh *lawd,*" J.K. crowed. "How's 'bout you and me go for a ride?"

"Ditchin' work I gather?" It dawned on me right as I commented.

"Cops've been searching the marina all morning. Lucky said it'd be best if I just cleared out for the day. Truthfully, I've been kinda waitin' on you in hopes of diverting my energy. Take my mind off this crazy mess."

"Did they find anything?"

"Not Jimmy."

"What do you mean?"

"He's gone missin'. Tried his cell about a dozen times but it bumps over to a recording. Stupid fool. Hiding'll give folks the wrong impression.

*

We motored over the metal causeway deep into Carolina country. Filled up on fuel and sweet tea at a gas station so ancient, paying at the pump wasn't an option. J.K. veered off at 210, a twisty winding road, lined with pine trees, budding cornfields, scattered modular homes and its share of malodorous chicken coops. Overcast skies subdued the June heat, so instead of cranking the A/C, J.K. unrolled both windows and let the wind whip through the cab.

Thirty minutes into the trip, we branched off on a rickety drive marked with dilapidated road signs too faded to read. Due to the narrow and rocky conditions, J.K. crept along. The trail opened up to a collection of scattered rusted-out doublewides and a warehouse baking in the Carolina heat.

"What is this place?" I tried deciphering another dusty billboard but the sun momentarily peaked though the clouds and blinded my view.

"Give me a second, Maggie." He reached over and kissed my hand before jumping from the cab and jogging into the building. Minutes later, the warehouse door pushed open and J.K. emerged carrying a couple of white gallon buckets. A short stocky dude with a killer tan, wearing loose jeans and a muscle t-shirt, followed him out. The two were talking amongst themselves. J.K. mentioned something and the short guy replied with a raucous laugh. Actions so natural, it was apparent that they'd been previously acquainted.

I stepped out of the cab as J.K. hollered over. "Maggie, I want you to meet a good buddy of mine. This here's Dakater Moon."

"Howdy, ma'am."

"Dakater? *Wait.* Is this a blueberry farm?"

"Sho' is."

"This must be the place Sarah was always bragging about. Said you had the most voluptuous berries in the county. Promised to bring me pickin' a few years back but the summer got away from us."

"Always does." Dakater cackled. "How is old Foxy?"

"Maggie roomed with Sarah in college." J.K. cut in before I had a chance to comment.

"And Sarah said my farm had voluptuous berries?"

I grinned. "That was a big word for us back then."

"Well she nailed it, darling'. Sho'nuff."

We chatted for a good ten minutes before Dakater mapped out directions to his *private stock* bushes. "These here grow the plumpest, juiciest pieces'a blue that money can't buy."

"Can't?"

"You heard me right!" Dakater chortled. "The Piggly Wig won't be shelving my private stock. No ma'am! These berries'll be savored by only the closest of my personal relations. Friends that 'ppreciate a top grade speci-*man* and don't mind a half-mile trek in a hun'erd degree sun to git'em sum'."

"You won't be disappointed, Maggie." J.K. added as we set out. "These are some sweet treats."

It was a lazy afternoon. Neither of us spoke about Sarah or Jimmy, or Lucky and his search for answers. For a few precious hours we picked fruit and relaxed, pretending to be just another couple in lust, ducking out for an afternoon of berries and sex, which we got to shortly after in a shady hollow just beyond the blueberry fields.

We headed home at sunset. I flipped up the mid-console so I could sit practically on J.K.'s lap, flung off my sandals and cruised with my right foot dangling out the window. J.K. testified that I was acting like a redneck, but stopped midsentence to bellow out the chorus of some country western song cranking on the radio. This gave us both the giggles and I settled in with my eyes shut, feeling the wind lick my toes as we maneuvered the curvy roads a little slower this time. It dawned on me that J.K. was harmonizing the newest *Filipino Cowboy* release; a musical rendition of cooking biscuits with a baby doll.

Maybe it was the music, the blueberry farm, or everything all mashed together, but I was back to thinking about Sarah and her end of summer promise. *Oh, and I still need to take you blueberry picking! Shoot! We never got to do that! But there's time, Maggie. Lots and lots of time...*

Thankfully, I was wearing sunglasses because my eyes welled up and I had to cough to clear an anxious tickle that rattled my throat. I didn't think J.K. noticed until he reached over and squeezed my knee. "I know, Maggie." He said softly. "I miss her too."

***

We arrived at the condo just as the first splat of rain hit the windshield. The radio had been squawking about afternoon thunderstorms, but the billowing congestion teetered offshore, taunting farmers and lawn lovers alike with the occasional gust and spit of precipitation. Tonight their prayers would finally be answered.

We'd been discussing body showers and a trip to Salty's, but as the skies opened up our plans shifted to another round of leftovers and Netflix. J.K. directed me to drop my stuff in the spare bedroom down the hall while he went into the kitchen to heat up another box of Chinese. I located my designated door and pushed it open.

The room was dim and cluttered. I tripped through the darkness until I found a table lamp and flicked the switch. Weird as it sounds, it was a black light, the kind that makes everything glow a weird purplish white. As my eyes adjusted to the eerie phosphorescence, I noticed that the interior was plastered with posters, mostly famous sports people, all with really bright teeth and glowing jersey numbers. A couple of shelves lined the far wall cluttered with trophies, ribbons and a couple of *Autobots*, namely *Optimus Prime* and my favorite, *Bumblebee*. I couldn't help but smile. This was J.K.'s childhood bedroom and, by the looks of it, hadn't been remodeled in forever.

The ceiling lit up like a New York City train tunnel, filled with graffiti scribbles written in glow-in-the-dark marker. Signatures, team logos, shit like *J.K. rules... Cowboys # 1! Susan Saint was here. Prom night! Class of 2002! Craig+Jeri, Jennifer+Ralph, Donna+Dale, Russ+Diane...J.K.+Sarah.*

I don't know why this irked me so, but I immediately moved to the dresser and scanned a jumble of framed photographs. Sure enough, I found what I was searching for. Five couples lined up in billowing prom gear, getting ready to board a limousine. My friends were the last couple on the left. J.K. wearing a black tuxedo and a shiny royal cummerbund. Sarah shimmering in blue taffeta, too puffy for her chubby features. J.K. didn't seem to mind. With arms wrapped awkwardly about her waist, he peered affectionately into Sarah's bouffant hair while everyone else posed for the camera. Even the snapshot boasted infatuation.

An overhead light flickered. I froze. J.K. was standing in the doorway, arms crossed, sipping a beer. I could tell he was embarrassed. "The *last* door, Maggie. The last door on the left."

"This is your bedroom?"

"Not anymore. I took over my folk's room about three years ago when they bought the new place up in Elizabeth City."

"Sarah never told me you went to the prom together."

"Well, we did."

"You were so young."

"It was a long time ago."

"You look...happy."

J.K. chuckled nervously. "I was stoned."

He reached for my hand and led me into the spare bedroom. Before I had a chance to drop my bag, he was gripping me from behind, kissing my neck and slipping his hands in my shorts. I let him rub and caress as I dropped forward onto the bed. He pulled me in from behind, aggressive at first, and then tender, as if even the sex conflicted him.

Or is it me whose conflicted? You're thinking too much Maggie. Stop it.

I twisted about and wrapped my legs around John's sweaty torso as he pumped and heaved in a frenzied rhythm, jarring me back to my senses. He nuzzled my neck and we both trembled at release, J.K. kissing me softly and stroking my hair.

Sometimes, I guess, it's best to just go with the flow.

Chapter 31

During our throws of passion Lucky had phoned my cell, but when I returned the call it tripped over to voice mail. I tried three more times before giving up. With each attempt J.K. circled like a twitching dog, no doubt anticipating more drama. Back in the living room, eating leftover chop suey, he finally confronted me."

"How is it the sheriff believes Sarah to be dead when there's no evidence of a body? What am I missing, Maggie?"

"What do you mean?"

"What do I *mean*?" J.K. huffed. "For starters, I'd like to know why Lucky's so dead set on persecuting Jimmy? And how the heck did Gallagher get involved? Or you, for that matter? Shoot, you haven't seen Sarah in a hundred years. Why is the sheriff keeping you, of all people, in the loop? "

"Maybe because I'm her friend."

"No, Maggie. *I'm* her friend. I've been her friend since the beginning of time. Daggone it, I want answers!"

Unable to look him in the eye, I focused on my next forkful of veggies. "You'd think I was bullshittin' if I tried to explain."

Annoyed, J.K. retrieved two beers from the fridge, cracked the lids and passed one over. "Yeah? Try me."

"Promise not to laugh."

"About what?"

"What I'm going to say. It'll sound ridiculous."

"Jimmy killing his wife, that's ridiculous."

"Okay, fine." Forgetting my very recent and horrific hangover, I took a sip of beer and was surprised at how refreshing it tasted. "Remember that night at the Tipp, when I fell asleep in the surf?"

"How could I forget?"

"I didn't pass out. I bet myself that I could swim to the buoy. It took less than two minutes, an easy ride out, but getting back proved to be a problem. The riptide was relentless. I got caught in a series of waves and...truthfully, I almost drowned. And would have if..."

"Crazy girl! I warned you about swimming the Tipp. And I don't care that you were a life guard. It's a daggone suici..."

"...if Sarah hadn't pulled me in."

"What?" J.K. stuttered, obviously stunned. "Wha...what did you say?"

"Sarah. She was in the water."

"That..." J.K. slowly shook is head, whispering. "That's not possible."

"Sounds crazy, I know."

"You were out of it, Maggie. Sarah was nowhere near the beach. It was them sisters who found you."

"No, John. Sarah *lives* in the water." I coughed. "She's a mermaid."

J.K. paused...and then chortled. "You little *bitch*! Had me going there for a second."

"It's no JOKE! Whether you believe me or not." My voice tumbled into a murmur. "And if Sarah's a mermaid..."

J.K.'s features convulsed in a rainbow reaction. First surprise, then angst and eventually disgust. "Oh, give me a BREAK!"

"I'm *serious*! Every girlyfish has at one time lived among us. *Real* people, J.K., from all walks of life. Viola swears to it."

"She's a NUT JOB, Maggie. Ever since that boating accident back in the sixties, when her father's ship sunk to the bottom of the Atlantic, Viola's been off her Caribbean rocker. I like the old fox, really I do, but *think* about it. You're putting way too much stock in a woman who chugs bush tea, relaxes to AC/DC, and believes in love beads and weather monkeys. Everyone knows the mermaid sightings are a scam! That's how the Sea Queen promotes her books!"

"There's more. Viola's under the impression that to become a mermaid one must meet an untimely death."

"How do you mean?"

"To be perfectly blunt—mermaids are murder victims."

J.K. pinched his lips together, jumped up and grabbed another beer from the fridge. He cracked it, chugged a couple of gulps, and then sat back down. Finally he said, "Is this a *joke* to you, Maggie?"

"Ask Lucky if you want."

"Lucky believes this horseshit? That's *absurd!*"

"I assure you the good sheriff is privy to Viola's secret. They're not lovers by the way. He investigates the mermaid sightings."

"STOP. Okay. Enough with the nonsense." J.K. flicked on the television, clicked through a few channels and shut it off, clearly agitated. "Okay, okay, so say I play into this mermaid legend. How does it work?"

"Well…after a sighting the witness is brought to Viola. They detail the incident and she paints accordingly."

"Viola paints mermaids. So what?"

"The creation depicts how the mermaid presents in the water, the storybook version, brilliant and beautiful. But then, well, the second painting isn't so pretty."

"Second?"

"That's the screwed up part. The big secret." I walked to the fridge in search of another drink. The beer was going down way too easily. "Viola claims that she loses control when this piece is created, like some external force takes over and does all the work. The second picture gives clues."

"What kind of clues?"

"When Sarah pushed me to shore that night on the beach, she wouldn't shut up, blabbing about Jimmy and school and our deteriorating friendship. She kept smacking me in the butt with a wand to enforce her point."

"Sarah carried a wand?"

"That's right. But it wasn't a wand. *That's* how Gallagher got involved."

J.K. glowered at me. "How does *that* involve the Ice Cream Man?"

"In the second picture the wand was repainted as a cooking spatula. Gallagher carries that burger spatula like a friggin' weapon. He had to be in on it."

"This is *impossible!*" J.K. shouted abruptly. "Nobody's going to believe it."

"That's the thing. Nobody has to believe it. It just helps direct Lucky to more clues."

"*I* don't believe it."

"Neither did I...at first. Not until I heard the Minny Justice story."

J.K. frowned. "Who the heck is Minny Justice? There's no Minny on this island."

"Take a seat. This may take a few minutes."

Toward the end of my narration, J.K.'s skin color turned a pasty gray. He jerked up, excitable, and dove in for a third beer. "But this painting of Sarah...Gallagher isn't the killer so it's wrong."

I sighed. "Ronnie *says* he isn't the killer. I don't think he is but, well, Viola said this could happen if I jumped to conclusions."

"How do you mean?"

The phone rang. J.K. jumped nervously and grabbed for the receiver. "Hello? Yeah? So?" J.K. paused. "You're *shitting* me. Damn." He held up a finger. "Okay, I'll tell her." J.K. dumped the phone and turned to me. "They found Sarah's fishing gear on The Foxy Princess."

"So?"

"Gallagher's tape was in the tackle box."

It was my turn to frown. "But...but wait... Why didn't Jimmy dump it? If I killed my spouse, that shit would've been tossed a month ago."

"Why would he *need* to Maggie? Sarah's been on The

Foxy a million times. It was his wife. It was *her* boat. So what if they're separated. Nobody can prove shit from a simple tackle box. But the tape…now that's a different story."

"Have they found Jimmy?"

"Not yet."

I reached for my sandals. "I gotta go check on Viola."

"Let it be, Maggie. I can't believe what I'm sayin' but Jimmy's in thick. He's a cooked bird."

"There's got to be more to the story."

"Why do you keep *saying* that?"

I buckled the straps and headed for the door. "The painting, it's not finished. And like you said…we still need a body."

Chapter 32

On account of the weather we drove J.K.'s truck. He insisted on coming, expressed that he needed to see the *evidence* for himself. In minutes, we sat parked in front of Viola's stilted cottage.

"You better wait here for a second and give me a chance to explain. I don't want to piss her off."

"Fine."

Bullets of rain jabbed at my face as I hurdled the steps three at a time. The sky had blackened and the trees bowed, the hovering squall now in full tilt. I banged loudly before letting myself in.

"VIOLA!? V?"

"UPSTAIRS!" Her muffled voice sounded far away.

I huffed up the second flight, as quick as the first, in urgent expectation. On entering the studio, a black silhouette caused me to jerk. Lightning flashed in the distance, momentarily illuminating the West Indian's rickety frame. A bewitching crack followed as Viola's voice erupted in the darkness. "Come, child. I am finished."

I edged closer, extremely fearful. A vision of Minny Justice, lifeless and sadistically ravished, tortured my mind. Did I really want to see what had become of Sarah Fox?"

Viola tched and clicked. Attempting to control her emotions she started to pace, muttering aloud, every few seconds returning to the canvas which only increased her agitation. Soon enough, she began to speak.

"*Sarah climbs out of de boat and jogs up de dock. She enters de side door at Larry's. She is hunting for somet'ing. Music. She recalls seeing it on de prep table next to a satchel of onions. Dat's right! Sarah understands de music is important to de mon, and wants everyt'ing perfect. Love is in de air. She smiles in spite of her conflicting emotions, wondering how life could go from bad to good in a snap.*" The old woman snapped her fingers. "*Sarah is happy.*"

Viola shifted her gaze and I could tell she was at the prep table. She pointed and then reached out. "*It is here. De tape! Sarah is excited. She calls out dat she has found it. But...somet'ing is wrong. There is a sound. A t'unk. Heavy and crushing. A groan. Sarah is frightened. She runs to de front of da store and...*"

Viola gasped and for a quick second held the features of her young granddaughter. "*A stranger stands over her mon as he lays face down on de floor. Out cold. Widt out t'inking, Sarah rushes de hooded intruder and jumps on his back.*

"*De stranger is bewildered. He rams his back into de wall knocking da wind out of her. Sarah's lungs feel tight but still she holds on. Dey struggle. Frustrated, de intruder reaches for a knife and swings erratically. His angle is off. He catches her forearm and it starts to bleed. Ouch. De stinging makes Sarah angry. She wraps her legs tighter and slaps at him harder.*

"*De stranger is furious. In one aggressive swoop, he drops forward and pulls Sarah over his shoulder. Instead of flipping completely and landing on de floor, her head hits de counter...*" Viola staggered. She reached up and lightly gripped her throat. "*Sarah...her neck... It is broken.*"

I moved toward the old woman but she halted me with a hand. "*Dere is more. De masked mon is in great discord. When he realizes what has happened, he drops down next to her...uncertain. He cries out and wrenches her into a hug. Dat is de final assault. Widt out realizing it, moving de body has caused de spinal cord to sever. Sarah takes her last breath on dis earth. De mon is heartbroken. He kisses her lips and weeps. After several minutes he lifts her body and, widt great attention, carries it from de room like a groom cradles a bride over de t'reshold.*"

Viola's expression washed in relief. She broke into a tired smile and slumped into a chair. I poured cold water and she sipped it thoughtfully. Kneeling next to her, I waited.

"It was an accident, Maggie. De mon who killed Sarah loved her very much."

I tensed and my skin flushed. *Jimmy.*

"He washes her face and says a prayer, kissing both hands as he does so. He buries her in flowers." Viola's voice trembled.

I gathered my courage and eased over to the canvas, once again mesmerized by Viola's talent. There was my old friend gazing out of the ocean like some kind of sea goddess. Long gone was her baby fat and frizzy hair. She was lean and muscular, with perfect twisting curls and a sculpted face. When I noticed the earrings my throat tightened. So it seemed that Sarah would spend eternity accessorizing her signature hoops.

I followed the tip of the spatula down a muscular arm inspecting the curve of the elbow and then up to the shoulder. The neck line was smudged, slightly distorted on one side. *The fracture.* I traced the neck to the other arm and discovered a laceration on her left forearm. *The killer is right handed.*

Sarah's underwater gown was nothing more than a striking metallic tail reflecting a golden aquamarine. The silky ribbons that twisted about her body had transformed into nurturing vines covered in lavish foliage and blossoming flowers.

"What is that behind her? Is that a...a net?"

Viola sucked at her teeth, clearly frustrated. "De flowers signify land and da net, dat's what I t'ink it is too, it signifies water."

"Well *that* narrows it down," I complained sarcastically. "We're pretty sure Sarah died at the restaurant, so maybe Jimmy loaded her up in a fishing net and dumped her into the ocean." I leaned into the painting. "What kind of flower is this?"

"Tis very common, dear. Dey grow all over de island."

"And these little ones?"

"I'm not sure." Viola waved a ruffled hand at the canvas. "I can't get any closer, Maggie. De foul smell is making me ill."

"The what?"

Viola pinched her nose. "Ever since I finished a nasty stench has penetrated me senses. It's coming from dere." She pointed at the easel.

"I don't smell anything."

"Lucky you. It reminds me of attics and yard sales, winter coats and..."

"*Musty*? Like old people?"

"Easy dear. I don't t'ink I reek dat badly and I'm about as old as it gets." Viola crowed.

"Perhaps her body is holed up in an attic or...or a basement?"

"Maybe. But every time I try and learn more dat odor makes me heave."

"Let me try."

On cue, Viola reached for my hand. "Go ahead Maggie, touch it."

The oil was still wet so I placed one finger on the edge of the canvas. I shut my eyes and breathed in. A fiery heat crept into my fingers followed by the smell of fry grease...fresh mown grass...flowers...Lilacs, perhaps? The pleasant aroma transitioned. It had an aseptic quality to it that reminded me of nursing homes...and...and over starched linen. A stench so pungent and overwhelming it caused me to release my grip.

My eyes whipped open as I pinched my nose. "I know this scent." I whispered. "Recently. I was just complaining about it...give me a sec. I need to think."

There was a faint knock on the wall and we both turned to find J.K. standing at the top of the stairs.

"Hello, John Kilian. When did you get here?"

"I've been here, Miss Viola, waiting on Maggie's signal. She tried to explain your special gift but I needed to see it for myself."

I stuttered and tried to apologize, pausing abruptly...*I remembered! Holy shit.*

Viola lifted a tired arm. "It's okay, dear."

J.K. entered the room, his movements jerky and erratic. He walked straight up to the painting and immediately turned a pasty white. I pointed at the markings just under Sarah's jaw suddenly stricken by the details. "She died of a broken neck. See here."

"We're trying to link de clues, Mr. Kilian."

J.K. stopped listening. Positioning himself no more than an inch away from the canvas, he inspected Viola's masterpiece. "Magnolias," he whispered. "Sarah's favorite. She always fancied a big pink magnolia." Tears welled up and he coughed. Shoving hands deep into his wind breaker pockets, John attempted to divert attention away from his broken stature.

"*Dat* doesn't help." Viola commented, and it took everything in my power not to kick her skinny arthritic leg. "Dere's a Magnolia bush on every corner."

"Maybe we should call Lucky." I cut in anxiously. "See if he's picked up Jimmy. They found Gallagher's tape on his boat, V. Jimmy's the perp like I've been saying all along."

Viola wasn't paying me any attention, still trying to explain the picture to J.K. "See this? We t'ink it's a fishing net but I'm absolutely positive Sarah was buried on land. If I could just nail dis odor. Maggie, dear, have you figured it out?"

"What odor?" J.K. questioned.

"I...uh...." For a brief second I flashed back to Ace, my old sex buddy, and the first time we did it on his basement couch. I bled all over one of his mother's decorative bathroom towels and Ace freaked, wondering how he was ever going to explain. When I offered a suggestion he cut me off. "*You need to go home, Maggie, before my mother gets here. I can already tell that you're going to blow it and fess up. You're way too easy to read.*"

226

I got mad and punched him in the nose. He started bleeding profusely and inadvertently it settled our dilemma. When I got ready to leave he reached out and squeezed my arm. *"I didn't mean that ugly, Maggie. You've got an honest heart is all. Sweet folks don't know how to lie."*

I concentrated on Viola, trying to warn her through mind telepathy that I didn't possess, afraid that eye contact with J.K. would give me away. "You misunderstood. I...I was telling you about Gallagher's tape."

Viola refocused on J.K. "You are correct in assuming dese are Magnolias. And dis is a vine of purple Pansies, I t'ink. Dese little white ones...you know what? I don't t'ink dey're flowers at all. I sense dis is where da smell is coming from." The old woman casually reached for J.K.'s hand. "Touch it dear. Tell me what you see."

Before he had a chance to react, J.K.'s hand was on the canvas. He stood stock still, in frozen horror for a good thirty seconds before jerking away. He twitched and skidded back. His skin, now milky gray, beaded up with sweat as he promptly vomited in a trash can. An aroma of stale beer and MSG penetrated the room.

Too busy wiping the nasty from his mouth, J.K. didn't notice the flash of alarm that washed over Viola's face when she touched his skin. I tried playing it cool, but like Ace had warned my body language was way too readable.

J.K. swung around, frowning, his gaze shifting between us.

"Tell me, son. What is it dat you see?" By the flatness in her tone, it was apparent that Viola already had her answer.

The room became uncomfortably silent. I averted my eyes by re-inspecting the portrait but could feel J.K.'s gaze burning a hole into my side. Quietly, he said, "I'm pretty sure we all know what's going on here. But go ahead, Maggie, let's see how smart you are."

My body shook from a mix of fear and rage, and yet I

maintained a steady tone. "It's not a net, V. It's a chain-link fence. Those are not pansies but Mrs. Walsh's favorite, Purple Passions. And the little white dots, I'm pretty sure they're mothballs." My knees wobbled. "Sarah's buried in J.K.'s backyard."

Before I could form another word, J.K. grabbed Viola and put her in a headlock. There was a clicking sound and a flash of metal. He planted a gun right above her right temple. His tone suddenly menacing, he said, "Ladies, I think it's time we go for a ride."

Chapter 33

On J.K.'s orders, we all piled into the front of his cab like teeny-boppers.

"You drive, Maggie, and don't do anything stupid or the old lady gets it. That means not mucking up my paint job either. Take a left."

The rain was coming down in sheets and the glare of street lights made it hard to see. In minutes the road transformed to dirt as J.K. directed me to the outskirts of the island, roads better adapted for golf carts than Ford F-150's. As I cautiously maneuvered the narrow passages, the list of magic-markered numbers on J.K.'s bathroom mirror flashed through my mind.

"HOW MUCH ARE YOU IN FOR?" I hollered over grinding gears and the flap of windshield wipers.

"What do you mean?" Viola asked.

"J.K.'s a thief, Viola. Needed the money for gambling debts. That's why he broke into Larry's. Let me guess? You're in up to your *ASS!*"

Viola hissed. "I would t'ink you were raised better dan dat."

J.K. jabbed Viola in the side as if to enforce his point. "Cherry fucked me in the playoffs. Heat and the Mavericks, game six. I bet the over and the points, but the line was dead on! A *PUSH.* Cherry said to win I had to be over the line not equal to it and that's just plain *BULLSHIT!* Not winning was bad enough, but to lose? What the fuck? *ON A PUSH.* I was down eighteen grand. Cherry gave me a week to come up with the cash before her father brought in the Boston boys. Those bastards don't play."

"Gambling? You killed me grand baby ON A *BET?*" Viola's pitch went shrill.

"IT WAS AN *ACCIDENT!*" J.K. bellowed. "SHE WASN'T SUPPOSED TO BE THERE!"

"Oh, *STOP.*" I cried. "You'd think Larry's would've been a lesson well learned, but Cherry said you have until Friday, which means that you're still in deep. Big money, I presume, or she would've kept her mouth shut. How are you planning to pay her this time? Gonna rob another friend?"

My jaw dropped as I answered my own question. "You little SHIT! You're the one who screwed up the wiring. Viola, he's planning to hit the store!"

"PAST *TENSE*, baby," J.K. crooned. "Old news!"

"*WHAT?*" Viola and I chimed in unison.

"Why do you think I offered to let you stay with me, Maggie? Hate to burst your bubble but it wasn't for your *protection.* When I learned that Marty had already started working on repairs I knew I had to act fast. Two nights ago, as soon as you fell asleep on the couch, I went out to pick up Chinese food, remember? I figured that was my last chance. If Lucky caught me snooping around, I had an alibi. You forgot your blow dryer or nail polish or some other type of girly mess and I came to pick it up." J.K. nudged Viola playfully. "Tough safe you got there, *grandma.*"

"What safe?" I asked.

J.K. cackled. "You know, under her desk. I've got to say, Viola, I was a bit skeptical about your net worth but *damn.* The sister knows how to bring home the bacon!"

I cringed visualizing the musty old humidor Viola referred to as her safe. The top layer full of Marco's now very stale cigars, the bottom half used for storing petty cash and bank deposits. Viola habitually hit the teller every Tuesday, but since Sarah's disappearance had missed more than a couple of bank trips. The money was piling up. I didn't bother asking how he knew about it. As J.K. liked to brag, he'd been friends with Sarah since the beginning of time.

"You're going to jail, son." Viola muttered.

"You think so?" J.K. spat irritably. "No, ma'am. Jimmy.

Jimmy's going to take the heat for this mess. Jimmy killed your granddaughter and tonight he's going to throw the three of us overboard. We found out the truth, you see. How Jimmy murdered Sarah when he caught her swapping spit with the Ice Cream Man. By the time Lucky figures it out, if he ever does, I'll be long gone."

"You have nowhere to go."

"I'll figure something out. Maybe take a drive down to the Florida Keys, shave my head, get a big tattoo, and hustle a job on a fishing boat. In forty-eight hours I'll be cruisin' though the Caribbean, and then off to South America where I can live like a king."

"What about the Boston boys?"

"Change of plans, darlin'. Wasn't expecting Viola's fucked up voodoo painting. Think I got a better shot at changing scenery. I'll be needing the cash for travel money. Cherry's outta luck."

"What about us?" I asked.

"I just told you. I'm going to throw you overboard out near the Tipp. Give you another shot at beating the rip, although we both know that that's highly unlikely."

"What if I make it?"

"Shoot!" J.K. laughed out loud. "Couldn't make it on a sunny day, how you 'spect to do it in a squall?"

"Where'd you get de gun?" Viola asked.

"Won it in a gentleman's game of poker down in the Bahamas. It's still registered to a guy named Sal Son-of-a-Bitch. Least that's what he called himself. With every toss of a card, Sal would mutter *son-of-a-bitch* thinking it would throw us off. Never worked. He was a terrible poker player—lost all of his money, the gun, his phone and a two hundred dollar pair of shoes. When he anted-up with a knock-off Rolex, we changed his name to Dumb Son-of-a-Bitch 'cuz that's what he was. After my last run-in with Boston I figured the metal might come in handy. Those bastards don't play."

"You'll never get away with this." I grumbled,

purposely steering the truck into a pothole.

"The hell I won't. Take a right and easy on the shocks."

***

On the way to our execution, J.K. detailed the burglary at Larry's Place. How he crossed the metal bridge and boarded the casino boat as he had been doing consistently every Saturday night for six months. "I usually carry about a hundred bucks and play craps for awhile to score the free drinks. If I win big, I hit the Black Jack table."

I scoffed, "Bet that happens...*never.*"

"Kiss off, Maggie. I win more than you think."

"That's what they all say, Viola. Gamblers only brag about the big wins and never their hundred losses."

J.K. ignored my comment. "So I get on the boat, grab a drink and socialize like a bastard. Wave and salute everyone I know, make sure to be seen. When we were getting ready to depart, I told Cherry that I forgot to hit the money machine. Nobody likes paying the casino ATM fee—*six bucks!* It's pretty common for a dude to make a last minute dash. Obviously I planned on missing departure. If Cherry questioned my whereabouts I'd blame a very long line. Thing is Cherry's a Black Jack dealer so she didn't miss shit.

"First I hit the ATM for my alibi, ya see. Then I went in the Crab Shack, parked at a corner table and ordered a beer and some clams-on-the-half-shell. I gave the waitress my credit card and opened a tab. I stayed an hour, waiting for the Saturday night crowd to get good and busy before slipping out the side door and climbing in my truck.

I hit the old Tipp Trail, a road folks used to frequent before the metal bridge. It's impassable now on account they had to dig it out for the intercoastal passage. 'Course with all the sediment and shifting tides, there was only so deep they could muster, hence the reason for a turn-style bridge.

I had my father's old *Sea Ray* hidden in the Gully Trap,

an inlet about an eighth of a mile north of the bridge. Stashing my wheels in the shadows, I buzzed across the intercoastal in total darkness. I jumped into my awaiting golf cart and made a beeline for Larry's. The trip from the Crab Shack took less than thirty minutes.

"Town was dead, too early in the season for a night crowd which helped. Not that there was anything unusual about a man sporting a Carolina ball cap, driving a golf cart 'round these parts. No matter, I didn't run into a single person.

"I pulled into Larry's just after closing, my timing impeccable, and parked in the golf cart line next to the others. I hid in the shadows 'specting the Ice Cream Man to hit the road, but *noooo!* Gotta pick a Saturday night to go fishing. From ten feet away I watched as he plunged into the back of his jeep, grabbed a cooler, and headed for the docks. Either Sarah wasn't with him yet or was already on the boat, I didn't realize…

"I waited another fifteen minutes, becoming more and more anxious as time slipped away. I peeked around the corner and scanned the docks. Gallagher's dingy was nowhere in sight so I snuck in the building.

"How'd you manage that?"

"Keys, darlin'. My old man's a silent partner, remember? Back in the day, when Gallagher was sick or couldn't be on island for whatever the reason, my father opened the store. The keys've been dusting a hook in our kitchen for over a decade. One day I picked 'em up on accident trying to open the shed. That's how I got the idea. I could waltz in anytime. I'd heard the rumors about Bubba and his fireworks. Shoot, it's been a Fourth of July conversation piece since the day it blew. Besides, Gallagher is another one of those sorry saps who believes this island is the safest place in the world. Hitting Larry's would be like a walk in the park." J.K. stopped short. "Take it slow through here, Maggie. You'll be needing to make another left."

The way J.K. abruptly changed the subject, I was sure his explanation was over. Surprisingly, he continued. I suspect it felt good to relinquish such a fatal secret.

"When Gallagher surprised me, I got scared and whacked him in the head with a cooking mallet. Out like a light, he was, blood oozing from his skull. My heart was revvin' faster than a jackrabbit beatin' feet from a coon dog. I bent down to check his pulse, and that's when Sarah jumped on my back like *Rambo*. I panicked. Didn't know it was her, ya see. Survival mode kicked in. I grabbed a knife and cut her arm. Blood spattered everywhere and still she held on. My adrenaline went haywire. I remembered an old Judo move from back in the seventh grade and flipped her over my head. *WHAM!* The counter...it got in the way. Fucking *SNAP!* And then I was like...*SARAH? What the heck?* I knew it was bad. Her breathing was all screwed up." J.K.'s voice broke suddenly. "I...I picked her up, wondering if maybe I could get her to a hospital. She died before I got out of the building."

Viola reached over and touched his knee. "It was an accident."

"DON'T *CONSOLE* HIM, VIOLA! WHAT THE *HELL*?"

"I was running out of time." J.K. said. "The casino boat was expected back in less than an hour, and now with Sarah involved I couldn't screw up my alibi. Sarah needed to disappear, at least from the crime scene. I ran down to Ronnie's dingy, grabbed her fishing gear and a blanket. I threw the tackle box in the golf cart and then went back for the...uh...body."

"Don't forget the money." I added sarcastically. "We all know that got taken."

"Fuck *OFF*, Maggie." J.K. snarled and then continued to narrate. "I rolled Sarah in the blanket and rode with her leaning into me like a lover. In my mind we were just another couple of snowbirds out for a Saturday night drive. I passed a few cars and each time my heart pounded furiously. Friggin' terrified, I was. The four-minute ride to my place felt like eternity. The mutts next door barked up a storm when I struggled through the gate but, thankfully, not a single light flicked on. Neighbors were so use to them smelly bastards, it kinda helped my situation.

"I didn't notice the tape until I got back in the golf cart. It was Gallagher's of course, but at the time I thought it was Sarah's. Figured it slipped out of her pocket when I picked her up. It's not easy, you know, heaving a dead person. I got tangled in the blanket and lost my footing—a shit show is what it was. I tossed the tape in with her fishing gear and come Monday, when I went to work, I dropped it on The Foxy. We have tons of Sarah's stuff on the yacht. What was one more bucket?

"I made it back to the bar when the first of the casino passengers trickled in. Everybody hits the Crab Shack after a gambling run. When I realized Cherry didn't miss me, I ran my mouth about a couple of decent hits on the craps table. Paid her some of the cash I owed but not all of it. I didn't need her old man catching wind. If I won ten grand on his ship, fucker'd be replaying the security tapes and then I'd be super screwed."

"But you left a trail," I said. "With your credit card at the Crab Shack."

"That's the beauty of a tab." J.K. clucked. "They keep it open with credit but if you pay cash they never run the card. Weighing my options, I decided on cash. Let the town believe I was in the middle of the ocean during the robbery, especially after what went down. It was a huge gamble but shoot... I thought Gallagher was a dead man. I couldn't go to jail for a double homicide. I'd be some gangsta's bitch in a matter of seconds.

"*If* Ronnie woke up, and that was a big "if", I figured he'd go to the cops. It was only a matter of time before they started asking questions and sheer luck when Gallagher's memory lapsed. It was me who spread the rumors that Sarah skipped town. Shoot, even Ronnie believed it.

"I hid Sarah's body in the shed but didn't bury her until morning. Risky for sure but I needed a solid alibi. Sleeping at Cherry's clinched it. The next morning, after a very visible diner breakfast, I stopped by Gargano's Lawn Supply and purchased a couple of Magnolia bushes. Claimed they were a surprise for Mother's Day seeing it was just around the corner. 'Course I picked 'em on account of Sarah. It was the least I could do for my oldest and dearest friend."

"Don't you *dare* call her *friend*!" I growled.

"And you were any better? Acted like her BFF when she let you stay at the apartment and got you a job! But when her marriage collapsed and friends were scarce, where the hell were you? Not *here*. Not answering your phone. Don't lecture me about friendship. If I could take back the accident I would!"

"You're so twisted, dude. I think you could rationalize anything."

"Screw OFF, Maggie, you second rate piece of SHIT. That's right. The whole time we were together I was dreaming of Sarah, just like during that super summer you're always glorifying. Back then, I knew you'd be an easy score but I never *wanted* you. The flirtin' was meant to make Sarah jealous and nothin' more. What...? No comment? *Lawdy Jesus*, Maggie Mack is speechless!" J.K. cackled. "That's because you remember, don't you little girl? How Jimmy hustled Cherry...Sarah pined for Jimmy...and I lusted over Sarah. *Nobody* wanted you."

Viola touched my knee. "He's lying, dear. Trying to separate for when he needs to t'row you off de boat."

I laughed in spite of the statement. "Oh, THAT makes it better. Thanks, Viola."

"You're very welcome."

J.K. signaled to turn on a road marked *DEAD END*. The rocky pot-holed street transitioned into a footpath. With it came sand, mud and bushy undergrowth.

"Stop!" J.K. ordered. "We'll be walkin' the rest of the

way."

Retrieving a flashlight from the glove box, J.K. commanded us out of the truck. Rain fell in buckets but lush semi-tropical foliage shielded the sky and momentarily kept us from complete saturation. We trudged along in shadowy blackness. A great rushing sound warned me that our destination was nearby. Within minutes, the path opened up to a small inlet and the intercoastal waterway.

"I know dis cove!" Viola acknowledged. "Dis is where dey used to sneak in whiskey during Prohibition."

"Shee-*iit*, Viola!   I   know   you're   ancient   but Prohibition?" J.K. jeered.   "Doesn't that make you like a hundred?"

"Reading, Mr. Smarty Pants, can prove quite educational. You should try it some time."

"You're right about one thing, grandma. This here secret lagoon is known as Pirate's Cove, and we just hiked up Liquor Lane. Frequented by many a scoundrel in earlier centuries and reopened for business during Prohibition. The dense vegetation keeps it well hidden. I leave my old man's boat here for that very reason, to save money on dock fees."

I could barely make out shadows of the cuddy-cabined vessel we used to frequent back in the day. Jimmy's father was pretty strict about taking the commercial boats, so we spent many late afternoons crabbing the coastal waters on J.K.'s beater. Sure, the cushions were faded and ripped (if you sat on a holey one, your ass would be soaked for hours). But as J.K. liked to brag, it purred like a pussy cat and the hull rode shallow enough to manage the grassy inlets.

A terrific wind pushed me along as we tripped through a shifting rain. I had never seen the intercoastal as white-capped and turbulent as it was right then, raging past like an angry beast, cracks of jagged electricity lighting the way. I spotted the Sea Queen as she climbed onto the rocking vessel, certain she would break a hip just trying to board.

J.K. ordered Viola to drive.

Bewildered I shouted, "BUT SHE'S LIKE *EIGHTY!*"

"SEVENTY-FOUR AND QUITE COMPETENT, T'ANK YOU VERY MUCH!" Viola positioned herself in the driver's seat and twisted the key.

"WHEN WAS THE LAST TIME YOU DROVE A BOAT?" I screamed over a deafening wind.

"MAY!" She yelled back. "DAY TRIP TO DE SOGGY DOLLAR IN JOST VAN DYKE! GOT A DRINK DERE CALLED A PAINKILLER! COULD USE ONE OF DEM RIGHT ABOUT NOW." She turned to our captor. "DESE ARE TREACHEROUS WATERS, JOHN KILIAN!"

"SHUT UP AND DRIVE!" J.K. bellowed. "NORTH!"

I have to admit, I was pretty impressed with Viola's nautical skills. She maneuvered the boat like an expert even with the pelting rain and ripping thunder. Personally, I wasn't doing so well. With every pounding wave, my body went rigid and I mumbled the only prayer I could muster. *Dear God…please don't let me fucking die.*

My stomach churned and twisted, the only reason I didn't vomit was because I had my arms clamped around the back of Viola's seat, crunched in a hug hold, too terrified to let go. The swells were steep, knocking the ship around like a cheap plastic bobber. A screeching wind, louder than a freight train, flattened every wrinkle on Viola's seventy-four year old face.

The craft rocked along for a good fifteen minutes in shadowy darkness. The rain momentarily slowed, offering the rare opportunity to marvel at a big black gaping hole we were about to enter—the tip of Tippany Ridge—a surfer's paradise and a swimmer's hell. I cringed and muttered another prayer. *Dear God…Let me live and I promise to never miss another session of Baptist Bingo!*

I focused on John Kilian, who suddenly clenched his fists and spewed a string of obscenities. Without releasing my death grip, I craned my neck to view the cause of his angst. A small light flickered in the distance hovering mid-intercoastal.

What is *that*? Is that…A BOAT! My heart soared.

J.K. angrily kicked the console and rammed the gun back in Viola's temple. "STOP THE BOAT, GRANDMA!"

Viola flipped the key and sat motionless, staring at the Great Blue as it lifted us into another tilt. This didn't seem to bother her much. Without moving a muscle she said, "YOU'RE OUT OF TIME, MR. WALSH!"

"GET UP!" He screamed. "NOW!"

Viola clenched the steering wheel and remained seated. I was surprised at how calm she appeared next to our frazzled captor. "I'M NOT GETTING OFF, DEAR. AND YOU'RE NOT GOING TO SHOOT ME BECAUSE YOU'RE *NOT* A KILLER. SARAH'S DEATH WAS AN *ACCIDENT*. WE CAN GO BACK. I WILL EXPLAIN EVERYT'ING TO LUCKY."

J.K.'s lip twitched as he muddled over Viola's comment. This brief lapse in concentration caused him to lose balance. With the next tremulous current, he stumbled sideways, flailing his arms as he slipped across the deck. Somehow, he managed to hold onto the revolver although, at the time, I was thinking a gun shot wound was the least of our worries.

That was when shit got weird. What I initially perceived as a shadow came charging out of the cuddy cabin. Hair wild and caked with mud, I couldn't tell who or what the heck I was visualizing, and yelped from sheer surprise. The creepy mud monster dove onto J.K. Only then did I realize that it was a man.

Not just any man, it was Jimmy Fucking Harrison.

For the first time ever, I have to admit I was overjoyed to see the stupid bastard. He roared like a wild beast as he charged my very recent lover, all the while screaming curse words and accusations, "YOU KILLED MY WIFE, YOU LOW LIFE SON OF A BITCH!"

Swinging furiously, they both landed on the holey cushion but were already too waterlogged to notice the seeping thrill of an oozing memory.

As I watched the scene play out in a kind of weird déjà vu altered reality, Viola had moved from the driver's seat and set to work twisting a rope around my waist. With diligence and great speed, she whipped up a couple of very intricate knots, talking directly in my ear as she did so. "We need to be ready, baby girl." She pulled some slack on the same rope and repeated the process of harnessing her own waist. There wasn't a life jacket in sight, so Viola ripped a styrofoam ring from the wall and hoisted the rope through the center before tying one end to a side of the vessel. This process took less than ninety seconds.

I could feel the force of the riptide as another debilitating undulation rammed the side of the craft. The boat rocked full tilt and we were suddenly perpendicular with the intercoastal. I tightened my hold as salt water poured over one side. J.K. screamed and momentarily broke free from Jimmy, reaching for the wheel that Viola had so abruptly abandoned. In his attempt to maneuver the small vessel one handed, (for he still gripped the Dumb Son-of-a-Bitch's revolver in the other), J.K. over compensated. As Jimmy lunged, the boat nose-dived in the opposite direction and the driving force actually pole-vaulted Mud Man into the air. My last vivid memory, one that I would reflect upon for many years, was that of a drenched and dirty Jimmy Harrison, mid-flight, in full attack mode—arms and legs spread wide, face contorted and eyes fierce.

A gun shot was the last thing I heard.

The Sea Ray capsized and the world went unexpectedly silent. My nausea replaced by a crippling all-consuming fear as I found myself immersed in gazillion gallons of water. Unable to make heads or tails of the gyrating current, I flipped into pure panic mode, kicking and thrashing, searching for a lit-up exit sign that didn't exist.

It's a crazy thing, Human Will. No matter how futile a situation, the body struggles to survive. Even as this little thought invaded my inner brain, I could feel my nervous system shift into overdrive. *Think, Maggie! There's got to be a way out! Yeah, right. What the fuck're you smoking? Maybe if I was Aqua-Man or a...or a mermaid...* My lungs burned from oxygen deprivation. *If I could just inhale!*

Something tightened around my abdomen and jerked me to one side. *Viola's rope!* I flailed my arms aimlessly in search of the nautical twine before remembering to check my waist. *And here it is! Yes!* Using all my strength I followed the line until I touched a foot. A leg! *WOO-HOO!* Before my mind could process another thought, a hand latched onto my shirt and forced me upward. My lungs were fucking *SCREAMING!* I kicked hard and felt my head hit an object but it didn't hurt. The styrofoam ring!

AAAHHHH AAIRRR!!! My lungs burst with joy as I broke the surface. The moment was short lived for I was immediately sucked back into the vortex, crashing into something painfully hard. *Holy shit! The boat!* The goddamned beautiful capsized Sea Ray. I gripped the side, kissing it like a frantic lover, at which time Viola surfaced. I reached out with my free arm, amazed at my surge of super hero strength, and reeled her in. Heaving and gasping, we lay haphazardly across butt of the overturned craft, every muscle burning and clenched, anticipating another intercoastal beating.

I had no idea what was going through Viola's head, but for me it was a bunch of random memories. ...Riding my father's back like a horse in the summer of second grade while Finn and Roman (naked except for Iron Man underwear and cowboy hats) chased after us shootin' *Spit-fire* water guns... Sitting on Mom's lap as she brushed through my hair verbalizing concerns about premature split ends... Scarlett being scolded in full clown face after attacking Mom's make-up bag... Peering up at Ace's scrawny chest as he shuddered through his first real orgasm... Sarah passing over the best damn jelly cracker I ever tasted...

It could've been five minutes or two hours, gauging time proved futile. I may have gone unconscious or fallen asleep but truthfully, have no recollection of holding on. Next thing I remember was a strange whipping sound.

WHIP,WHIP,WHIP,WHIP,WHIP,WHIP…

I peeked through slitted lids to check Viola, who lay squeezed in next to me like a sardine. My body went taut as I noted an empty vessel. The Sea Queen was gone.

"VIOOOOLA!" I screamed into the swallowing blue. "VIOOOLA!"

A horn blew. *HOOONNNNKKK!* Flood lights. An echoing voice vibrated from the sky. "STAY CALM!"

So startled by the loudness and lights, I yelped and my mind uttered a string of obscenities. *How the hell do you expect me to stay calm! I'm in the middle of the friggin' ocean on a capsized boat very close to becoming shark bait. Stay calm my ass!*

A slimy yellow alien hovered above the water. At least that's what it resembled in the flickering light. It took a second for my hypoxic brain to comprehend the actual image. A man dressed in a rain slicker swinging from some kind of…of *hook*? When he touched down on the boat he babbled through his mask, but all I could hear was a jumbling mumble. He tied me into some type of harness, securing me like a wiener dog in a very narrow bun.

I was flying.

Next thing I remember was the helicopter. The pilot yelled out from the front seat as the alien unstrapped me from the harness, furiously rubbing at my skin before rolling me up in a scratchy wool blanket. I went from wiener dog to sausage king in a matter of seconds. "ARE YOU OKAY?"

I choked out a response. "Viola! I…I lost her."

"I'm fine, Maggie."

I cranked my neck to the sound of her voice and found a second sausage bundled up in the corner. Viola offered a weary smile. My emotions shifted from elated joy to shocked surprise as the slicker man, doing all the harnessing and rolling, pulled off his hood.

"*Lucky*? But…but how did you *find* us?"

Lucky wiped his brow and sighed tiredly. "We'd been literally hunting Jimmy down for two days. I was getting discouraged thinking someone must have tipped him off." At this comment he threw an irritating glance at Viola. "I sit down for the first time in twenty seven hours, starving and ready to dig in to a bowl of beef stew, when the phone rings.

"Lo and behold, it's Jimmy! First he apologizes for not answering his phone. Says he's been laying low. You'll never guess where?" Lucky crossed his arms and glared at the cocoon shape next to me. "Said he was chillin' at *Viola's* place."

"I told you de mon was innocent." Viola replied smugly. "I just needed time to prove it."

Lucky winked, clearly relieved to find the Sea Queen alive and well. "He was reading in Viola's bedroom when you came bursting into the house with J.K. on your tail. How he explained it, you were up in the loft with Viola, J.K. was on the stairs, and he was at the base. Each one spying on the next. Jimmy replaced J.K. on the stairs when he entered the room, and when John pulled a gun and started squawkin' about taking a ride, Jimmy ran ahead and hid in the truck's cab. When the truck entered Liquor Lane Jimmy put it together. He knew about J.K.'s secret discount dock. That's when he called me. I immediately hung up and contacted the Coast Guard.

"Jimmy said that if I didn't hurry he'd deal with the situation on his own. With the storm and all, I knew we'd never make it by boat. "

The pilot scoffed at the deputy sheriff. "And that's the *only* reason we took the chopper?"

Lucky grinned, "Well...that and the fact I don't *do* boats."

I laughed in spite of my predicament and then remembered. "Oh, my God...Jimmy! J.K.!"

WHIP,WHIP,WHIP,WHIP,WHIP,WHIP,WHIP,WHIP...

Lucky shook his head.

Chapter 34

During the wee hours of the morning, Deputy Sheriff Louis Stacks was forced to make a string of very distressing phone calls. The first to Dr. and Dr. Fox in Cary and a second to Mr. and Mrs. Walsh out in Elizabeth City. He then contacted the judge and spent hours filling out paperwork, obtaining proper jurisdiction and authority to exhume Sarah's body if in fact it was buried in J.K.'s backyard.

According to Lucky's boss, Doug Stevens (or Dingleberry Doug to most folks), who rarely got involved in field work unless there was a possibility of making a television statement, boldly announced that only police personnel were allowed at the crime scene. This, of course, seriously pissed me off.

"They wouldn't have a crime scene if it wasn't for us." I stewed at Viola's kitchen table while she offered to boil up a batch of calming brew. "Don't waste your time, V. Calm is not on my list of emotional options for today."

Not thirty minutes later, the phone rang. It was Sergeant Dingleberry calling to report that his staff had counted twenty-four Magnolia bushes in the Walsh's back yard alone, and whined that it would be hours before he could get a rental sniffer dog in from Wilmington.

"It appears dat your assistance will be needed after all, Maggie." Viola passed me the phone. "Be careful, child. Death is not to be glorified."

Of course I knew the exact location of the body, in the southern corner under Mrs. Walsh's Mother's Day plants. But even after Viola's warning, I played dumb and said, "I'd have to see the yard, sir, to be absolutely positive."

Stepping through the gate, visualizing the combustion of activity as detectives and suited officers gathered data in a frenzied collection, my knees buckled and fear circumcised my abdomen. *Is this fun for you, Maggie? Are you having a good time?* I suddenly questioned my insistence on being present for such a horrifying task. Would exhuming Sarah's decomposed remains offer the serenity I so craved? Or would it haunt my dreams by casting a shadow over her memory?

With a trembling finger I pointed to a string of Purple Passions that crawled up the fence behind the bushes in question. Lucky reached for my hand and tried leading me closer to the dig site but I stayed rooted on the spot. Shaking violently, I noted mothballs scattered throughout the yard. Technically, the snake story was probably bullshit but it gave me an excuse to clear out.

I quickly determined that Sarah's life, not her death, is what I wanted to remember. How she rambled that first day of school, going on about Tippany Ridge and her entourage of rock concerts. The way she ran barefooted at the surf, arms spread wide. Dancing with her pool stick at Felci's, shooting the perfect combo. Scrambling for French fry boats during a wicked wind. Sarah laughing. Sarah clowning around. Sarah in love…

I shut the gate on my way out.

***

J.K.'s body washed up near south pier four days later. His skin was bloated and blue, tangled in seaweed like a damn monster, but according to the coroner absent of bullet holes. It was Fatty Faye (Minny's Aunt) who stumbled upon the body. She was alone, thankfully, and not accompanied by her twin ten-year-old daughters.

Faye presented as a stranger when she barreled into the store soon thereafter, in search of a fresh ear no doubt to recount her recent beach find. The smudges of blush triggered a passing memory, as did the pronounced caked make-up, but I was completely unprepared for her new and improved physique. Frustrated by futile attempts at fasting and crash diets, Faye turned to Weight Watchers and purchased a pair of cross trainers. She attended weekly meetings and trekked the beach four miles at a time, slowly shedding years of cumulated baby fat. Last I heard she was down a hundred and ten pounds. All I can say about that is *Go Faye!*

As for Sarah's husband, well...his body never surfaced. Viola and I determined that it was Jimmy who took the bullet. And a bloody corpse floating the waters of Tippany Ridge disappeared almost immediately. Viola never actually said the words, shark bait, but some things didn't need to be explained.

***

I traveled to Tennessee for Christmas. Mom finally got Dad to buy a real house. In light of the purchase I bequeathed my parents one of Sarah's original paintings—a hitchhiking mermaid very much resembling Sarah's street sign of a young and vibrant Viola Fox.

Our evenings were filled with Christmas gatherings and festive affairs while days were spent fixing up the house, taking breaks only to hit *Lowe's* and *The Home Store* for additional decorative supplies. We deliberated over furniture and throw rugs, scoured and repainted cabinets, wasting no less than two full days trying to hang wallpaper. (Not a pretty sight.) Before I could think, ten days had passed and I was packing my bags and hugging good-byes. It was time to go home.

Yep, I decided to stay on Tippany Ridge. Gina's cousin, Bart, had a girlfriend named Autumn, who landed me a job at the Tippany newspaper. In a snap I was back in the trenches, pushing paper and editing meaningless stories about turtle eggs and changing tides, awaiting my big break. It didn't take long.

Viola, you see, has agreed to let me write the adult

version of *The Mermaid's of Tippany Ridge*. We spend evenings in the studio, Viola laying flat on her back, meditating with eyes open, offering secret details only she can recall. I leaked this information to my boss during a casual conversation in the break room and watched her jaw go slack and saliva drip from her sixty year old jowls. She immediately started squawking about a weekly column. *Perhaps, Maggie, you could introduce the Island's legend, you know, one mermaid at a time?* What killed me was the way she brought it up in a meeting like it was totally her idea!

Just yesterday, I got a second peek at the *Miss April* painting. This time I touched the canvas and *holy shit!* You would DIE if I told the story! (And by that I mean literally.) True novel material. Of course it's never going to happen. Viola refuses to let me release the secret of Norma Jean.

"But why?" I had whined.

The old woman sighed, blowing the heat off yet another brewed concoction. "Some secrets, Maggie, are best left in de closet."

***

As for Ronnie Gallagher, his custody battle ended and the witch didn't win. He gets the kids every weekend and a month in the summer. As a matter of fact, he's taking the team cross country next year, clear out to California, and asked me to tag along. We've been hanging out a lot together, fishing at the pier Friday nights and hitting Baptist bingo on Tuesdays. We're just friends, of course, but...well, let's just say I've relocated the Van Halen poster to its original position over my bed.

***

The Fox family organized a memorial service for Sarah and Jimmy that following spring, two days before Viola's trip to the Caribbean where she anticipated hours of Carnival dancing. Since Sarah's body was part of a murder case, it took weeks for it to be returned from the coroner's office, at which point the Fox family agreed to have the remains cremated.

The task of scattering was performed on a late Saturday in April, at the very spot Sarah deemed *totally incredible* my first day on island many years before. The tip of Tippany Ridge. The weather a blustery seventy-five degrees as mobs of locals huffed and puffed, climbing the rickety steps that kissed the sky. We gathered on the edge of the surf as Captain Gary, an elderly fisherman and pastor, who married and buried most seaworthy individuals, offered a brief yet sentimental sermon.

It wasn't like any memorial service I'd ever been to. C.J. and Peko built a huge fire, while others lugged chairs and tables that were immediately garnished with an entourage of vittles. From crock pots of barbeque, to burgers and dogs, skewered vegetables, fruit salad, and dozens of cakes and custards, the choices were endless. There were gallons of sweet tea and lemonade, a rum punch that could put hair on the scrawniest of chests, and of course a cooler of canned beer chillin' in icy salt water. Big Mikey passed around woo-woo filled Dixie cups and the ceremony ended with everyone's drink high in the sky, hooting and hollering in fisherman fashion.

Shortly after the salute, shit got weird. I turned to Big Mikey who was standing close by sweet talkin' Cindi (they're an item by the way) and said, "Do you hear that?"

"Hear what?" Mikey and Cindi both paused.

Gallagher also inquired. "Anyone hear what I'm hearin?"

Peko held up an authoritative hand. "QUIET EVERYONE! *Listen!*"

By now, the two hundred or so guests huddled in dozens of random groups were curiously peering about.

"It…it's *music!*"

"Is it the Cowboy?" Gina chirped.

"The Filipino Cowboy!" Sudsy finished.

Gallagher turned to the surf. The sun had descended and the water twinkled a silvery orange. "IT'S COMING FROM THE OCEAN!"

Awestruck, the beach crowd stood stock still, frozen in disbelief, as the melodious rhythm of the country funk singer echoed across the Atlantic. We listened in rapt silence as the music shifted and changed, transforming to the more eerie and lurking sounds of Jim Morrison.

"I'll be shit-shined!" Savanna Skip howled. "A school of Dolphins off the coast of the Ridge in the middle of spring!"

My heart soared as I raced to the edge, desperately searching... The music was everywhere now, loud as a rock concert, vibrating off the waves in perfect rhythm.

"*THERE!*" I screamed. "IT'S *THEM!*"

***

Viola wasn't the slightest bit surprised to find Jimmy swimming fin to fin with Sarah. He was Sarah's true love, after all, and had died at the hands of another. (And you know what they say about murder victims 'round here...)

So it went that Sarah Harrison got her fisherman back. And while the rest of us danced under an enchanted moon, I was absolutely certain that Sarah was lighting Jimmy's fire a hundred leagues under the sea, in a Fisherman's Paradise where the rum is always spicy, the fishing bountiful, and mermaids voluptuous.

THE END

AUTHOR'S NOTE

If you enjoyed this story, please...do me a favor. Pass it on to a friend and WRITE A REVIEW ON AMAZON. As a self-published author, my greatest chance at success is through you!

I would also like to thank a few very awesome friends, most notably, Marcy May, who took time out of their extremely busy schedules to peruse my scribblings and offer grammatical assistance. Lastly, a hoot-n-whistle to Molly Mack for the final polish, Ken Lane for his PDF abilities and to my husband, Mike, for putting together the cover! Thank you all!

P.S.
I bet you believe in mermaids now...

A sneak peek at my mermaid sequel...

PIRATES, WITCHES AND DIRTY MERMAIDS

...I climbed out of the mermaid mobile and stumbled toward the sea, not quite sure what to expect. The shoreline echoed. Whispered cries bounced in every direction causing me to slow and restlessly shift.

Taking heed of my instincts, I soldiered on, wide stepping through the squishy sand. My eyes scanned the coastline as I concentrated on listening. A roaring wind made the screaming sound like an urgent whisper...sometimes DEAFENING...other times lost and disconnected...

"Heeellllpppp meee! Anyone! PLEAAsssEEE Helllpp!"

All of a sudden, a shadowy apparition burst violently from the breakers.

On any other beach in the world, this observation would sound strange, but on Tippany Ridge my first instinct was to check for a tail.

Nope. The victim had legs.

It was a woman.

She attempted to stand, but without success. Plunging forward, she dropped face first into the surf. Fluorescent waves crashed violently in all directions, covering her body in white foamy bubbles. The victim pushed up, emerging on strong arms, coughing and sputtering. She kicked violently, thrashing about, clawing and crawling her way to shore. Long and stringy hair strewn across a shadowed face, clothing stretched and drenched, clinging tightly to upper body parts, hanging like a smock over curved hips, making her legs appear malnourished and stick-like. I advanced cautiously.

"HEY! ARE YOU OKAY?"

Not sure that the stranger even noticed me, but the sound of my voice made her jump. She let out a wailing shriek. The girl shifted directions, mumbling and staggering, tripping about. "OH MY GOD OH MY GOD OH MY *GOD!*"

"I'M HERE TO HELP!"

This time there was no doubt as to whether or not she heard me because the woman launched herself in my direction, vaulting into my lap, straddling white legs about my waist. I held on tightly, hugging her back, confused at my next move.

Eventually, I forced her to stand. Pushing sodden clumps of tangled hair out of her face, she displayed wide frightened eyes that I immediately recognized. It is my turn to freak.

Images of the travel stone coincided with Viola's very recent warning rushed to the forefront.

A storm was a brewin'...
... Trouble is on the way.

Made in United States
North Haven, CT
08 June 2023

37516107R00157